P9-CDE-697

SHOOTING THE HEART

SHOOTING THE HEART

PAUL CODY

VIKING

VIKING
Published by the Penguin Group
Penguin Group (USA) Inc., 375 Hudson Street, New York, New York 10014, U.S.A.
Penguin Books Ltd, 80 Strand, London WC2R 0RL, England
Penguin Books Australia Ltd, 250 Camberwell Road, Camberwell, Victoria 3124, Australia
Penguin Books Canada Ltd, 10 Alcorn Avenue, Toronto, Ontario, Canada M4V 3B2
Penguin Books India (P) Ltd, 11 Community Centre, Panchsheel Park, New Delhi – 110 017,
India
Penguin Books (N.Z.) Ltd, Cnr Rosedale and Airborne Roads, Albany, Auckland,
New Zealand
Penguin Books (South Africa) (Pty) Ltd, 24 Sturdee Avenue, Rosebank, Johannesburg 2196,
South Africa

Penguin Books Ltd, Registered Offices: 80 Strand, London WC2R 0RL, England

First published in 2004 by Viking Penguin, a member of Penguin Group (USA) Inc.

10   9   8   7   6   5   4   3   2   1

PUBLISHER'S NOTE
This is a work of fiction. Names, characters, places, and incidents either are the product of the author's imagination or are used fictitiously, and any resemblance to actual persons, living or dead, business establishments, events or locales is entirely coincidental.

LIBRARY OF CONGRESS CATALOGING IN PUBLICATION DATA
Cody, Paul, date.
    Shooting the heart / Paul Cody.
       p.   cm.
    ISBN 0-670-03309-X
    1. Psychiatric hospital patients—Fiction. 2. Missing persons—Fiction. 3. Married
people—Fiction. 4. Amnesia—Fiction. I. Title.
PS3553.O335S47 2004
813'.54—dc22   2003062138

This book is printed on acid-free paper. ∞

Printed in the United States of America
Set in Spectrum
Designed by Carla Bolte

FOR LIZ AND LIAM AND AUSTIN

ACKNOWLEDGMENTS

I'm deeply grateful to Martha Collins. To Julie Schumacher and Steve Marion, Harry Segal and J. Robert Lennon. To my agent, Noah Lukeman, and my editor, Paul Slovak. With love and longing: Jack, Michele, Mary.

"Turn to the right, it was a wall," the Misfit said, looking up again at the cloudless sky. "Turn to the left, it was a wall. Look up it was a ceiling, look down it was a floor. I forget what I done, lady. I set there and set there, trying to remember what it was I done and ain't recalled it to this day. Oncet in a while, I would think it was coming to me, but it never come."

—Flannery O'Connor, "A Good Man Is Hard to Find"

.

Whatever thou hast to say, be it more or less, forget not to utter it in a low soft tone of voice. Silence, and whatever approaches it, weaves dreams of midnight secrecy into the brain.

—Laurence Sterne, *Tristram Shandy*

SHOOTING THE HEART

ONE

That spring I thought about it. About things, about what I had done or what I might do. At night, after she was asleep.

Outside, everything was turning green and you could smell the earth and almost hear moisture move in the veins of leaves and plants, in thickening buds and in the shoots of grass and weeds.

Cars were moving, too, on thin dark roads, their headlights like yellow eyes.

But inside, in the room, I'd lie in bed and listen to her breathe, and go over all of it, all of everything, a thousand different ways. The shades would be down and the curtains drawn, but there were still slits of milky moonlight at the sides and bottoms of the windows. I could see Joan's hair spread over the white pillow, and I could see the oval of her face. Air whistled in and out of her nostrils and down the length of her throat.

I didn't know and couldn't even begin to tell if I'd ever do anything. In the press and push and whirl of words and thoughts. The feeling of swim and panic, the swirl of thinking scary things, then not knowing for sure if that was a thought or an action, a memory or dream. Because if you could think a thing, you could do the thing. Couldn't you? Then faster than a blink and a blur, it was more rushing words and thoughts and times, and that question: Could you do that to a person you loved? Did you do that or think that?

But as I lay there next to her, so so close to her sleeping form, to the sweet heat of her body, I thought of how we were together in bed. I thought of how the nights and weeks and years would go by, and we would always be lying there, even after we were both dead.

We'd be in the ground somewhere—in boxes maybe, possibly in urns, but still side by side. And for a few seconds—lying in the dark, that weak light seeping in at the edges of the windows—I felt like I wouldn't be able to last, to contain these things inside myself, in my brain and heart, and I wouldn't be able to keep my hands still. I was afraid, really really scared, and almost sure and unsure at the same time, that I'd have to do something that would make everything stop.

I wouldn't be able to help it. It wouldn't really be my fault. Somewhere in the *DSM-IV,* the *Diagnostic and Statistical Manual of Mental Disorders,* it said, "A **delirium** or a **dementia.** Schizoaffective Disorder. Number 295.70. Mixed Episode. Depression and hypomania. Severe with psychotic features."

Joan would gurgle in her sleep, or almost sigh words, words I could never understand. I'd put my hand lightly on her neck or on the back of her warm head, and I'd want then to protect her, to never let anything or anyone hurt her. She had such soft hair. As soft even as a little baby's hair. Shhh. Sigh.

She loved when I whispered in her ear and told her I loved her. Sometimes I asked and she would tell me about her boyfriends, from before. What they thought about and did together. Which excited me. And made me mad too. Thinking later, afterward.

I'd lift my hand away and slide it under my pillow, which was always very cool. Then I'd take deep breaths, trying to make my heart and my head slow down.

The red numbers on the clock winked silently by, 12:52 or 1:27 or 3:11—always later and slower and darker each time I looked, and even more silent and lonely. I'd tell myself to hurry up, for God's sake, to get to sleep, you jerk, you stupid nothing, or I wouldn't be any good at work in the morning, teaching the boys.

Not that I was much good anymore anyway.

The breathing worked for a while. In real slow.

Way slow—through the nose and all the way to the bottom of my lungs, and then farther down, to my hips and legs and toes.

Then even slower, out through my mouth, past my teeth and lips, everything inside going flat and flatter.

I'd imagine riding slowly down an escalator, counting backward from twenty to nineteen, eighteen, seventeen—until I reached the bottom and zero.

Nothing. No thing.

I'd say to myself, You're tired, you're getting sleepier and sleepier. Your muscles are relaxed, you feel calm.

C'mon, stupid.

But somewhere in the middle I'd feel people behind me on the escalator, or I'd say, You're tense, your leg is twitching, and this picture would come into my mind of driving at night on an undivided highway, somewhere in Brockton, Massachusetts, or Venice, California, or anywhere, and there would be headlights coming toward me, faster and faster. And I couldn't stop it or help it or do anything else. My arms and hands moving, moving, doing the thing, the thing. Until I had turned the steering wheel all the way, all the, all the way into them. Then blood and tissue and whatever else.

On my face, hands, all over. Glass sprinkled everywhere like salt. After that, after a, after a long while, the whole of everything, all of it—the world, the universe—trees, bugs, plants, leaves— mashed up, was, blasted down, to almost nothing, then, were— just—turned white and frozen: then.

.

I pushed the covers aside and stood up. As I was going around the side of the bed, Joan whispered, "Earl?" and I whispered, "It's okay, honey."

"You can't sleep again?"

"I'll read," I said, and patted her foot under the covers. And be-fore I was even out of the room she seemed to be drifting back to sleep.

I closed the bedroom door behind me, and everything in the hall was washed cool by that moonlight. Pale. Almost sick in a way.

In the kitchen I opened the refrigerator door, closed it, then looked in the freezer. I could feel the cold. Even after I shut the freezer door there was a space of icy air for a few seconds.

The windows in the sunroom looked onto the backyard, and beyond that to Commonwealth Avenue. There were no cars pass-ing, but there was a string of yellow-orange streetlights along the road as it went up the hill toward downtown Boston. I saw one car's headlights at the top of the hill, hundreds of yards away, and I followed them down the long curve, until they came to the flat stretch, a hundred yards from our house. The window glass was right in front of me, and when I touched it with the tips of my fin-gers—barely touching, more like tapping lightly—it was cool, and I tried to guess the temperature. Thirty, maybe thirty-five.

The phone was on the counter in the kitchen, and I picked it up. The dial tone was loud, and I pressed seven numbers, listened to the rings. There were nine or ten rings, and then a groggy voice, a woman's voice, said, "Hunh," and I didn't say anything.

"Hello," the voice said, and I breathed evenly into the mouthpiece, and the voice said, "You jerk. You. You sick son of a bitch." And the line clicked.

Maybe I thought of going back to the bedroom, of lying for a while in bed. Sometimes I folded my hands on my chest and thought of waking Joan up. "How do you sleep?" I wanted to ask her. "How can you do it like this? So easily? So simply?"

Probably she'd say, "Earl, please see someone."

I'd shrug, look away from her eyes. Look below or up above, look for cracks in the darkness of the ceiling.

"You're not the same, honey," she'd say. "Something is happening. You're not like—you're not who you used to be."

I opened the bedroom door, careful of the small click the doorknob made, and I saw her dark lump in the bed. She was asleep on her side, one hand under her chin. I stopped breathing for a moment so I could hear her breathe. We'd been married, I guess, I don't know, six, seven months, couple of years maybe.

"This can't keep up," she said more and more. "It scares me. I need to be away from us. For a while. Get space, get distance."

Then, after looking at her sleeping, I closed the door without a sound, without Joan knowing I'd been watching, and I lifted the phone from the counter again. I pushed seven numbers, and this time an old man answered on the second ring. "Yes," he said in his old man's voice, dry and scratchy like used-up sandpaper, and I could tell he had been awake, so I hung up.

The couch in the living room was white, and it sat in front of a window that looked onto the chain-link fence, a streetlamp, the houses across the street. I lay down, adjusted some pillows under my back, and without turning a light on, I took the book from the coffee table.

There was a picture of him, of the guy, on the cover. He was a heavyset man in his mid-thirties, and just from the light from outside—from the streetlamp and moon—I could see his eyes, and the things in his eyes.

He was already executed in Illinois. That's what the newspapers said. But that could have been just a story they put out to fool people. To make them feel safe. Maybe he was still alive. Maybe he was in an institution right now in Illinois, was there tonight, locked in. Locked down. And I wondered if he was asleep. I thought of him sleeping. Sleeping tonight. Then sleeping back then for five or six years with all the bodies of boys, young boys, in the crawl space under his house. Even with lime, with layers of dirt, the bodies of the kids, the teenagers, had begun to smell.

Like sheep they were laid in the grave. Death had fed on them. Their way was their folly. He said, had read. Bible.

Neighbors had said things, to him, to other neighbors, in some cases to authorities such as the mailmen and once or twice even to the police. Someone even called the city, somebody phoned in to the Department of Sanitation.

People who went near the house—to read a gas meter, maybe to deliver the newspaper or mail, maybe even to drop off a package, leave it between the front storm door and the inside door—they noticed the odor. The stink. It was a smell both strong and weird, something they could neither place nor forget. Winters the smell wasn't so bad, in the cold, with the windows down.

But summers—summers were something else, especially in the last year or two.

The police weren't sure at first how many boys. They had no idea at all.

When he died he would carry nothing away. His glory did not descend after him. In the Bible. Where you go for solace.

Something like this. Normal neighborhood. Houses, cars,

lawns. People raising families. Kids on scooters, kids with training wheels on their bicycles.

Fathers worrying about mortgage payments, about if they were paying enough attention, say, to a younger son. A mother worrying about a three-year-old girl with a sore throat, with an ear infection. About remembering to give the kid the pink medicine they kept in the refrigerator. Give it twice a day. Morning and bedtime, until all of it was gone. Tasted like bubble gum. Would make you better in no time.

Away from us. Distance and time, is what Joan said.

Pressure, pills. White wine. Green bottles. Rhine wine.

In the crawl space, under his house, in the neighborhood. Back then. Not too long ago. There were twenty-seven, thirty-one, maybe thirty-five. Bodies of boys. Some had been there a long time, and the space would flood during heavy rains, and with water and lime and all the years, many of the bodies were in pieces. There were parts. When the police dug, the smell was wicked strong and the pieces so decayed they had a hard time telling.

There were scraps of heavy paper bags that had contained lime. There were pieces of leather belts. T-shirts, blue jeans, a sock. A black sneaker with the lace double-knotted.

I set the book back on the table and watched a car whoosh by on Commonwealth. Its taillights were pinpricks of light on dark skin. This was at two. This was on a Sunday morning in April. I knew that much. I was sure of that.

Still, I wondered about who was in the car and what he was doing on the streets. What sort of person would be out and about at that hour? I pictured him looking at the windows of the houses, at the shapes of bushes and trees, and thinking about the people behind those windows. The old and the young, the sick and the well, in pajamas, in T-shirts and shorts, lying in beds, sleeping fitfully, dreaming of children stolen, of parents dead, of orgasms so convulsive they couldn't—for days—walk or think or feel anything but the wave of nerves in their groins.

Maybe they dreamed of flying. Maybe they dreamed of fields of flowers and trees.

The book was on the table, and I looked at the shape of it, maybe twice the size of a cigarette pack, and then I thought of the boys. The boys nobody had known about. It was as though I could hear their screams, and see and imagine the way the slowed flow of blood when he tightened the rope around their necks would do things to their faces, the way their eyes would change, and the differences in the way each boy's face would look when air was cut off.

Not the kind of boys in the school where Joan and I taught. Where we met. Those were clean boys, loved boys. Joan was a boarding-school kid. More like them. Everything I was not. Which appealed so much to her.

She, Joan. She shifted in bed in the next room, and I thought of this woman named Claudia. I knew her during graduate school, when I was twenty-four. Back a while. How she smiled and asked me about my work, and I began to call her and she began to be busy. Then I stayed in my basement apartment on weekends, waiting for the phone to ring. She had very short hair and light eyes. She wore dangly earrings. My apartment had pipes in the ceiling, water seeped from the kitchen wall after it rained. The linoleum cracked on the floor in the bathroom, and whenever I shaved the black bits of beard floated for hours because the sink wouldn't drain.

Something clanked in the basement, and I stood up and went to the door in the hall that led down there. To the basement.

It was quiet and empty when I pressed my ear to the wood of the door. Then I unlocked the door, opened it, and without turning the stair lights on, I closed the door behind me and went softly down. Stood at the bottom of the stairs for a while.

Light came in through the small high windows of the base-ment. Pale moonlight. And I saw the big shapes of the furnace and water heater, like crouching beings. I opened the door to the stor-age room, and it was suddenly real cool and damp in there, even with carpet on the floor. There were no windows, and the ceiling was a drop ceiling, made of acoustical tiles. I couldn't stand up straight. Someone had built this room for their children in the six-ties, I bet, probably to play in. But there was no electricity or heat. Joan and I, she and me, we had never done anything but store boxes there. Crap. Old backpacks, a broken fan, framed pictures of Venice and Greece, wedding presents we would never use.

I sat down on the floor and pushed the door closed until the latch clicked. Then I kept my eyes open and listened slow and real carefully, but there was nothing. I held my hand in front of my face, but I couldn't see anything. That's how dark, how utterly lightless, it was. I could smell moisture and feel the damp in my bones.

If you want me again look for me under your bootsoles. Said Whitman.

This was April, and this was during the spring. I think it was two in the morning, though it might have been three. You have to understand how dark and silent and cool everything was. What pressure there was. How unmoored.

·

"Get up, Earl," Stephanie whispers, and I can see her on her hands and knees next to the bed, her cheek pressed to the linoleum floor. Her face is upside down to me, and I want to tell her she looks funny, like she's the only one in the world for whom gravity doesn't apply. But I'm not sure of this, or of a lot of other things either. I almost reach over to touch her, reach to make sure she's there, and that it's really her. Stephanie, and not someone else.

"It's okay," I whisper back, and then I start looking at the springs and wooden slats above me, at the underside of the bed.

"You're supposed to be in bed, Earl." She smiles, but her smile, her whole face—it looks weird from down here. "In bed," she says. "On the bed, not under the bed."

"Don't worry," I tell her.

She reaches in and takes hold of my wrist. Stephanie has three kids and she's divorced from her husband. She works the overnight because that lets her be home for the kids when they get out of school. She watches TV with them in the evenings. She's in her late forties, and she's overweight. Twenty, maybe twenty-five pounds. I know cause she's told me. I listen. I see and hear quite a few things.

"Please," she says, and tugs on my wrist.

I weigh 224 pounds, and Stephanie knows I won't move anywhere until I decide to. Mostly. She could have security here in five minutes, big fat bastards with sticks and radios, and there are shots, injections of one thing and another. But she won't take that path.

Stephanie winks, and we both wait a little while longer. Then I begin to slide out, and crack! Shit. Fuck. I bang my head on the nightstand that's next to the bed. The spot is above my right eye, and I can feel it tingle and throb at the same time. Makes me woozy. Dreamy, dumb as a stump. Kind of lopsided and stupid. Throbbing out big flowers of pain.

"C'mon," she says. "This is silly." I can hear her talking to her kids. "What in the world," she begins.

Stephanie wears glasses with brown frames, small rectangles that look like little windows on the front of her face, on the bridge of her nose.

"I think I was maybe dreaming," I say when I'm finally on my feet. "It happened, this weird dreamy stuff. This. This very deep dream shit. When I was asleep."

"Earl," she says and smiles. "Talk to me, Earl. Don't be telling me stories."

"How's the night? You having a good shift?"

She turns and motions with her head for me to follow her. It's quiet and late. Very late. Dark mostly too. Look for me under your bootsoles. Under the grass he loves.

The lights in the hall are low, and as we pass other rooms, I can hear the sounds of sleep. The shifting bedsprings, the snores, the low, whistley sounds of air going in and out of people, of life keeping on in the dark. After the rest and true as any on the shadowed wilds, the Bible said.

We get to the nurses' station, the office, and Stephanie tells Walter, the other night person, that I was right there, right under my bed. He looks up from something he's writing. He says, "Earl." He smiles and moves his head from side to side. Walter goes to Boston University. His hair is thinning on top even though he's only twenty-three or something. Walter lifts weights, and there's a tattoo on his forearm. A globe with crossed swords on top. Walter was in the marines before college. He tells me. I hear.

Stephanie points to a chair next to one of the desks. There are loose-leaf notebooks, papers and coffee cups on the desks. Pencils, pens, a gray speckled rock the size and shape of an egg, a red hair clip. There's a picture on the wall—a great white shark, its jaws open, rising out of the water. Underneath, in black letters, it says RELAX. Fuck you, too.

"So tell me," she says.

She's wearing a loose maroon chamois shirt over a navy blue sweater. Neat.

"Tell you what?"

"What's under the bed?"

"Dust," I say. "Floor, tiles." I look at her. "Usual things."

There are streaks of silver in her hair, and her eyes are brown. The rims of her eyes are red. Hasn't slept enough or very well. Too much on her plate.

Stack of dishes.

"You don't remember going under there?" She crosses her legs. She's wearing white running shoes that have blue stripes on the sides. The stripes are shiny, would reflect light in the dark.

I shrug.

"Say," she says.

"It was this—all this dreamy stuff."

"What stuff?"

"Such stuff. Stuff such as I wasn't sure, couldn't tell if anything was really happening. Like I'd touch things, put my fingers out and on things to make sure they were there."

"What things?"

"Everything," I tell her. "Every thing." Then I put my hand out in front of me. My fingers are spread, and I can see blond hairs on the backs of my fingers. I put my hand on the desk, and then on Stephanie's forearm. I lift my hand slowly, touch my face, push hair lightly off my forehead. Touch. Just touch.

To tingle.

"What's today?" she asks.

"Sunday night, Monday morning."

"What's the date?"

"December, January."

"What year?"

"Ninety, twenty, something."

"And this is what city?"

"Boston, Massachusetts, U.S.A., earth, Milky Way."

"Good." She smiles at me like I've spelled a whole list of words correctly. One plus one equals a warm pile of shit.

"How long you been here?"

"What's green and slides on ice?"

"How long, Earl?"

"Peggy Phlegm."

"What is this?"

"What is what?"

"Where are you?"

"A hospital."

"What kind of hospital?"

"A bin, Stephanie. A barn, a bane, a bed. A place for Looney Tunes."

"How long you been here?"

I don't say anything.

"How long, Earl?"

I shake my head.

"Two days?" she says, and my head keeps moving from side to side. "Two weeks? Two months? Two years?"

"Don't know, don't know, don't know," I begin saying, and she says, "How come? How come? Why not? How come?" over and over.

Says the "Why not?" to confuse me.

She stops, and for a long while—for what seems a long time, at least—she looks from my hands to my face and back to my hands. "Where's Joan?" she asks, and I move my head from side to side. "Where is she?" Stephanie asks again.

"I don't know," I say. Joan, Jean, Jane. Starts with J.

"She's gone you know." You know. Know, see, believe. To see is to believe. Seeing is believing. I think therefore I. Did, am, thought.

"You did something. She left. You think you did something," she says, her voice low and whispery. She leans so close to me that her nose is two inches from mine. "Or she left, and then you think you did something to her. Said or did something." Failed to do. "To the woman you lived with. To your girlfriend. Your wife."

I'm not saying anything. I'm picturing blood, and pieces of brain and bone on the wall. Then I'm not picturing it. I'm trying to be sure, but I'm not sure either. Things go too fast. Too scared, I don't know.

"Tell me, Earl," she says.

Then Walter says, "Stephanie," and I am crawling under the desk. I don't know what month, and I'm not wearing a wedding ring, and there are scars on my knuckles, white and red crescents and lines and spots of flesh that have healed over.

My name, I think. It could be John or Lee. Should. Maybe. It could be Charlie or Charles or Angelo or Albert. My name is Dean or Ken or Ted or Earl. At 2:00 or 3:00 or 4:00 A.M., and I don't know how long or why or how or when. Or even if—possibly, don't—it matters.

TWO

On Friday afternoon the sun was out, and I watched the street in front of our school. Mrs. Cronin, our teacher, talked about the American Revolution, and big-finned cars passed outside on Nevada Street. There was a knock on the classroom door, and Mr. Casey, the janitor, was standing in the hall. He whispered to Mrs. Cronin, and we could see his belly hanging over the front of his brown leather belt, and the strands of hair trying to cover the bald spot on top of his head when he bent to whisper. He wore dark green pants and a tan short-sleeved shirt. His forearms were covered with black hair.

Mrs. Cronin whispered back, and then she began to sniffle and her hand went to her mouth, and she said, "No." She put her hand over her mouth, said, "No, no," then she started to gasp for breath, and Mr. Casey stepped into the classroom and said to us,

"President Kennedy has been shot in Dallas," and the whole room was silent except for Mrs. Cronin and the noise of her crying.

Mrs. Cronin had dyed red hair, and her glasses hung from a black ribbon around her neck, and whenever we passed the teacher's lounge during lunch or after school, we could see her inside, smoking cigarettes and laughing in such a low and smoky voice that we began to laugh just from hearing her.

Mrs. Vara, from the room next to us, appeared behind Mr. Casey, and she and Mrs. Cronin whispered together. Mrs. Vara bent her head, and her shoulders began to shake. Her shoulders trembled like a leaf in a tree in the wind, and she started to suck air into her mouth in gulps.

After a few minutes the two teachers and the janitor opened the door that connected our room to Mrs. Vara's room, and we filed solemnly into their classroom next door. The television was on, and Walter Cronkite, who wore glasses and had a serious and sad gray face, was talking and his voice was so careful that we knew something very bad had happened.

The whole fifth grade was together in Mrs. Vara's room, and I watched Marian Singer from their class. She was tall and already beautiful and out of reach. Far away and way past us and still in the fifth grade only. A goddess. She sat near the window, and there was an astronaut pencil box on her desk, and she wore red knee socks and pretended not to see me or any of the other boys who stared at her. She kept her eyes on Walter Cronkite, and he said things to Dan Rather, a younger man with black hair. Dan Rather was in Dallas, Texas, and he stood in front of a hospital. Parkland Hospital was written in white letters at the bottom of the screen. Walter Cronkite was in New York City.

Friday night was when they had boxing from Madison Square Garden on TV, and I knew there would not be boxing tonight.

We heard crying from the classroom across the hall, and Walter

Cronkite said, "November twenty-second, 1963. Dallas, Texas." He paused and looked down at a paper in his hands. Then he raised his head. "A tragic day in the history of our country," he said.

David Schwartz made faces at Marian Singer. He crossed his eyes, he stuck out his tongue, he pressed his nose flat with his finger, but she watched the screen.

Larry Spoto, a fat kid who never took a bath, leaned toward me and said, "They gonna let us out early?"

I shrugged and looked at the doorway. Mr. Casey and Mrs. Vara and Mrs. Cronin talked in quiet voices, and Miss Monroe from the third grade came up to them, and Mrs. Cronin put her arms for a moment around Miss Monroe. They leaned together until Mr. LaRoche, the principal, joined them. Even Mr. LaRoche's eyes were wet. He lifted his hand to his face to brush away tears, and that's when it became even scarier. Because he was the principal and he wore a blue suit and a red tie and he was almost always very serious. He had wet eyes too. A grown man in a suit. That's when we knew for pretty sure that bad things could happen to our lives.

∎

The cars were parked everywhere, and a door opened, and the small skinny man was surrounded by big men, all of them in suits. This was on television. This was real and live on television from Dallas, Texas. One man wore a white hat. They walked toward the camera, surrounding the small skinny man, then another man in a dark suit crossed in front of the camera, and moved quickly at the skinny man, and we heard, *crack crack crack* like the Fourth of July, and the men were shouting, and the announcer was shouting, and Mom had her hand to her face and she said, "My God! Oh, Jesus!" I looked over, and her hand was next to her mouth, and she said, "Please, oh, oh, oh."

"Oswald has been shot! Oswald has been shot!" the announcer said.

"It's TV," my brother Ed told us, but we didn't see the body lying there, its eyes closed like in sleep, the mouth set. Men shouted, and we saw the light and dark suits, the white-hat man. We saw men rushing and bending over, and someone screamed and others yelled, and they all lay jumbled in heaps like at a football game. And the announcer's voice seemed to jump. It said, "We're with you live. We're with you live from the basement of the municipal building. Shots have been fired. Several shots have been fired. We know that."

.

The horse was black, and there was a single shiny black boot in the stirrup, pointed backward. The horse moved slowly, its hooves clopping on the street. In Washington, D.C., our nation's capital. It was a very old horse. The black boot in the stirrup, pointing backward, that meant that the leader had died. Like in old wars. So even the horse was sad.

.

Late at night, as we lay in bed after the lights were off, I asked Ed when the wife of the president and the two children would have to move from the White House.

He said he didn't know. He said they might give them time to find a new house, but he wasn't sure.

Ed was a year and a half older than me, and he usually fell asleep before I did. There was a window between our beds, and I put my hand on the glass and thought about the eternal flame, and how it had been lit by the woman in black with the dark veil across her face. The wife of the slain leader, the beautiful widow who was in grief.

"You know the flame?" I said to Ed. "At the cemetery?"

He was silent.

"Won't rain and snow make it go out?"

"It might," he said.

I thought of layers of snow lying across the cemetery in January and February. I thought of the flame burning and melting flakes. I wondered if someone would stand there in case it went out, or what they would do when the wick burned down. Then I wondered if there even was a wick, and I pictured his handsome face, and the diagrams of his head on television, and how arrows showed where the bullet went in and took off the back of his skull.

His wife was wearing pink, and there were dark splotches of blood on her suit. Now she was alone with two small children who would probably not even remember their father. She stood there on the plane. They held the Bible on the plane, and the man from Texas became the new president. His wife, the new president's wife, held the Bible, and the widow of the dead president stood with them. I watched the new president's sad face, the big ears and nose. I knew he would be different from the dead president, the way a stepfather would be different. It would be very hard for him, no matter what.

·

The leaves had fallen from the trees, the branches were black and bare like the legs of spiders, and I went next door to the small green house with uncut grass where Brandon lived with his mother, Mrs. Maloney. Mrs. Maloney said it was because he was Irish and because he was a Catholic like us. That's why they murdered him.

Brandon was growing a mustache, and he had a thing called Down's syndrome that made his face round and wide and his eyes a little slanted and his small finger, his pinky finger, was short. Brandon was born that way. Short neck, short arms and legs too.

"They hate us," she said. Her face was the same as the new president's face, big nose and ears, thin lips, only she wore glasses with heavy lenses so her blue eyes swam behind them like they were underwater and drowning. Her hands were huge. She'd raise her hand and put her big forefinger in front of my face.

Sometimes she was nice, sometimes she was mean. She always had something baking—butter cookies, scones, brownies, cakes, chocolate chip oatmeal cookies with walnuts and raisins and cinnamon. And Brandon had more toys than anybody. An Erector Set and Lincoln Logs and wooden blocks with numbers and letters on them. Army guys from every war, cowboys, Indians, trucks, planes, bulldozers, a walkie-talkie. He let me play with everything, and Mrs. M., she fed me and fed me—but she could turn in a blink. Scare you so fast and deep you almost didn't think it happened.

Brandon sat in his enormous burgundy chair, and his hands were small. They stayed there folded in his lap. Those short little fingers. He wore a white corduroy shirt with big blue checks, his sleeves rolled to his elbows, and there were brown spots on the backs of his hands. He licked his lips. He seemed to swallow something.

I stood and followed Mrs. Maloney to the kitchen. She signaled for me to follow with her hand. Down low. This little movement, so Brandon didn't know. She took a towel, opened the door to the stove, and I could feel the heat make my eyes water.

"Where's your mother?" Mrs. Maloney asked.

"Out," I said.

"Out where?"

I watched the cake inside, browner than the bark of a tree. I said, "I don't know."

What you did was, you went downstairs, out the back door, two steps over that strip of lawn, in through the fence gate with white chipping paint, the catch broken, then five, six, maybe seven steps up. And their back door to the hall, it was never locked. It was always dark, and there were coats hung there, and rubbers and boots, and a mat to wipe your feet. And that smell. Cabbage, potatoes boiling, wet dog, maybe bread. Brownies, cookies with M&M's, old tea, cat pee.

Always the TV, the radio going. "My stories," she said. Mrs. Maloney's stories, the soaps. And poor Brandon. Body of a man, kind of. Short. Mind of a child, but pretty nice. Or something.

She looked in the oven and put her fingers in the hair on the back of my head. They moved lightly on the back of my skull, and I saw the air move in waves from the heat. Mrs. Maloney's face was red and there was fog on her glasses.

Her fingers tightened in my hair, and she began to push my face toward the oven.

"This is what they did to the Jews," she said, and my face was so hot it was almost cold, like the wind blowing hard on January nights. My eyes watered, and I could see brown stains on the bottom of the stove.

"Feel that," she said, and you could hear a little Ireland in her voice. The wild west of Ireland. Connemara, mountains and rocks. The rain, the wind blowing. And the roots of my hair burned and stung.

The coils on the sides of the oven were red. "The only way out, they told them, was through the chimney, or through work. Work will make you free," she wheezed, the air barely making it through her throat and nostrils. Her bright face, her blue blue eyes.

"Mama," Brandon called from his chair in the living room. "Where're my glasses?" Where ma glusses?

Thick Brandon tongue.

"Look in your coat pocket," she called back. Then in a hiss she said, "Feel what they did," and pushed my face to within a foot of the oven. "They'll do it to you too. Here, or after you die and go to hell."

She pulled me away from the oven, took her hand from my hair, and placed it on the back of my head. Moved her hand in a circle around the place where the roots of my hair throbbed. Then patted the place, soft at first, then harder and harder.

She smiled. Her teeth were perfect and white. The dentist pulled all her old teeth when they were rotting, she had told me. Then he made her new ones that were perfect.

Picture of the Virgin Mary on the wall. Crucifix over the sink, crucifix over the kitchen table next to the clock, picture of Jesus with his chest wide open and his red heart glowing, just about holding his heart in his hands.

Sacred heart.

She licked her lips. Just like Brandon. "You'll want cake," she said. "When it's done. You tell me what kind of frosting you like."

Then she said, "Little friend." Is what she called me. "Good boy. Smart fella or a fart smella," Mrs. Maloney said.

She wore a white dress with blue clocks on it.

"You like orange frosting," she said. "How about orange?"

I nodded.

"Cause Brandon's all I got, and you come see us. I don't know what I'd do without you." Kissed the top of my head. The hair. The cushy front of her. My head on her pillow. The nice Mrs. M.

"It's our secret about the oven, about the Jews." Her hand on my shoulder, the oven door closed. She put her hand inside my shirt, and rubbed the skin on my chest. Her fingers were warm. They touched my nipples, pinched them lightly.

"Our secret, Earl? Don't ever try to tell nobody."

I watched the floor.

"They'd know you're lying. Brandon would be heartsick, and you don't want to break his heart. He's all I've got, you know."

The floor was white and black squares, with silver speckles.

"Earl?"

I nodded again.

∙

Michael Williams has hair so black it's almost blue, and dark eyes, and when he smiles his slow smile his teeth look white as a cloud. He gets a pack of cigarettes a day—that's the ward rule—and he smokes all of them by dinner.

We play chess next to a window in the dayroom, and Michael always wins. He played all the time in Danbury, the federal prison in Connecticut, and he says the best chess is played at federal rather than state prisons.

"Half the assholes at Walpole can't read," he has told me. "They're fucking animals—barbarians—like the jungle."

Has my queen pinned, and I'm trying to force one of his bishops out of my territory. Jean Higgins, she, who is an aide, wheels the blood-pressure machine up to him, and without taking his eyes from the board, he unbuttons the cuff on his shirt and rolls the sleeve almost to his armpit. Jean wraps his upper arm, pumps the ball, and air hisses from the tube.

"Who's winning?" she asks. Jean is tall and heavy, and has glasses with curvy earpieces. Designer.

She unwraps his arm, writes something down in a small note-book.

"He is," I say.

"That's cause he looks like Elvis," she tells us as she moves away.

I stare at Michael, and he does look like Elvis. The young Elvis, before he went into the army and then came out and made a bunch of shitty movies for his manager, Colonel Tom Parker. Then started doing drugs and getting fat. Playing Las Vegas, throwing scarves into the audience of screaming women.

Michael's still got his eyes on the chessboard.

He moves a pawn to king five, and I'm looking at the board too, imagining horses on a battlefield, whinnying and wheeling, clashing armor and clanging swords. Roger Novak, the nurse, says, "Time for meds."

We shuffle out and into the long hall and line up in front of one of those doors that are cut in half—the top open—and when I reach the front, Roger says, "How is it, Earl?"

"What?"

"Tricks. Everything."

"Okay," I say.

Roger can't be more than twenty-three or -four. He rubs alcohol on my upper arm, and when the needle goes in and he presses the liquid into the muscle, it's like a small hot sea spreading through me. Going all over. Into bones and tendons and the hidden scary parts of my brain, where neurons and synapses flash and crackle in the darkness like lightning at night in deep space.

.

The *PDR,* the *Physicians' Desk Reference,* has a red cover and is thicker and taller than the Bible. It sits lopsided on a shelf in the nurses' office, next to books named *Latency* and *Nurses' Drug Handbook.* Near the *DSM-IV.* It says, "Prolixin Decanoate is the decanoate ester of a trifluoromethyl phenothiazine derivative. It is a highly potent behavior modifier with a markedly extended duration of effect.

"Prolixin Decanoate has activity at all levels of the central nervous system as well as on multiple organ systems. The mechanism whereby its therapeutic action is exerted is unknown.

"Prolixin differs from other phenothiazine derivatives in several respects: it is more potent on a milligram basis, it has less potentiating effect on central nervous system depressants and anesthetics than do some of the phenothiazines and appears to be less sedating.

"Prolixin Decanoate is a long-acting parenteral antipsychotic drug intended for use in the management of patients requiring prolonged parenteral neuroleptic therapy (e.g., chronic schizophrenics).

"Outside state hospitals or other psychiatric institutions, Prolixin Decanoate should be administered only under the direction of a physician experienced in the clinical use of psychotropic drugs, particularly phenothiazine derivatives.

"Prolixin Decanoate may be given intramuscularly or subcutaneously. A dry syringe and needle of at least twenty-one gauge should be used. Use of a wet needle or syringe may cause the solution to become cloudy."

■

He worked at night, I know, at two or three or four in the morning, when everyone normal in the city was sleeping, when most of the traffic lights blinked in the dark, and cats and dogs and rats moved in the alleys, and raccoons bit through the green trash bags and spilled cans and bones and greasy paper onto the pavement. There was broken glass in gutters, and empty paper cups, and when a car passed its lights shined for an instant over the shards of glass and lit them up like sun on water.

He sometimes drove whole nights without stopping, drove from Beacon Street in-town to Massachusetts Avenue—over the silently stinking river—and into Cambridge. From the Cambridge side he could see downtown Boston on the far shore of the river, could see the Hancock and Prudential towers and, farther to his left, the towers downtown, the Federal Reserve Building like a giant washboard.

He followed Massachusetts Avenue through Cambridgeport, into Central Square, where pizza places were still open sometimes and cabbies hung out and leaned against their cars, looking, and maybe talking a little to each other. Then toward Harvard Square, where the rich girls slept in buildings with security locks and alarm systems, and where every hallway had lights. Warm safe cunts.

He drove into Arlington and looked at windows, and he noticed the way parked cars glowed under the streetlights, like boats underwater. He lit cigarettes and watched the shadows, and sometimes he'd see someone on foot, someone nearly always male, someone young and high on something, and he'd slow down. And if they looked, he waved and slowed still more, and even then it had more to do with what was inside him, with how long it had been there, and the size of the feeling. The itch that got bigger and bigger, and made him want to growl and groan, and get his nails into the itch, at the skin, and scratch and scratch and scratch. Maybe until blood came.

He'd reach under the seat to where the handcuffs were, and the new white clothesline, and the small snub-nosed gun with the gray duct tape on the handle.

But on that one night in April, I knew, because it was me—this disturbed, private-high-school teacher of history and literature— teacher of boys—thinking this, imagining this—on that one night, that Sunday night in early spring—when the temperature was barely above freezing—he just kept driving and driving, past Arlington and into Lexington and Burlington, and he finished one pack of Kools and opened the second pack, and kept the window cracked an inch or so.

Drank white wine, swallowed pharmaceuticals. Pressure inside, building and building. Going faster. Wanting to go faster. Trying to slow it all down, keep it in.

Even with the window a little open, his eyes burned and watered as though he'd been reading all night, and when he reached a place called Nutting Lake, it was nearly four in the morning.

He parked under some trees and shut the engine off and listened to something under the hood go *tick-tick-tick*. Then he closed his eyes and put his head back against the headrest, and as he pressed his fingers to the side of his head, he thought that this is what a salesman would do in some town somewhere, driving for a long time to get back to his wife and daughter, say. Drive at two or three in the morning, and near four, when he was past exhausted and had walked through mirror after mirror in his mind, seeing himself, seeing nothing but darkness, into deeper tiredness, then alertness, then more tiredness—he, the salesman, would stop under a tree near a small lake and think of his wife and daughter. A normal person. Sleeping at home, in their bedrooms in Highland, Indiana, in Middle River, Maryland.

And as he sat there he thought too of the long shadowed figures of boys lurching home. He couldn't help this. This is where his mind sometimes took him, even if he tried not to go there. To that dark part of his brain. But he did. He always did. He thought of seventeen-year-old boys with skinny asses so white that he would lick them like smooth cream, and with the cuffs on he could take the surgical scissors and cut away their underwear and see their limp curled cocks lying like a bird before flight.

And he'd lick and stroke and suck until they grew in his mouth—these thin, proud boys—and, seeing this, knowing they'd grown hard for him, they had tears in their eyes. Tears of shame, of humiliation.

But the cuffs would be on them by then. They were always so tired and drunk and wasted from one drug or another. And the cuffs would be tied to the handle on the back door of the car, and if fear and adrenaline suddenly kicked in and made them clear-headed and shit-scared and alert for a moment or two—then if the handcuffs did not calm them, he held the cool barrel of the gun to their foreheads, just above their eyes. He whispered what he would do to them. And they sometimes trembled and shook like they were very cold, but they did what he told them. They didn't fight.

He made a small noose of clothesline and slipped it over their balls and tightened it enough to hurt a little, and they let him lick more, and when the white explosion came, when the white gobs spurted from the slits in their cocks, he knew he had them— deeper and for longer than they would ever know.

Then mostly he didn't do anything else. Just unlocked the cuffs and took off the noose, kissed them on the forehead or nose or eyebrow—tender, with love—and told them to get out of the car and forget about everything. Get a good night's sleep. Sweet dreams, gentle prince. Flights of angels sing thee to thy fucking rest. For there was love there. A certain kind of love.

.

On the ride home he did not smoke or drive too fast, and when he finally pulled into the driveway it was as though he had just come home from work or maybe even from a vacation somewhere. A brief step or two off and out of his regular life. Then back to normal.

.

In the basement apartment when I was a graduate student of American studies, I could hear music and conversations in the apartment above me. I heard a boy break up with his girlfriend, and later that night I heard her talking to her mother, saying over and over, "I love him, I don't care."

The front door and hallway to the rest of the apartments in the building were directly over my bed, and in the winter people stamped the snow and slush off their boots, and chips of paint from the ceiling fell on my pillow.

This was from sometime before. After college maybe. I'm pretty sure. But before Joan, I think. Grad school: Jonathan Edwards. Human soul suspended by God over a pit of fire by a single strand. Strand of human hair, strand of a spider's web. Some such. Pretty fucking precarious.

One night—at four or five in the morning—a woman who was spending the night woke me up and asked how I could stand it.

"Stand what?" I asked.

"Beyond the wall," she said. "The noise."

It was the furnace rumbling.

"I like the sound," I told her. "It helps me sleep."

Her name was Kirsten or Karen. Maybe Ellen too. She probably had brown hair. Small breasts, pink-brown nipples.

•

It's still morning, and I see, observe, this young woman with dark hair cut to the nape of her neck standing down at the other end of the long hallway on the ward, smiling slightly, looking around her, almost shyly. She, this young woman, is wearing a long black coat. A coat you'd see in a movie. I watch, and even though she doesn't look like anyone I know, she is somehow familiar to me. Sort of the same size as Joan, maybe a little taller, or possibly similar to Claudia—who I knew once. And the face is almost. Very fair skin, almost black hair.

This young woman on the ward. Here. Younger certainly than Joan. Jean.

I would say her name could be Erin. She has brown eyes. An almost, a slightly, just barely, an upturned nose. Very attractive. Long legs. The black coat comes to her knees.

She is an outsider, surely. She is wearing black pumps and has a folder, briefcase, pocketbook, bag—bigger than, say, a large manila envelope. But dark brown. Reddish dark brown leather. She holds the thing—briefcase maybe, under her right arm, then as I watch—down here at this far end of the quite long hallway—cracks in wall, pipes along the high ceiling, many many closed doors on both sides of the hallway—then I observe, I see as she switches, moves the briefcase thing from her right hand, arm, to the front of her.

Folds both arms around the dark leather folder thing, holds it to her chest. Stands, is quite tall.

Then someone on the staff—a person of the male persuasion, with keys, comes out of the nurses' station, which is to say office, way the hell down there, stands in front of this tall dark-haired really quite attractive and really lovely you would have to say.

Staff person says something—gestures, moves lips, face—and the woman says something. They turn, those two. Go away and toward the front dayroom. Way the fuck down there. Many many feet away.

Past pipes, cracks in ceiling. Patients, crazy fucks pacing sitting standing in dayroom—to the alcove past the dayroom, this long long look going away, getting smaller, more and more distant. Then pause, unlock door, both exit. Marriages fail every day in every way.

So many come. They go. Did not see me, the person I am. And he dreamed yet another dream. In the Bible. These are the sons. The sun. Reigned in his stead.

.

My father opened the door to our room and leaned in, and I saw the outline of his head from the light down the hall.

"You okay?" he asked. "Everything all right?"

Ed was asleep, and I didn't say anything, so after a minute or so he went away.

Later we heard our father scream in his sleep, and we knew he was having one of his nightmares. I heard it I know. I heard it for sure.

"Why's he do that?" Ed asked, and I could tell Ed was still mostly asleep. I never knew what to say to him. Me and Ed were just kids then. Six, seven, eight years old. Maybe five. Maybe four or nine. Younger or older, long time ago.

.

Joan slept deeply, and I got up from the couch and went to the kitchen. I took a pickle from the refrigerator and ate it while I looked out the window behind the sink. In all the time we'd been together I don't think I once went to sleep before Joan.

There was moonlight on the lawn, and even though some of the trees had buds on them, I kept picturing the way they looked in the summer, and how the wind moved through the leaves and made that faint raspy sound, like someone trying to breathe. But having a hard time. Emphysema, years of smoking. The wind soft and quiet. May. Say, late of an early May night.

I opened the bedroom door and went quietly in and around to my side. Pulled the covers back and got in bed, and Joan said, "Earl," in this real low voice, and I patted her hair and felt her skull underneath.

Kept still and closed my eyes, and pulled one of the pillows over my face, and pictured the ocean and waves curling up on shore, then I was lying on the sand and the waves rolled over me, and salt stung my eyes.

The mattress was hard, and I turned from my back to my hip and pulled the blankets to my neck. Everything began to slow down, and I could feel the edges of sleep. There were sounds far off—voices and songs and laughter, then birds and wind and a gunshot—but they were in dreams, I thought, then I wasn't sure. They were within or without. It didn't matter.

Joan shifted, moved an arm so that it rested across her forehead, and I was awake, this Earl person who was I, a big nervous trembly guy, and nowhere near the country of sleep. The quiet place on the other side, where I had to get to if there was any hope for me. Awake like an exposed nerve.

And her. Saying she couldn't take this, that she'd have to leave. Because I was not the person she'd fallen in love with—not the person she'd married. That if I wouldn't see someone, do something, then she couldn't say or guarantee anything. Couldn't hang in there forever no matter what we'd said or promised. People turned into other people. And I scared her. These books and the sick stuff and all the crazy stories about evil creepy people— and their secret lives, their invisible urges. Secret and hidden desires. And who and what was I turning into?

After a few more minutes I got up and went to the kitchen again. I took the phone book, and found the number in the Yellow Pages under "Suicide." I dialed and she picked it up, this woman I didn't even know from a hole in the side of a tree or a building, she picked up and said hello on the second ring.

"My name is Earl," I said, and in a voice so calm it almost sounded drugged, she said, "Hello, Earl."

"I know it's late," I said, and was careful to keep my voice low. Maybe because Joan would hear, or because I was pretty afraid by then myself. One part of me really afraid of these other parts.

She listened, and when I didn't say anything more, she said, "It's okay. We're here all night."

"I don't know why I called," I said.

"Any hunches?"

"No."

"You're not feeling so good," she said.

"Right."

"Are you afraid you'll hurt yourself?"

"Yes."

"Do you have a plan?"

I could hear voices talking softly in the background on her end. I carried the phone into the living room, sat on the couch, felt the carpet under my feet.

"Lot of plans."

"You want to tell me about them?"

"Like what I'd use?"

"Sure," she said.

"Sometimes I'd be driving in the car, and I'd go fast, really fast as hell—eighty or ninety—and I'd drive off the road, and that would do it, that would stop everything."

The car bouncing and flying, turning over and over, maybe splitting in half on a tree or pole, then sparks and the gas in the gas tank. *Poof.* Red and orange flames and deep deep billowing black smoke.

She breathed slowly and said, "Stop what things?"

"Everything. All of this."

"All of what?"

I thought I heard Joan sigh in sleep in the bedroom. Maybe she'd not yet gone, or I hadn't done anything. A car passed on Commonwealth, and I said, "What's your name?"

"Paige."

"How old are you?"

"Thirty-five," she said.

"You're a year older than me."

"Do you work?" she asked.

"Sometimes."

"What kind of work?"

"I can't tell you."

"Can you tell me your name?" she asked.

"I already did. It's Earl."

"And you don't feel so good, Earl."

"I can't sleep."

"What do you do when you can't sleep?"

"I think."

"What do you think about?"

"About razors and knives, about terrible things. Sometimes I want to cut myself. I want to take the razor and drag it across my chest. I want to see the skin separate, and I want the blood to flow and cover me over like a red sheet."

"But something keeps you from doing that?"

Sometimes.

I nodded, my head moving slowly up and down in the dark. I was curled up on a corner of the couch by then. I said, "Yes."

"Do you know what it is?"

"The something?"

"Yes."

"I don't."

"But you called us and that's a good thing."

"How come?"

"Because it's doing something that doesn't hurt yourself, and it's something that can probably help."

I curled up tighter on the couch and listened to the sound of the phone line. The faint faint hum of life, of live wire running for miles underground and overhead—and just this living quiet hum between us—between me and Paige.

"Who calls you?" I asked.

"All kinds of people."

"Old people? Young people?"

"Both."

"And you talk to them?"

"Sometimes all night."

"You like doing it?"

"Yes."

"You ever talk to people who've killed people? Who want to kill people?"

"Why do you ask?"

"That's what I think about," I said. "At night sometimes, when I can't sleep. When I try not to think about things like that."

"Have you killed people?"

"You know about the one in Chicago? The one with bodies in the crawl space?"

"No, Earl."

"You want to know?"

"Why would I? What's the point?"

"It's what I think about, what I can't stop thinking about. It's like I'm in love or something."

"Then maybe you should tell me."

"Are you married, Paige?"

"Yes." Her voice was low and tired, her voice was rich and deep with possibility. It was past four in the morning. Paige, you could tell, had heard so many things in her life. My knees were almost touching my chin.

"You have kids?"

"No," she said.

I waited and listened to the phone line, to the live humming space between us.

"You love your husband?" I asked softly. "You like your life?"

"Very much. I'm very fortunate."

To speak of the woe that is in marriage. Bob Lowell. Crazy locked-up fuck.

I didn't say anything for a while, and she kept listening. This open line going from me to her, her to me. Every breath, every beat of our quiet hearts.

Finally I began to talk. Slow, evenly. I knew too much, even if I didn't want to know. "He was heavyset, this man, and he used to dress up sometimes as a clown and visit sick kids in the hospital," I said. Paused, and could tell she was listening. "He felt for the kids, knew how tough it was for them to be so sick, so little and to have such pain. They were little soldiers. The ones with burns and leukemia, the tiny kids like plucked chickens with holes in their hearts." I knew so much about this. Had read the newspapers and magazines, had read and reread the books.

"He dressed up as a clown. He called himself Pogo. He brought balloons in every bright color they had. Yellow, red, orange, pink. Sometimes he'd cry when he saw the kids. So sad, it hurt his heart. They'd be wrapped up like mummies, or they'd be bald and have the big black circles around their eyes, and they looked like old people—maybe because they knew they were going to die." Little kids no more than three or four sometimes, I thought but didn't say to her. Kids who barely knew what it was like to be alive, even.

"He'd put on the big floppy shoes, and the long wild orange hair, the red nose, and all the paint on his face. Huge red lips, great black eyebrows, green rings around his eyes. He'd fight back the tears when he saw them in their beds and chairs, the parents nearby, some of them looking as bad as the kids almost, what with no sleep and half dead with worry. And he always said later that seeing the kids finally break into smiles and then laughter filled him with this warm feeling. This big warm feeling that flooded though every part of his body."

I stopped and listened and could tell she was still there. Quiet, but live. I could also hear voices in the background on her end.

"He did other stuff too. Organized a big parade in Chicago, a parade for Polish people and the Democratic Party in some neighborhoods, in a northeast suburb of Chicago, Norwood Park. West Summerdale Avenue. There's a picture of him shaking hands with the first lady. He's almost smiling, and she's smiling, and he was proud of that picture. He hung it on the wall in his den, along with paintings of clowns.

"He had a business, a kind of maintenance and handyman business. He'd clean up, do small carpentry projects and paint, do repair work, odd jobs around people's houses. He hired teenage boys, kids without many skills and not much direction in life. Within a few years of starting up, his business was worth hundreds of thousands of dollars."

I paused, and I could still hear voices in the background.

"Paige?"

"Mmm."

"You with me, Paige?"

"Yes."

"This boring you?"

"No, Earl."

"How's he sound so far?"

"The clown man?"

"Pogo," I said.

"Okay."

"He was."

"I'm almost afraid to hear the rest."

"You should be."

"What's his name?"

"Pogo," I said. Somewhere in the distance, on my end, I could hear trucks pass, probably on the Massachusetts Turnpike. I thought of white lines running at headlights, and the lights of towns along the highway. Dark houses on hills in the distance. Maybe a light on in an upper room. Someone sick, someone couldn't sleep. Someone having trouble breathing. Bad dreams. Poles, trees, telephone wires, power lines.

"What's his real name?" Paige asked.

I thought and thought, then said, "How about we call him John?"

"Okay."

Pause.

"So what happened to John?"

"He had this business," I said, "and it was getting bigger and bigger. And as I said, he needed help. So he hired kids, high school kids mainly, to help. Kids who were around, who didn't have much to do. He paid higher than minimum wage, and he was a nice guy. He'd have them over to drink beer and smoke dope a little, watch sports and cartoons on TV. He lent them money now and then. Ten here, twenty there. Whatever.

"The kids liked his house because there were no parents around, and they liked the pictures of clowns on the walls, all the sad-faced clowns. And sometimes they'd bring their friends over, and they'd all get high together. Sometimes John would give them advice about doing something with their lives. Getting good grades and working hard, and that's when he seemed most like their parents, weed or no weed. Seemed like he cared but wasn't going to kick them out of the fucking house for drinking beer and smoking dope and not going to school."

I stopped and took a slow, deep breath. All the way in, then held it, then all the way out. Still curled, the side of my face against the fabric of the couch.

"You okay?" Paige asked.

I made an okay sound without even opening my mouth.

"You?" I said. "You sure you want to hear this? It's something—it's not what I like to think about."

"But it does bother you?" she says. "Am I right? It bothers you and scares you and makes it hard for you to sleep?"

I say, "Yes, absolutely."

"Then I think you should tell me."

There's the live hum for a while and no background noise. Not on her end. Joan way under. Just shadows and silence and the smooth clean surfaces of things in the dark.

"So this guy, this John guy," I begin in my whispery voice, then stop.

"It's okay," Paige says, soft and deep, and we've never been closer. She'll go with me.

"So he went out late sometimes too. When he was restless, when he was angry. When he was up and playful. Just too damn much energy. Fit to be tied. He'd get in the car, get the heat on low, and drive and drive. One of the rock stations on low, just for background. Drive past all the stuff you see in the world. Clotheslines and fire escapes and Dumpsters at night. Through some neighborhoods with the nice houses. Lawns and fences, big trees, even. Could tell how big the trees were over you even in the dark and the night.

"But usually, eventually, he'd drive to downtown, to the bus station, sometimes to the gay bars, and he'd park on the street and leave his window down. Looking, watching. Minding his own business. And once in a while he'd give a kid a ride, some kid who had run away from home, or who was drunk or high. He'd tell them about his being in business, the painting and plowing and cutting grass, and how he hadn't always gotten along so well with his father either, but how you couldn't let that rule your life. Sometimes you just had to be away from each other. Do a little growing up on your own, give your dad some space to breathe, for the love of God.

"John would look over. He'd say, 'Grown-ups are human, too, you know. Even moms and dads.' "

I stopped to listen and hear the hum on the phone line, and Paige—she was there—Paige was in and on this with me. We were together. We were a team.

"Sometimes he pretended to be a cop, and he'd accuse the kids of hustling, of prostitution, of trying to sell drugs. He showed them a badge he'd gotten from a thrift store. Shiny silver metal, leather case like a wallet. He'd lean them against his car, or against a wall, spread their legs and frisk them. This was kids who were fourteen and fifteen, kids in tight jeans and fake leather jackets, kids who were pretty lost, pretty fucked up to begin with.

"He'd get them in the car and he'd pretend he was gonna arrest them, and he'd call them assholes and liars. He'd say, 'You lying little fucker! You fuckwipe! You know what you're doing with your life?' And then he'd go from bad cop to good cop. Sit silently for thirty, forty seconds. Then he'd be understanding. Said he knew how hard it was to be a kid, especially these days—the drugs, the pornography, the crazy motherfuckers out there who'd kill you for looking at them the wrong way. Wasn't easy trying to grow up, to be a man, all this confusion. No boundaries.

"So many people talking to you all at once, giving you directions, telling you what to do and what not to do. Then nobody talking to you at all. Leave you in a room for hours and hours to listen to water drip somewhere. Insects go *chir chir chir.* Paint chips. Water stains on the wallpaper. And John, God. He went back and forth between rage and understanding in seconds. He could perform. This is what he loved.

"John fed the kids, too. He'd sit them down at the kitchen table when he got them to his house, and he'd make sandwiches. He set out jars of olives and pickles, and he'd ask them if they liked mustard or mayo. He liked being a nice guy to them, even when it was one or two or three in the morning, even when he knew what he was about to do."

I heard the furnace down in the basement, while I was on the phone with Paige. And I thought of how cold the glass on the window had been, earlier, when I touched it. Under your bootsoles.

"You don't have kids, you said?"

"I don't," she told me.

"That's lucky."

Silence. Only the hum. Live wire.

"So, John, this guy out in Chicago, he'd get them in his house, and the thing then was to get the handcuffs on them. After the cuffs—then . . . well. Don't ever let anyone put handcuffs on you."

Paige was quiet.

"He'd tell them it was a trick, part of his clown routine, or it went along with him being a cop, like he claimed. Just a joke, a trick. These weren't regular handcuffs, he'd say. But once he had them cuffed, he could do anything he wanted to them for as long as he wanted. And he was so fucking angry, so fucking humiliated.

"After everything was found out, after they caught him, neighbors started saying how on certain nights dogs howled and whined for half the night, and these neighbors would wake their husband or wife up and say, 'Listen. That sound? Is that an animal? A baby?'

"Like no sound they'd ever heard. But nobody knew. They thought it was a baby, or animals—maybe raccoons or bobcats or something.

"We're not talking about out in the country," I whispered to her. "Not some farm on the side of a hill somewhere. This was a neighborhood in Chicago with quarter-acre lots, TV antennas, bushes, squares of lawn people watered after work. You know what I'm talking about?"

"I do."

"And this wasn't in some storybook somewhere. It didn't happen in Germany with goblins and black knights, or in Salem three hundred years ago. And it wasn't some guy with a tail or some subhuman with an IQ of seventy."

"I know, Earl."

"Because the thing is, Paige, the thing I can't leave alone, the thing I can't get away from—"

Then I stopped. Just stopped. Closed my eyes in the darkness. The phone was still live at my mouth and ear. John gone, John shot, John lethally injected. Gone John.

If you want me again look for me.

He was God almost. Master of Death, King of Life, Servant to None. And they encamped against it and fought against it. In the

Bible. But he was unto Him. A Master. None but unto Him. John. So long, John.

The beginning was the word.

I stopped. Listened, paused.

Heard Paige breathe at her end of the line.

Paige, Earl.

Two people.

Two human beings, alone but together.

Look for me.

"Paige," I whispered very very low. "Paige," I said again. "This thing I'm telling you about—this was in Chicago, the Windy City, and it wasn't too too long ago. And this was a guy who visited sick kids in the hospital because he wanted to cheer them up. You know what I'm saying?"

"Yes."

Outside the windows the bare branches of trees looked like webs.

"A bunch of them had rags or underwear stuffed so far down their throats that during the autopsies they had to use forceps to get it out." I needed to blow my nose. I felt like I needed a handkerchief.

"He'd take a rope, and he'd tie it around their necks. Then he'd put the handle of a hammer on top of the first knot, and he'd tie off the handle. It was like a tourniquet for the neck. A twist or two and the rope began to sink into the flesh, and they'd be coughing, and he'd say, 'This is just a trick,' and sometimes he'd wait."

I stopped and waited awhile.

"I hate to say this," I said to Paige, and then I was crying, even though I was pretty sure she couldn't tell from her end of the line. "I hate that I know about this.

"He'd fill up the bathtub, and he'd grab them by the hair and push their heads underwater. He liked to watch the bubbles coming up, and then he'd let them breathe a little. He'd wait for hours, sometimes even till five or six in the morning before he finally killed them. Keeping them barely alive, keeping them with him, close and still a little warm."

Some freckled boy. Boy with pebbles and twigs and a spider in his jeans pocket. Could barely wait to show you. Lovely excited curious boy. Know what? Guess what? Hey, you wanna know? Boy with light in deep eyes.

"Total power, total control. And then he'd carry the body into the crawl space. He'd climb down, dig a trench, pour lime, cover the body over."

I stopped and breathed deeply to slow myself down, and I could hear Paige breathing.

"I'm sorry," I said, and she kept breathing deeply. I was crying, and she and I, we were together on this. But she didn't know I was crying.

So it came to pass. You will hardly know who.

"Five years he did this. There were something like twenty-nine under the house, and they think he may have killed five or ten more."

The refrigerator made a clicking sound.

"And all the time he slept there, and everyone else in the neighborhood slept."

Paige blew her nose and said, "You lie in bed at night and you think of this?"

"I can't stop."

"You don't sleep?"

"Not much," I told her.

Water from my eyes dripped down the telephone and went over my fist holding the phone and hit the front of my T-shirt and fell on my lap. To pass, it came. I am or what I mean. What you could take from a boy. A simple boy, stolen child.

All the souls that were therein.

For a long time we stayed on the phone without making any sound. The two of us.

THREE

I was sitting on a radiator, which was in front of a window, a cup of tea in one hand, a cigarette in the other. I watched the smoke float slowly up, turn blue, then gray, then disappear near the ceiling. I sipped, and looked at the woman kneading dough at a table next to the sink.

This was so long ago it might have happened to somebody else, to somebody named Ted or Dean or Charles. The borders are skewed, the boundaries porous. There are films and veils. Smoke, mist, mirrors, sand.

A desert of mirrors. Sea of sand.

We had known each other only a short while. Both of us taught at a school for boys. Private high school. St. Jude's. Boys in white shirts and ties. She had come up to me in the teachers' lounge. She said I looked a little lost, looked like I could use a friend, looked like a person who needed a person to talk to. Looked like a person who might listen, might really hear.

That was so rare in this world. Someone who listened and really heard. Looked and actually saw. Took it in. Listened, looked more, slowly, carefully. Didn't just wait for a break in the spiel so he or she could begin to run their own spiel back.

She began to ask me questions and to tell me about herself. She was from New York City, Manhattan, but went to college at Berkeley, spent a year as a teacher in Oakland, lived for several years in San Francisco.

Lemon-colored houses. Fuchsia, orange orange. Hills and ocean. Cedar, air. The fucking Pacific Ocean. Big. Huger almost than God.

This was her kitchen, her apartment in Boston, her present life. It was a big room with lots of bare space. Dark woodwork, white walls. A lamp on the far side of the room, near the pantry, made a circle on the linoleum floor. There were shadows. There were snapshots on the refrigerator door, held by magnets that were shaped like fruit. An apple held a photograph of three kids, kids maybe four or five years old, laughing kids. There was a picture of a woman with long black hair, smiling, a thin gap between two front teeth. The woman in the picture wore black, she looked at the camera. There was a picture of a man, wearing glasses, in sunlight. He might have been thirty years old, and he was not smiling. A pear held his picture to the refrigerator.

Joan saw me looking and said, "That's Chuck." I didn't say anything or look away from the photograph. "From San Francisco," she said.

Then I nodded. "You lived with him."

She said, "Yes," and her hands continued to work the dough.

I stubbed out my cigarette in an ashtray, sipped more tea and watched her.

She was small—a few inches over five feet. She had short hair and wore a white T-shirt, tan chinos. She had no socks on, and her feet were small and pale. I could see veins near the ankle. She danced, she had said to me, and I could tell. You could tell too if you looked. I could see the muscles in her arms as she worked the dough. Ropes of it rose under the skin, there were long threads of tendon in the forearms. She had a dancer's posture. No slouch or sag. The curve of the back, the butt, the legs— were all a taut line, a tense sure curve.

The window behind me was open, and I could hear the wind in the trees. Rippling lightly, fanning September leaves. It was Friday night, after eleven, and I listened to the wind, felt the air on my back. I'm in Boston, I thought. I'm in a kitchen in Boston, and a woman named Joan is making bread. She used to teach kids in Oakland, she lived for three years in San Francisco, maybe in Berkeley.

Fix the place and the time. Draw a line. Black line on white paper. Trace a stick in sand.

"What about you?" she asked. "Tell me about you," she said. "Tell me about your girlfriends," she said. "Were they pretty?" In a voice that was light and low, dark, high. A voice I could swim. In.

This woman, this Friday-night room. She knew some things about me.

.

In class I made my students close their eyes. Sit up straight. I read them a haiku by Bashō. " 'All the stones are dead, / the waters withered and gone— / winter and nothing.' " Told them to take three slow, deep breaths when I finished reading. In slowly through the nose, all the way in, slowly, down to the toes, then hold, and think of the particulars of the haiku—stones dead, waters withered and gone, winter and nothing—breathe out slowly through mouth. Breathe three times. Then read it again. Same haiku. Same three breaths. Then again. Then a second Bashō haiku. " 'Grass for a pillow, / and a dog also crying, / howling all night.' " Three breaths. A second and third reading with breaths after each. Third Bashō haiku, all translated by Sam Hamill. " 'At breaking sunrise, / glistening whitefish—an inch / of utter whiteness.' " Same thing. Breaths, reread. Picture the details. Breaths. Reread. Breathe all the way in, breaking sunrise, whitefish, utter whiteness—exhale. Looked from boy face to boy face to boy face. Their closed eyes. Open still spaces in their minds. Concentrated, relaxed, balanced, calm. My sweet hooligans. My barbarians.

Said open your eyes. Wake up. Be here now.

Told her. She looked. Saw, smiled.

.

She lifted the dough in her hands and slapped the shiny ball. She stepped through the circle of light on the floor, took a metal bowl from the pantry, put the dough in the bowl. Then she covered it with a dish towel.

Looked at me and crossed to the stove. Opened the oven door, put the bowl inside, closed the door.

"The towel's gonna burn," I said.

She looked at me again and smiled again. I saw things in her eyes. Light, color, heat, depth, shine. Memory and longing.

"The oven's not on," she said. Ago.

"Then what're you doing?"

Smiled. So much. There too. That smile. Teeth.

"Bread has to rise."

"Why the oven?"

"Because there's heat from the burners up here," she said to me, and pointed to the top of the stove. I saw cords in her arm.

.

She sat at the kitchen table and asked me for a cigarette. I fumbled one out of the pack, tricky fingers, and watched her hold it to her lips. Flicked the lighter, leaned, held the flame to the end of the cigarette. Smoke streamed from her mouth and nose. Billowed, bloomed.

"How long's it take to rise?" I asked.

She shrugged, eyes wet from the smoke. "Forty-five, fifty minutes."

I looked at my watch, and it was nearly midnight. Leaves outside. Boston night. Breezy air out there.

.

She asked if I wanted more tea, and I said, "Yes."

"Same kind?"

"What else you got?"

She looked in a cabinet over the stove, and I could see the arch of her foot.

"Lemon," she said. "English Breakfast, Constant Comment."

"English Breakfast. Maybe that."

"Sure," she said. "Why not."

.

She set the cup down on the table in front of me, and as she did, her arm brushed my shoulder. Touched skin on fabric.

Me.

Oh.

I was still sitting on the radiator, but it was so close to the table that it could have been another kitchen chair. She sat in a chair and took a cigarette from the pack.

Outside, the wind was still moving branches in the trees.

"You cold?" she asked.

I shook my head. "You?"

"A little." Cool.

I turned to close the window, but she said, "No, the air feels good." Fall air.

Felt good also? What? Room? Light? Me here?

She stood up, left the room, through a doorway into an unlit hall. Rustled, ruffled. Came back holding a gray sweater. Gathered the sweater at the waist, lifted it over her head. Which disappeared. Saw her head reappear, then her arms snaked into the sleeves. She straightened the sweater at the arms and waist, smiled at me.

I lifted the cup to my lips. Blew away some of the heat, watched waves on the surface. Sweet heat, neat heat, ripples and waves.

·

She reached into the oven and took out the bowl. The dough had risen so the towel looked like a balloon. She turned the oven on, then brought the bowl to the table by the sink, took out the dough, and began to knead again.

"How long you do that?" I asked.

"Few minutes."

"You want help?"

"No, no," she said. "You mind watching?"

I shook my head. "I'm fine," I told her. Said, thought, I like watching.

·

She. Joan crossed the circle of light again and took two bread pans from the pantry. Dark room the size of a refrigerator. She got a can of shortening, reached into it, and her hand came out with a white glob of grease. Shiny, nearly half disgusting. Slippery, sex wet. Sheath. Watched her grease the insides of the two pans, then she went to the sink.

I heard water run and watched her wash her hands. Her hands were small and strong. Water and soap and that knowing of hers. How she knew what to do and where everything was and where to reach to turn water on and take transparent bar of amber soap and lather up on pale fair skin and after where exactly and how to reach for a towel and efficiently and capably dry her hands. Knew precisely who and where she was.

When she turned she stepped surely. Got back to the table next to the sink, she took the dough and separated it into two loaves. Her hands shaped the dough. They slapped and patted and stroked.

·

She taught math and biology to the same boys I taught. St. Jude's. Boys named Joshua and Sean. Nicholas and Michael and Matthew. They loved her, flirted with her. She was strict and tough, and still they adored her. I'd see her in her room when I passed in the hall—in a dress and sweater—the boys in neat rows, looking up, and she moved sometimes down the rows, amid the boys. They wore ties and blue or white or yellow dress shirts with button-down collars. They had begun to shave and some of them had acne, and some still had braces on their teeth.

·

I was still sitting on the radiator, the windowsill and window screen at my lower back, and could feel the warmth from the oven and cool air on my back from the window. Then she said, "Almost done."

And I could sit like all of time was here, was right there in the room, sitting, air, her, the saying and turning. What she did. Maybe what she said. Possibly what she thought as I watched, as I thought, and her so sure. Each tic and movement. Knew exactly and precisely what and when to do. Dark air, Boston night, near midnight, within, without, outside, just on the other side of the screen.

She brought the pans to the oven, opened the door with a dish towel, put the bread inside. She wiped her hands on the towel, sat down at the table, lit a cigarette.

·

The kitchen was growing warm. The whole room was beginning to fill with the smell of baking bread. I looked at my watch, and it was after one. Three thin arms on the face of the watch. Under the crystal, ticking.

"It's getting late," I said.

She shrugged. As though to say, What's late?

"Tell me when I should go," I said.

She nodded and asked me if I wanted a drink. Something different and stronger than tea. Something other. "I'm gonna have some wine," she said. "You game?"

"Why not." Or, Sure, absolutely.

She took two long-stemmed glasses from a cabinet, then got a bottle from the refrigerator. She set the glasses on the table and poured. I saw red light, dark red liquid, called wine, in the glass. She handed me one, tapped glasses—*ping.*

"Isn't the radiator getting uncomfortable?" she asked. Drew attention to me and to what I was doing and not doing. Which is to say. Just sitting. My observation post.

I sipped, then stood up. My legs were stiff. I slowly walked the length of the kitchen. She stood next to the table. I was a head taller than her. I sat down at the table, watched her bring the glass to her mouth. How the red liquid swayed. Caught light. Her lips. The thin rim of the glass. Pursed, touched.

·

She stood up, took a towel, opened the stove door. The loaves were beginning to brown. She saw that, I saw that.

But she closed the door again.

She stood by the table and poured more wine into our glasses. Stood. A long strong line from heels, balls, toes of her feet. Ankle and calf and so on. To the top of her head. Her shoulder was inches from my face. I could see the threads in her sweater, a piece of lint at the elbow. Curly lines of gray wool woven and interwoven in the sweater. Millions of very tiny curls that held air between and among them and was why wool was warm, why wool was soft, could provide solace. How cats loved to lie on wool. Close their eyes, knead.

She wore small gold earrings, and the skin at her neck was flushed. Thought of petals, of milk, of sheets on a clothesline. Sunshine and cotton. Hung clean, windblown.

"How much longer?" I asked.

"You getting impatient?"

I shook my head. "Curious." Liked to know, inquire, ask, if that was all right. No harm meant nor offense taken. No crime, no foul.

"Ten or so minutes," she said. Then she. In Boston. She picked up the pack of cigarettes from the table. "Okay?" she asked.

"Course," I told her. "No need to ask."

"People like to be asked," she said. "It's important." Then she smiled, and the smile went to her eyes. And again. The shadows, depths, mysteries, light plus heat, years and miles, the fucking infinity there. In her. Mirrors to the soul.

Could go anywhere and forever, and did.

.

"Can I use the bathroom?" I asked. Because you drink tea, wine. Over time.

She. Hand lifted, finger or two or three, pointed to the hall outside the kitchen. She was sitting on a chair, her knees drawn to her chest, her feet on the edges of the chair.

By this time in the night. There in that room, that exact place.

Oriented in all three spheres. As to time, place, person. Could name the last five presidents in descending order. Could interpret—reasonably, responsibly—an aphorism, such as: A bird in hand is worth two in the bush. Such as: A rolling stone gathers no moss. Such as: Strike when the iron is hot.

.

Not say some inappropriate thing such as sucking chest wound or ligature, or juxtapose sexual and violent imagery—for example, naked young woman and glistening knife, the interpenetration of anything anywhere. Mingle, intermingle.

Just shut the fuck up. Keep it zipped, as it were.

That small smirk.

.

In the bathroom I looked at myself in the mirror over the sink. My eyes seemed dark, I needed to shave, I didn't like the way I looked.

This was so long ago that I was somebody else. I'm not who I was, nor will be.

How the thought and the action. Reaction, interaction, impulse, desire.

.

When I got back to the kitchen, I was in the kitchen. At that time and place. That person. Oriented in all three spheres—as to person, place, time. Criteria for sanity. Who are you? Where are you? What's today's date? What they asked you in the emergency room. And if you couldn't answer all three correctly, up to the ward with you.

And what I did was: I started thinking how I was in Boston, and how most of the city was asleep. I pictured the Charles River, and the brownstones on Commonwealth Avenue. I saw the winos sitting outside the library in Copley Square, on the ledges of the library building, in the sun, facing the open cobblestoned square, and I thought of standing in the Park Street subway station waiting for the Harvard train, a woman with long shining dark hair playing the cello near the stairs, two levels down. Way under the ground.

Winos in sunshine, and Bach—such sorrowful strains—so far underground, and the clacking metal on metal shriek of trains and trolleys moving.

"It's strange," I said to her. To Joan. In kitchen.

"What?"

"Being here."

．

She stood up, took the dish towel, opened the door to the oven. I felt waves of heat, warmth, watched her bent form.

She took first one bread pan from the oven, then the other. She brought them carefully to the table next to the sink. Knew each moment, each second, each movement. So confident. So precise. Almost planned. She turned the pan upside down, tapped, and lifted the pans from bread.

"There it is," she said, and patted the brown loaves.

"Honest to God," I said, and took a cigarette from the pack. I flicked the lighter, drew smoke in.

Thought, Christ on the cross. Sweet Jesus. Smiling damn Buddha.

"It has to cool," she said.

"How long?"

"Few minutes," she—in the kitchen, at that late hour, but early in my knowing her—told me. "Not long."

．

Thought how soon there'd be a day when we were walking along the Charles River—her and me—just walking like two citizens, two people, and she took my hand. So simple. She took my hand in her hand and held it as we walked. So basic and simple. Her hand holding my hand, walking. The brown river moving past. Held my hand with strong soft light fingers, dry warm palm and heel of hand. Hers. Mine. Together like that. She just reached— simply—took and held my hand. Human contact. No big deal. But so tender. So kind. And I fucking started to cry. She saw that. Knew. Squeezed my hand. Said, I think, something like it was okay and not to worry.

Fool. Damned fucking fool. Me, girl, young woman takes hand, and he had the tears running down his face. Sorry sad fuck. Touched Earl's heart in there. Jesus, it pierced him.

.

Then—fuck—I swear as the day is long.

What she did was:

Took butter from the refrigerator and a knife from a drawer. She laid them on the table with the bread. She touched a loaf and pulled her hand quickly away.

.

The boys for a while loved me too. Loved that I swore sometimes, loved that I cared so much, was passionate about history and literature and texts. Loved that my moods cycled up, and the pressed words rushed from me, and I told them to get their thumbs out of their mouths and their hands out of their pants. Said, "Shut the fucking television off. Don't be a mouth breather. Open a book. Read with a pencil in one hand. Read slow. Then slower still. Underline. Write in the margins. Back up. Read again.

"Go very slow. Then slower still. This is not TV. I repeat, this is not TV. I'm not a fucking television. What we do when we read is sacred, it's holy. It will make you come alive, it will animate you, not deaden you."

Held a book over my head. "Walt Whitman. 'If you want me again look for me under your bootsoles. / You will hardly know who I am or what I mean, / But I shall be good health to you nevertheless, / And filter and fibre your blood. / Failing to fetch me at first keep encouraged, / Missing me one place search another, / I stop some where waiting for you.' This is sacred text. This can, this will, transform you."

.

She looked at me, and asked, "You okay?"

I nodded and shrugged at the same time.

Okay? Like, what was that supposed to mean? Like, what the hell was with that?

"What is it?" she said. Wanted to know.

I looked at her short hair, her small features, at the gold earrings in her ears.

"I was thinking of a dream I had."

"Bad dream?"

I nodded, slowly. Just as slowly shook my head.

Could still hear the wind outside, but other than that there was no noise anywhere. No luffing wind, no tick or shiver or hum. Circle of light still near the pantry, pictures on the refrigerator as well. Gap-toothed woman, Chuck from Berkeley, Oakland, San Francisco, California, apple magnet, three kids. Whoever they were. Some other side of continent. Time ago.

"You don't want to talk about it?" she asked in a quiet voice. Looked closely at me. Observed carefully.

Not like most people.

I. What I did was. Shook my head, felt her eyes on my face. Thought of Boston, where we were then. Then pictured her in Berkeley, California, earlier. Possibly in a room, or walking in the streets late at night. Lemon trees, eucalyptus trees.

Then she stood up and went to the table near the sink. I looked at the bare walls, the high ceiling. I heard her cutting bread, then scraping from the stick of butter.

Steam rose from the loaf, and I thought how this was Joan's kitchen. We were in Boston. It was ticking away. Three thin arms of my watch. Was in fact two in the morning, and we had known each other two weeks.

She walked toward me, a piece of bread in each hand. I smelled the bread, saw melting butter. Her eyes were on my face.

Again, that smile. The things therein.

She handed me a piece, and the bread was warm. "Here," she said.

I brought it to my mouth, bit, and she was watching me.

"What was the dream about?"

I shook my head slowly.

She took a bite of the bread. Her piece. Separate. "Someday," she said, "you'll tell me."

Then we sat. Ate bread. Listened to faint wind in the trees outside.

·

The cat was warm and soft, the cat smelled faintly of musk, and I loved to press my nose into the fur on his back. He purred loudly, and sometimes it was like a crazy motor inside. How purring was like wool. Cool nights.

He climbed under the bureau in the bedroom, and sometimes into the laundry basket. When I woke up in the morning, he'd be stretched out next to my pillow, and he'd open his dark eyes and rub a paw across his face.

He sat on my stomach as I watched television, and late at night, when I couldn't sleep, I'd wake him and pick him up in my arms, and I'd stroke the spot on his neck that made the purring start.

One night I couldn't find him, and I looked out the window at the moonlit night, and I saw him lying on the lawn, his head twisted at an angle.

I went outside, swimming, sliding, as it were, and picked him up, and his head. As though it was attached by string, and somewhere nearby—in bushes, in woods, in shadows—I heard soft laughter, and I kept looking and looking. Then felt my hands—wet and sticky. Looked down, and there was a hole, an opening, where one of the cat's eyes had been, and blood was flowing from the socket.

Seemed as though the sky itself was red, and rain was scarlet, was redder than all the wine of the world. I tried, know I tried. To swim. Felt somehow, some way. Was underneath, flailing. Drifting—only slow—farther and farther. Deeper down.

FOUR

Nothing's working tonight, no matter what I do. I turn over again
and again, keep my feet inside the covers, then outside until the
air cools my toes and I can breathe better, breathe like I'm in air-
conditioning on a July day.

They've got these rubberized mattresses, in case you pee in the
night. So the sheet won't stay in place on the mattress and is always sliding off and around and all over, bunched up, and your
skin sticks to the mattress, and it's noisy every time you move.
Even a little. But very quiet if you keep still. You don't blink and
you follow every breath in and down and around, then out slow as
snails and syrup and shit trying sloooowly to flow uphill.

But then the noise starts up again across the hall. Claire Hite
moaning like she's having sex, only it's dreams because Claire's
husband has been dead fourteen years—I heard this, they talk—
and the only nights she spends away from home are when she's

here or with the Carmelite nuns on retreat. Nuns with the big robes and habits. Veils and wimples and what have you. Clacking rosary beads, pale faces.

Hath anointed. Lo.

Things slow down for a while, then this big vent over the doorway kicks on, and I start to picture the air flowing through the vents and pipes and blowers and screens, from one part of the hospital to another, through miles and miles of dusty ducts and pipes, blowers, screens, in and out of every room and hallway and passageway in the buildings, like ghosts, like shadows, wraiths. Then I start to wonder if this is the same air that was here a week or a month ago, and then I'm wondering if it's the same air all over the world, from hundreds of years ago. From Alexander conquering the world to Jack the Ripper eviscerating prostitutes in foggy London. Jesus and Hitler and Babe Ruth and Joan of Arc could all have breathed the same air, and now it's blowing through the vents here. Blowing through sleeping rooms, and over and in and around and on—everybody, everything, as it was in the beginning, is now and ever shall be—earth everlasting and beyond and before. Amen, be men.

C and Tree men.

Alicia Powers comes down the hallway, her flashlight beam bouncing on the walls and ceiling, her feet scraping the floor like fine sandpaper. She leans in the door, and her beam catches me with my eyes open. I'm jacklit. Wide, bright, frozen, caught.

"Earl," she says, and I say, "Alicia."

"Why you up?"

"Can't sleep," I say. "Can you get me a shot?"

"I'll look at your chart," she tells me. "C'mon if you want."

I follow her down the hall. She's—Alicia—in her forties, I think I would guess. Always looks like she just woke up. Hair and face puffy, clothes wrinkled.

She goes into the nurses' station, pulls a notebook from a shelf. The lights are bright here. Peter Elledge comes down the hallway toward us, his flashlight beam on the ceiling. He clicks the light off when he reaches us. He pats my shoulder when he passes. Touches me on the shoulder. Nice man, nice man. Doesn't say anything.

Your basic human contact.

Simple as.

Light travels. Light. Travels. Speed of.

"I can give you a shot," Alicia says.

She gets up, goes to a cabinet, takes out some things, then comes to me. The smell of alcohol makes my eyes sting. She swabs a place on my upper arm, cold, and I look down at floor, other side of room. She says, "Ready." Says, "A pinch." Slight sting. Then pops—fuck—the needle. In. Pushes the plunger. It's out it's out so fast. Blink open, blink your eyes open. Okay. Already over. Quickjustlikethat. And it's like I can feel heat spreading through me, like air in vents, through screens, pipes, behind walls, over ceilings, underground.

I go to the dayroom, which is dark, and I light a cigarette. It glows, and I blow smoke in the dark and picture how it would drift up, would collide with the ceiling, the walls. Smoke is the same as air and light and God. That same way. You know. You think you know.

This thing that is faith. So as to move mountains. So as to bear all. Is patient. Does not boast of itself. You can't really see it or hold it in your hands like a knife or a piece of bread, but it is still there. You know it even if you can't taste it or touch it. Nobody living has seen Jesus or Jack the Ripper, but we know they have been here. We know it by the pictures and stories. We know the fog, and the smile, the knife pressing into flesh. Jesus bleeding from the thorns on his head, from the nails, the wound in his side.

Stigmata. Where you bleed where He bled. Feel as He felt. Faith so as to move blood. Cathexis. Focus as mental energy. All brought to light, to bear, bring to bear. Draw bead on. As to light. Laser. Concentrated light. Bear left. Two men went hunting. Two Irish men. Two Italian men. Two Polish men. Went to woods. Saw sign. Bear left. Went home.

Ho.

Man in a suit and a tie sitting in a tree. What do you call him? Irish man? Polish man? Black man? Branch manager.

Ha.

Say to an Italian man in a three-piece suit? What to? Will the defendant please rise.

I draw more smoke in, and Alicia comes to the doorway. "That shot doing anything?" she asks.

"Not. Yet." Did she notice? Pause.

"It will," she tells me.

Then I lean back in the chair, and I do—indeed I do—begin to feel it. As she has promised. She spoke truly. She was right. And it's. Warm and heavy, and I start being young again. Think hard, think soft. Concentrate. Bring mind to bear. Bear down. Not bear left, nor right. Leave the woods. Go home. So: I start when Ed and I were in the backyard, and Dad was watering the grass and he squirted us, and we laughed at how cold the water felt.

Start again, back there. With love. Warmth. Collect. Recollect. Inside, outside. Now and then, there.

It was later, then, and the bedroom was too hot, so we had spread sheets on the living room floor. They, the sheets. They were cool beneath us. Air passed in and out of the windows, blowing the curtains out like sails, then sucking them back to the screen. Hot thick summer night. Could cut the air.

Much later—that summer night then—when Ed was asleep

and all the lights were out except the one in the kitchen, I heard the crack of beer cans, the foamy pouring. My father said the name Ida Irga, said she was a woman who lived on Grove Street, on the wrong side of Beacon Hill. She was seventy-five, lived on the fifth floor of a brick apartment building. I heard my father sip, and in his late-night, half-drunk voice, he went on. Kept saying.

Close your eyes. Listen. Faint. Then clearer. Low but quiet and quite clear. Careful, ears cocked.

"She lived alone, and when they got there, she'd been dead two days already. She was on the living room floor, a dress completely torn away from her body, her legs wide apart and propped up on two different chairs. He had put a pillow under her butt, and there was a pillowcase tied around her neck."

Breeze in curtains. Cool sheet. Night so hot, heat and humidity. Fry an egg. House collects the heat all day. Holds and stores it like a cell. Memory.

"Was that . . ." my mother began, but she spoke so low I couldn't hear the rest of what she said.

"No," Dad said. "With his hands. He apparently used his hands."

Strangle, strangled. Neck, throat.

Old lady, chicken neck. His strong hands.

My mother said something else, then my father said, "When they came in the front door, the apartment door . . . well, this was what they saw." Spread there. Manager of the apartment building. Passkey, then cops. Two days the phone unanswered, mail and newspapers not taken in.

"Her wallet wasn't touched," Dad said. "Even though there was money in it, and there was a gold watch on a bookcase. No sign of forced entry, nothing broken, so of course he must have talked his way in."

Words from Mom. Light on in the kitchen. Fly caught and dead in the white glass of the orb around the lightbulb, light fixture, in the middle of the kitchen ceiling. Black speck, lying curled inside white glass. Former fly. Deceased. Cease and desist.

"She's the fourth one," Dad said.

"Who is he?" Mom asked. My father didn't say anything.

"Why's he doing this?" Mom, she wanted to know.

One of them got up. I heard a few steps, then the refrigerator door, then another crack of a can. Foam.

"He has very powerful hands," my father said, and I pictured my father's big hands, the thick knuckles, the blue veins on the back of his hands. Then I thought of Mrs. Maloney and her hands, and I wondered how strong hands had to be.

"This nurse on Boylston Street. In Boston, in town," my father said. "She called the cops." He paused, and I heard pouring.

"She got this package in the mail. A doll with string around its neck, and a note that said, 'You're next.' "

My mother said something I couldn't make out.

"Just—you never know. Just be very careful," Dad said.

Mom said something, and Dad said, "No, I don't think so. I'd rather they didn't know before they have to."

The breeze filled the curtains, and a car—lights on ceiling, walls—went by out front. Was driving by. Hot night. Just out for a spin.

I heard footsteps, and I closed my eyes tight and felt my mother standing in the doorway, looking down on us. Glasses, hair like wires sticking up and out all over her head. Glasses, arms at her sides, hands dangling down.

Footsteps went back toward the kitchen. She said, "They're fine."

.

The weather was unusually warm the July that Joan Millis and I lived in Brookline, near Boston, the summer before we were married. It reached into the high nineties near the end of the month and was so humid that when we touched the walls in the kitchen our hands came away wet.

Sometimes it got so oppressive, the air almost greasy, that we'd leave the apartment at ten or eleven at night, and we'd drive around town, across the river, then out toward Watertown and Belmont. We'd keep the windows all the way down, and the air moved over us, and Joan said, "It can't last forever."

We didn't have air-conditioning. We didn't have much money hardly. Plus being nervous about someone gaining entry.

Many of the windows in houses and apartments stayed open, and lying in bed late at night, we'd hear a phone ring, and radios and televisions going, and conversations sounded like they came from the next room rather than from down the street. Traveled across air, branches, telephone poles and wires and electrical cables. What have you.

Whatever. The fuck.

I'd wake up sometimes at two or three in the morning, and people would be sitting and talking in low voices on the front steps of the buildings. Not too loud either. The heat, and it being late outside. You could still hear them nonetheless. You were careful, kept your ear and nose to the ground.

Listened, paid attention.

We talked often about how we would get married, me and her. Some nights we decided on a big wedding in New York City, with a country-club reception and champagne. What the hell. The nine or ten yards. Then the next day we talked about going to a courthouse and having a judge marry us, with one or two friends as witnesses. Friends such as we had.

Manner of speaking.

She had been working at the school a year longer than me. That meant something. Both of us pretty young yet. Kids not much younger than us, really. Ha. Me a teacher. Those fucking kids. So for the summer we were lazy, shared most of the cooking and cleaning, and I stayed up till one or two some nights. Sometimes really late. Sometimes later even, later than late.

I'd read in the papers about bodies found in the woods or behind warehouses or in the trunks of abandoned cars. This was then. But every day in the newspaper, every day. In New York that summer—this was some time ago—a man who used a .45, which is to say a big fucking gun, a handheld cannon—was shooting young women who had shoulder-length hair. There were articles in all the magazines, and hairdressers said so many, so very many, women wanted their hair cut short. And who is to blame them?

Sitting in a parked car on a city street very late at night. The happy couple. Leaves and shimmering light. Whisper almost, love like that. Long hair of the woman.

And he. Smile, that smile.

Boom.

Cry for help.

The city wept.

Once in a while she asked me how I spent my days, and I wouldn't be able to tell her. I took walks, and one time I went to the Gardner Museum by the Fens and brought home a postcard of a Rembrandt self-portrait. In the painting, not a painting, a sketch really, Rembrandt was in his early twenties, and already he had light around his head, almost like God. And the painting, it was just this tossed-off little sketch, really, just a pen-and-ink thing on paper from when he was a kid almost, no more than twenty-one or -two maybe, and it was tiny. It was the size of a fucking cigarette pack. But shit. Christ. There on that small piece of paper. Fucking H. Rembrandt. The nose, the cheeks. The boy. You talk chops, you talk life. You got an eye, a soul, a fucking tingling piece of vibrating humming life there. And so quiet. Just still as a. Not showing. There, like there. Alive. Mouse. Glory of simple life, being alive.

We finally got married in August. We did. I didn't tell my family, so to speak, or any of our friends, such as they were, so few, we didn't have too many, just about none, you want to know the truth, and Joan had a woman from work and her husband there as our witnesses. You had to have a witness, to say they'd seen it. To sign on the dotted line and make it official. Commonwealth of Massachusetts. Wherein, declare, city on a hill. Afterward, we ate lunch at a restaurant near the Common. The friend's name was Joy and her husband was Maurice. They had a summer place on a lake in Maine, and they told us we could visit them at the lake whenever we wanted. Nice guy, but French. Always complaining about the bread.

"You call this bread?" he said. Maurice. "This is not bread." Maurice the Frenchman said.

Later, she, Joan cried, and I asked her, asked her why, she said that she had always thought she'd wear white at her wedding and have bridesmaids and cake.

Like we snuck off and it didn't mean a fucking thing. Under the cover of darkness. Ashamed of something or something. She out of deep pity for my utter fucking loneliness. Had never thought to see, isolation. Such.

"We can do it again in California," I said, and she said, "No, it's okay." She told me that no matter what we had done, she'd have always wondered if the other way would have been better. Do this, do that.

"Doesn't matter," she said.

Don't mean a.

Profound compassion. As it were. Form of love.

Give a good goddamn.

When she was in bed late that night, wedding night, ha, I brought her a bowl of coffee ice cream.

"You're sweet," she said, and her eyes shone, and we told each other that we would be great together. We two form a—what—a what—multitude.

After she was asleep, I reached over, lifted slowly her left hand in mine. Felt the ring on her finger. Kissed it. Light lips, touch. Barely. As though nothing bad could ever happen to us, even if the whole world burned. We were steel, metal, granite, we were— fuck yes—more solid than stone.

.

Jane Sullivan was sixty-seven years old, I know, and a nurse. She lived in Dorchester, about five miles from Beacon Hill, from where Ida Irga had been found. She had been, Jane, Sullivan woman, dead for some time, maybe more than a week. Maybe eight days.

She was in a partly filled bathtub, her clothes pulled away, exposing her. You know. Two nylon stockings were tied around her neck. She had been killed about the same time as Ida Irga. She was the fifth victim.

A Boston newspaper printed an appeal on the front page. How they love it. Psychos and the newspaper people and the citizens too. Love love love it. Tingles all over. Printed, front page. "Don't kill again," the newspaper said. "Come to us for help. This appeal is to you, the man you were before this terrible urge overwhelmed you. You don't want to kill again, but you know you will unless you give yourself up." The newspaper said.

Very serious. Very caring. Public interest and what have you. This terrible urge. This thing inside.

Another newspaper—you bet—ran an article about Jack the Ripper, how he would send letters to Scotland Yard. Back in merry old England. Whitechapel. In one, he sent a human kidney. "I ate the other one," he wrote. "It was delicious! Yours in Hell, Jack the

Ripper." Jack killed seven women. With Jane Sullivan, in Dorchester, the Strangler had now killed five. One woman was in her mid-fifties, one in her mid-seventies. The other three were in their sixties.

In the public interest, public spirit.

Hey, come on up and see us sometime. In Maine. My apartment, you want.

The newspapers printed maps that had black circles where each victim had been found. Victim one, victim two, victim three, victim four, victim number five. Four in Boston, one in Lynn. On Gainsborough Street, on Commonwealth Avenue. On Newhall Street in Lynn, north of Boston. Lynn, Lynn, city of sin. Then back to Boston proper. Back within the boundaries. On Grove Street and Columbia Road.

John F. Kennedy, who had been born on Beal Street in Brookline, was the president of the United States. At the time he and his beautiful young wife lived in the White House. John McCormack, from South Boston, was Speaker of the House of Representatives. He was tall and thin, had white hair. Two small children played in the Oval Office. There was a pony on the White House lawn. Macaroni. Called it Macaroni.

Was the Strangler killing his mother? His wife? Why didn't he steal anything? How did he get into his victim's apartments? Why did he ransack drawers yet never seem to take anything? Why were each of these women so brutally exposed? Why no fingerprints, no traces of semen, no hair or blood from the killer? Why no sign of struggle?

For three full months, September, October and November, nothing happened. And wait. Hold your breath. Wait. Not yet. Hold. It. Just a. No arrests, no leads, no new killings. The Salvation Army bell ringers stood on Summer and Winter Streets in downtown Boston. On the Friday after Thanksgiving, they stood near

Filene's and Jordan Marsh, and the people who passed by put coins and sometimes bills in the red pots.

Ring-a-ling-ding, ring-a-ling-ding.

.

"Earl," Alicia Powers says, and I say, the person here says, "What?"

"You gonna stay there all night?" Here.

She's standing about ten feet away.

"What time is it?" I ask.

"It's after three."

I don't say anything. I am a silent witness.

"Did that shot do. Anything?"

I lift. Shoulders. Shrug.

"I can give you another," she says.

I get a cigarette and light it, smoke goes, smoke goes, flick and flick, and she says, "You want another shot?"

"That would help," I tell her.

"I'll be back," she says, and I draw smoke in, with my throat, lungs, bronchioles, little wavy tiny cilia in there, deep down. And I, out here, listen to her shoes scrape out of the room. *Scritch. Scrape. Scratch. Slide.*

Everything moving slow now. Here. Can. Slow slow down. Just feel the night, the dark and quiet, on every side of me. Shhh. Claire Hite isn't making noise anymore, and I can't hear vents or air or even people breathing. Not a single. A. Puff of. Air. Breath. Not moth. No small wing even. There's just the dark and the slow sweet noiseless feeling inside me. Within.

Then I. Start to wonder where Joan is. If she was still with us, still part of the plan, wouldn't she visit me? She could be visiting one of her sisters, or maybe they told her not to come. That part. Maybe they thought it would upset me. Him.

Rattle his cage.

Ruffle his.

We've been married, together, a long, some, a certain—time. She's—was—at one time—my wife. She loves, loved, me. She did when she was around. Where she is, I wonder, I picture and feature and try to focus and fix—my mind—in, on, her face.

You're not the person.

Alicia comes back, I pull up the sleeve on my T-shirt. Smell the alcohol, feel the cold spot on my skin. Upper fucking arm. Muscle, such as it is. Alicia says, "Hold on, Earl."

I, Earl, feel the tiny bite, the heat spreading, then she pulls the needle out, swabs the spot with more alcohol. Fast.

"You should. To bed," she says, and I tell her I will.

"Just one more cigarette," I say. Tell her. The room there.

She moves slowly from the room, here.

It must be after four by now, and way off somewhere I hear engines. Hums, thin high whines—so so far. Cars or planes or trucks—maybe factories, possibly something, the air, the earth, the sky, your eye—I don't know. Picture. I picture the Massachusetts Turnpike, almost empty, except when the lights approach, roar past, and become a clean fading whine somewhere on a distant edge of the dark. So black the dark. So long and wide and empty. So huge, expanding always.

The warmth is going through me some more, and I'm thinking of the whole world out there, and past and before that too, and how in a few hours the buses and trains will be running. And I don't want to move or sleep. I don't want. Would like not, prefer. But to smoke forever in the chair, here, with shots each hour. Just this knowing.

Then I'm thinking of air—again that air—moving through vents, and what Jesus must have thought on the cross as He looked down, as the blood seeped, and life by drips and drops slipped from Him.

Said, "Father, why have. You forsaken me?" As though He

wasn't God or the Son of God. As though the pain, the rage, the alone, the dark, the blank dark were more than He could handle.

"Why?" He asked, and no body or no thing answered. No voice thundering, no bolts of light from the sky.

"Earl," I hear, and when I look up, Peter Elledge is standing in the doorway. "Bed," he says, smiling. My father almost.

And when I stand up, there is a tincture, an amount, a such, of such warmth inside me that I want to be like this for all the years, times, nears, nows, heres—of my and in my only life. Amen.

FIVE

The first time they took Dad away, Ed was ten and I was almost nine. Dad had been lying on the couch in the living room for a long time, ever since he lost his job at the supermarket. Mom kept saying, "Your father's not feeling well." He was having what Mom called "one of his spells."

He grew a beard that had flecks of red and gray in it, and sometimes he called Ed and me into the living room and made us kiss him on the cheek. "Right here," he said, and pointed to a place on his cheek. "Show the old man you still love him. Useless though he be." Pointed to a place between his ear and the side of his mouth. Smelled like wet dog, like sour grapes. Like Old Granddad, Blanchard's Bourbon. "Four years old or more," the label said. Dad said that was pretty fucking funny, you thought about it. Four years old or more.

"Fucking A," Dad said. "Nothing but the best."

"Stick with me, youse kids, you'll see the finer things in life."
Is what Dad said. Then said nothing hour after hour. Eyes wide
open, but nothing there. Then the tears. Face scrunched up in
a ball.

There were large green bottles in the kitchen, and Dad would
get up sometimes and fill a plastic cup with white wine from the
bottles. Sometimes with four years old or more. He wore a gray
sweatshirt and blue pajama bottoms, and his feet were always bare.
His toenails were long and yellow, and once I asked him why he
didn't cut them.

"Why cut the soul from the body?" he said, and his eyes looked
like they were covered by waxed paper, and couldn't see out, and I
left the living room.

He walked real quiet without shoes on. Dad moved like air and
light.

Late one night I woke up at one or two in the morning, and he
was standing at the foot of my bed, staring down at me. His eyes
were almost white in the moonlight. I looked at him a long time.
He looked at me. Then he smiled and walked out of the bedroom
without a sound, the way Indians walked in woods.

I woke up a lot during the nights after that. I thought that my
father was standing and staring, and that he asked me who I was.

"Who are you?" he asked, not in a mean or angry way, but in a
way that showed he was confused and needed to know.

"I'm Earl," I told him.

"Earl who?"

"Earl your son," I said, and his face changed.

"Don't lie to me," he said. "Don't start lying now, or you'll
never be able to stop."

"I'm your son," I kept saying, and then he changed into Ed and then into Brandon next door with his short neck and stumpy arms and legs and then into my mother.

I kept saying, "I'm your son," over and over, but he did not understand that. When he changed back to himself, he had no way of telling what that meant.

.

Mrs. Maloney got me in a corner in her back hall where the cats peed, and she leaned her hip into me and said, "What'd your mother do to him?"

"Nothing," I said, and her hipbone was pressing into my chest.

I looked up and saw faint light on the lenses of her thick glasses, and there were beads of sweat on her upper lip and forehead. All I wanted was some cookies and brownies and to play with Brandon's toys. That's why I went over there. Something sweet and warm to eat, not like at home. And Mrs. M., for the sake of starving Jesus, was going into orbit. I should have been more careful.

She took my earlobe between her thumb and forefinger. She pinched it and then began to twist my ear.

"How old are you?"

"I'll be nine," I whispered.

"When will you be nine, feces?"

"December."

"Your mother dropped you into the world near Our Savior's birthday."

I felt her nails on the back of my neck.

"Is that right? You and the sweet Baby Jesus were born the same month?"

"Yes."

"And now you and your mother put your father on the couch

to harm him. And my own boy is a moon calf, a driveler, a brain like a jelly doughnut."

I shook my head.

"Lying child," she said.

There was light from the small window in the door that went out to the porch. There were red-and-white-checked curtains on the window. The walls were cracked, and in one spot the dusty slats showed where the plaster had fallen out.

Mrs. M., not me. But couldn't say. Whoever it was did it to you, I swear to Christ on the cross, it wasn't me. Nor did I make Brandon the way he be.

"Where do you think you're going, little man?"

"To visit," I said.

"To visit," she said, her voice imitating my voice. Then there was the wild west of Ireland in her voice. "To visit whom, may I inquire?" Mayo and Clifden, and the Twelve Pins by Slyne Head. The great long hunger. Potatoes rotting in the fields, and eyes as big and haunted by the hunger and the hatred. The hills of Connemara. The bay at Galway.

"Brandon and yourself."

"And then go where, may I ask?"

"Out."

"Out where?" Her face was red, and she breathed as though she'd been running.

"You chase little girls, don't you?"

I shook my head.

"You want to do something to them, don't you?"

There were beads of sweat on her face.

A fingernail dug into the back of my neck.

"You'll go telling your mother, boy."

"No," I whispered. "I don't tell."

She smiled, and I saw the silver wires that held her teeth in.

Time passed with neither of us moving. Hours passed. Minutes and seconds passed. Time went by without any sound from either one of us. And our faces so close. And then we heard footsteps in the kitchen on the other side of the dark door, Brandon's slippers shuffling across the linoleum, and he said, "Mama," and waited for a long time, with me and Mrs. Maloney barely breathing. Then louder he said, "Muummma whearaarr youuu?" Thick fat tongue.

Mrs. Maloney took her hands away from me and stepped back, and then the door to the hall, the door from her kitchen, opened, and Brandon stood in the doorway, squinting to see us, his cuffs rolled up on his red checked pants.

"What the . . ." he began. Whut duh. And she said, Mrs. Maloney said, "What's the problem now?"

Brandon didn't say anything, just looked at us like we were television or a stain on the wall. Saw just nothing. Flat behind his slanted eyes. And Mrs. Maloney said, "For the love of Christ nailed to the wooden cross." For the bleeding damn wounds of Jesus Himself.

.

Dad stayed on the sagging couch from mid-January until the end of March. He slept most of the time, and I would sit on a chair opposite the couch and watch him. His mouth was always open when he slept, and I'd watch his chest move up and down with the air inside. Waited for bubbles to rise from his mouth and from the black holes of his nose. Waited for his breath to stop.

Once he opened his eyes when I thought he was sleeping, and I was so shocked that I stood up fast, bent over, and started to go sideways like a crab from the room.

"Earl," he said loud and clear. "Back, back."

I came back and sat on a chair and he said, "What's wrong with you?"

"Nothing."

"Why'd you try to sneak off?"

I told him. I said I didn't know, and he said, "Get the fuck out of my sight." Something like that.

.

It was like fever, those days after I met Joan. Back then. It was like the flu, only half the aches were whispers and strokes, were melting pains like sinking into a long sleep.

"Okay," she always said. "Okay, honey," she told me all the time. Like I was something sweet. Like she liked me, too. Sweet. Imagine. Me sweet.

I wouldn't sleep or eat, wouldn't read books. When I walked up and down the aisles of my classroom, the kids asked me questions, and I wouldn't hear them. It was like I'd gone away, though I was standing there. Me in a schoolroom with the youth.

I will open my dark saying upon the harp. My mouth shall speak of wisdom.

They wore ties to school, and came on the subway with backpacks and book bags, and only a few of them had begun to shave yet. Their cheeks were red, and most of them were awkward and skinny, elbows and wrists and knees sticking out like knobs, like parts they hadn't found a use for. Remembered kids, misremembered kids. Kids trying to grow up, to come of age, to come into their own, not such an easy thing to do. Easy to forget how hard. How fucking painful.

Fast fold thy child. His eyes behold.

They knew about Joan and me within a month.

"He's got a girl," they said. Ho. Ha. Ms. Millis.

All the Johns and Matthews and Jims and Bobs and Charlies. Josephs and Richards and Dans. One Lee, one Walker, one George. All Catholic boys from big families that loved them, that wanted them to go to college.

For their voices lifted unto them. And the song was. The song.

There was a Bob whose father drove a cab, and a Dan whose mother and father were divorced. I talked to Joan about them, and she laughed at the stories. She told me about her students. She had mostly ninth and tenth graders. A Rufus, a Linus, a curly-headed brilliant Elias. I had juniors and seniors. My students said, "Can we come to your house? We want to have supper with you and her, Mr. Madden." Ha.

And they made bells of pure gold, and put the bells of the pomegranates upon the hem of the robe.

They saw her in the long polished halls. Through windows in the classrooms. They'd ask questions, and in a way I'd tell them about her, I'd introduce them to the idea of us.

"Is she beautiful to you, Mr. Madden?" they'd ask, and I'd look, frown, and they'd laugh. Freckles, white teeth.

"Yes," I'd say.

"What do you do? Where do you go?"

"Out to eat, to movies. Sometimes we just sit around and talk. We sit at the kitchen table. She makes bread, and I smoke and sip tea, and we talk."

"What do you talk about?" Matthew Burns, who was sixteen, wanted to know.

"Anything," I'd say. "Everything." Nothing.

"Baseball?"

"Sure."

"Her old boyfriends?"

I'd frown.

"Sex?" Joe Meehan asked, and the kids were silent, tense, a little afraid. The book. For my head is filled with dew and my locks with the drops of the night. Are as the eyes of doves by the rivers of waters. Are as a bed of spices.

"Time for the Civil War," I'd say, and they groaned.

At night Joan wanted to hear my stories about them. "What does Walker look like?" she'd ask. "Is he the tall one? Black hair? Green eyes?"

I'd tell her about Abraham Lincoln the writer or the Great Depression, or I'd repeat a question John Boyle asked about FDR. "Did he really betray his class? Like Judas betrayed Jesus?" So there was division among the people because of him.

Joan and I walked up and down the aisles of Purity Supreme, the supermarket. Sometimes at midnight, at one in the morning. We saw other couples, we saw mothers, we saw old men with shopping lists in their trembling hands. Can of soup. Can of cat food, pint of skim milk, box of crackers. Lips parted, lips almost purple and blue. Shaky old men, fingers as straw.

The next day I'd be walking up and down the aisles of my classroom, and I'd look over the heads of my students and think of the night before, of the bright aisles of Purity Supreme, and Joan and I touching each other, a hand, an elbow, our sides brushing, her head for an instant on my shoulder.

Or I'd wake up late at night and she'd be awake too, and we'd talk. As outside, high above us, a plane crossed the sky, droning like a mosquito, and we talked about where the plane had come from, and who was on board, and where it was going.

I said, "Someone's father died, and he, the son, is going to claim the body."

"No," Joan said. "A woman's flying across the country to meet her lover. She aches for him."

"A man with a bomb," I said. "With a pocketknife."

"A doctor bringing a heart for a transplant," she said.

"An old man visiting his daughter," I said. Maybe that.

"It's three thirty-seven," Joan said. "Some of them are sleeping. Most of the overhead lights are out, except maybe for an old lady, an ex-nun, who's trying to read, but who's worrying instead about her brother who drinks too much."

"She hasn't seen him for seven years," I said, "even though they've written letters, even though they've talked on the phone."

Joan shifted, adjusted her pillow. She put her hand on my hip.

"He lives in a room in a house in Brighton, a few blocks from Comm. Ave.," I said.

"And his landlady drinks, too," Joan added. "Sometimes they watch the soaps together, sipping wine from jelly glasses and commenting on the lives of the characters."

Her, me. Then, there.

Then we'd lie there, and the noise of the plane would be gone, and neither of us would say anything, as though we could picture the tiny red taillights, growing smaller in the vast black sky.

∙

That goeth down sweetly, causing the lips of those that are asleep to speak.

∙

Kirby Meade, a kid from my class when I was small, drowned in the Charles River in February. This I knew for sure. He had been walking on the ice and fell through, and Tom Marion from the grade above us said that when the divers found Kirby's body they weren't sure at first if it was human or the body of a pig. "Bodies swell up," he said to us on the playground.

I went to the wake with Darryl Webster and Darryl's mom and dad, and when I saw Kirby in the casket in a dark suit, he looked not bloated but small and old. Both at the same time. Maybe it was the suit and tie, or the satin lining of the casket. Maybe it was all the adults in dark clothes, and how serious everyone was. By dying, Kirby was suddenly a different person. Like a grown-up. Only a midget. Not one, not the other. Both and neither.

At school Kirby used to pretend to pick his nose and wipe his finger on someone, and now he was the cause of all these dark clothes, these unsmiling faces.

When I saw my father on the couch, I'd look hard for movement—for his face to twitch or his chest to lift or bubbles to rise—because I'd start to picture him being like Kirby, with his hands folded, waiting for someone to close the lid.

Mom rolled the television on its stand and set it up at the foot of the couch. Dad watched game shows, and he whispered answers to the TV.

The gray light was glowing on him. And they shall go into the holes of the earth.

"You fucking morons," he said. "Got shit for brains," he told the TV.

Mom came to our room one night, after Dad had already been asleep for a while, and she sat on the edge of Ed's bed. She put her hand on my shoulder, then she put her hand on Ed's hair, and she combed his hair with her fingers. Mom had gained weight and she had lost a tooth on the bottom in front. There was this dark space. She tried to cover her mouth with her hand when she spoke. She knew but she didn't know either.

"Your father doesn't mean what he does," she said. "He's been very sick lately."

"Will he die?" Ed asked, and Mom said, "We all die, Eddie."

"But soon?" I asked. "Like Kirby Meade?"

"I don't think so."

"Why's he lie there?" Ed asked.

"He feels bad," Mom said. "He loves you kids, and he's ashamed he can't work to support you guys. He can't give you the things he thinks you should have."

"What things?" I asked.

"Things boys want."

"Like bicycles?" Ed asked.

Mom nodded and kept combing Ed's hair with her fingers.

To shake terribly the earth. I will give children to be their princes.

"Guns and toys," I said. "Maybe a horse."

My mother kept nodding.

"He could get a job," I said. "Then he'd get us stuff."

For a while Mom didn't talk. I watched her and I watched Ed. The wallpaper was stained above his bed. The stain looked like a butterfly. Flicker and fly, in the dark, go by.

"If your father seems hard sometimes," Mom said, "it's not because he doesn't love you."

She shut the light off and then sat on Ed's bed for a long time. The mattress sagged under her weight.

After I went to sleep I thought I felt her hand on my head. And much later I felt the wet liquid spreading from my middle onto the blankets and sheets. I could smell the pee, and later, as the wet turned cold and I was partly awake, I couldn't get out of bed, couldn't go to the bathroom like I was supposed to. All the time the darkness was changing outside the window. Black and wavery. Shadow shifting. Trembling, light breeze, damp.

∎

Joan slept more deeply than anyone I ever knew. She wore night-gowns that had designs of flowers and stars on them, and even when the temperature at night never went below seventy, she still wore the nightgowns, still wrapped herself with sheets.

With the windows wide open and the moonlight spilling in, her hair would be a dark flower against the sheets, her neck a stem.

I'd prop my head on one hand, and I'd look at her some nights for hours. If she woke up—even for an instant—and saw me staring, she never seemed surprised. She'd smile, turn over, go back to sleep.

Go under and away to somewhere nice.

Joan had one brother and four sisters. I knew that because she told me. I was always careful to listen. And I never forgot. Even when she didn't think I was, I heard every little thing. The brother was the youngest, then two sisters, then Joan, then two more sisters. In photographs all of them were fair and striking. They had white teeth and shiny hair. They were posed at the side of a lake, or at a graduation. In sunshine, dressed mostly in white or in pale summer colors. Long thin arms and legs. The brother wore a tie, and slouched and smiled. You could tell how much his sisters loved him.

When Joan was young, her parents owned a house on a lake in the Adirondacks. Each June, when school ended, her mother and the six kids moved north to the lake. They spent the summer in shorts and sneakers, with the smell of insect repellent and charcoal embers glowing, with sunsets and lapping water, with her mother rubbing cold cream into sunburned arms and legs, and logs burning in the fireplace on nights when the temperature dropped below fifty.

Spokes of light. Sunlit water. Flew in fleeces tinged with violet.

"Mom read us stories," Joan told me during our nighttime car rides. The air moved through the car, and Joan blinked her eyes in the wind and said, "Beth and Karen got to light the fire because they were the oldest. The rest of us searched around the house for twigs and small branches.

"When it was halfway dark and all the dinner dishes were done and put away, Beth would say, 'Can we, Mom?' And Mom laughed and said, 'Sure,' and one of us would let Todd sit in our lap, and the newspaper would burn first, then the twigs.

"There'd be that crackling, and before anyone noticed, you might look up and the outside had gone completely dark.

"Then bigger pieces of wood caught fire, then logs, and Mom read books to us. *The Little Lame Prince, Charlotte's Web, The Black Stallion.* Sometimes we'd have popcorn or ice cream, too, and Todd would always fall asleep before Mom was done, and would have to be carried to bed."

Todd was the youngest. The smiling one. Most loved, most dear to their hearts.

We would be out in Wellesley or Weston or Natick by then, me and Joan, and we'd pass fields and big houses with huge lawns and porch swings. I'd look over at Joan, and even after she'd fallen silent, she had a distant look on her face, as though she was in New York, and it was twenty years ago.

And me, Earl, with her then: lout, oaf, block, crank.

"Dad came up sometimes on weekends," Joan said. "He was still at the New York office then, and he'd leave late Friday afternoon and get to the house at eleven or twelve or one.

"We'd be asleep by then, but I remember half waking up and hearing Mom and Dad talking in the kitchen. Dad telling her about the drive and Mom telling about the week, about Beth tipping the canoe or Todd having a virus. And I'd lie there in bed, and the lake would be sloshing and slapping against the dock in this quiet way, and I'd stay awake as long as I could. But it was like falling into clouds of warmth."

In Natick I'd get on the Mass Pike going east, and we'd pass through the Newton tollbooth, and I'd go all the way to the Allston exit, and we'd go slowly through Allston Center to our apartment in Brookline.

She knew that I was kind of starved, and very scared and nervous. Rushes of thoughts. Needs no sleep. Up at all hours. Reading and thinking. Hypomania, that infectious energy. Almost dancing around the house at 2:00 A.M. Climb to stars. Pharmaceuticals. Sip wine, sip wine.

What I had not had. Did not have. But had worked. And loved my students. Who were dear to me. Was pretty gentle underneath. But then so fucking angry. My thick-skulled boys. "Turn off the television," I would say to them. "Take your hands out of your pants." Looking up, mouths agape. Mr. Madden. The Madder. Madman.

Did he say? Did he mean?

Fuck? What? Huh?

"Open Father Walt. Mr. Thoreau." Held the book up, pacing, in front of them. My tie loose. Big boots, big guy. Voice that went soft, then loud.

" 'I was a self-appointed inspector of rainstorms and snow-storms,' " I said to them, voice full, pages of the text flapping, not even looking at them, but speaking from my head, from memory, maybe getting it wrong. Missing a word or two. " 'And reported to no one.' " Stopped, paused. Looked from one upturned face to the next to the next. Red cheeks, eyes lit, clean heads of boy hair. Black blond brown. Curved curling, lank and straight. " 'I am well-traveled in Concord.' "

Then looked at them, held the book over my head. The text, the holy book. That which is sacred. That which will lead thee, free thee, lift thee from thy ignorance and darkness and unknowing.

Then Joan and me. For she knew I loved them and loved her, loved the word, wove the word. Create in me a clean heart. Re-store in me. Open thou my lips.

Everything would still be hot when we got back, the walls damp, the curtains swaying in the hot breeze. But we—Joan, me—we felt like we had escaped, even if it was just a car ride, just a story by then about a lake in New York.

.

Dad said he wouldn't go, and Mom said, "Do I have to call the police?"

"Just wait," he said, and she sighed, and we saw her in their bedroom, sitting on the side of the bed, silent and heavy. Face grown fatter and fatter. Water leaking from her eyes.

Me and Ed, though Ed said. Ed said so little. Did not look as I did. Did not hear. I think, am pretty sure.

He saw or said he saw. Ed. Heard or said he heard, thought he saw or heard to remember. My brother Ed.

Dad called me into the living room one night when I had gotten up for the bathroom. I don't know why I didn't just wet the bed like usual. Warmth spreading. And quiet. Still. But after he said my name I went and stood in the doorway, and he just looked at me for a while.

Dad who had not shaved. No bath, nor brushed his teeth, such as they were. Eyes gray stones set in the bones and skin of his face.

It must have been two or three because there was no traffic outside and no noise anywhere. He was covered by a green sleeping bag that was unzipped to make a quilt. He lifted a corner of the sleeping bag and said, "Get in."

I got under the covers with him, and he curled around me. He was warm and heavy and smelled like a stove, and he put his hand on my face and said, "Earl, honey," and he began to shake and cry.

"I'm sorry," he said. "I'm so so sorry," he told me. I felt the heat. Stove smells. Thought, This is what a bear feels when he sleeps in a cave all winter, and I pictured the snow almost covering the mouth of the cave.

"Forgive me," he said and sobbed, and I felt his tears on my neck and shoulder.

Then he began to talk. Whisper talk, slide words. About being in the army and riding in trucks through Germany and Poland at the end of the war. Piles of human hair that were bigger than barns. Piles of shoes and clothes, and in pits the size of drained ponds there were bodies so white and thin they looked like small branches without bark. Mud and mud and broken trees and trucks and broken walls, and bloated bodies like balloons, stretching the uniforms. Rain falling. A hand, boot. Smashed stumps of trees, towns. Splinters, pieces and pieces.

Then he slid over in his brain and he told about being at Carson Beach in South Boston when he was eight years old and seeing the body of a drowned woman.

"She was blue and green," he said, "and you couldn't make out her eyes or her nose."

"Will you die?" I asked him, and he moved his hand from my face to my shoulder.

"Everyone dies," he said. "You know that."

"What happens after you die?" I asked.

"They drain your blood, then they embalm you. They put you in a suit and paint your face with makeup. Then they stick you in a pillow box and put flowers all around you."

"How come?"

He stopped. His hand on my shoulder. Old stove, smell of grease, onions, cooked meat. Steel, yellowing insulation.

Said, Dad did. "Flowers for the smell. Sweet smell. For beauty, life. Flowers are alive, and smell nice. But they don't last long." Hid other smells. Alive so you didn't think, Dead. Not flowering. Just dead and gone. Old meat that would rot and have decomp. Maggots. Save for the blood drained out. From an artery. Long hollow needle. Called trocar. Pump in Formalin. Formaldehyde mixed with water, alcohols, emulsifiers, so body didn't turn brown, shrivel.

Then paint. Nice suit, satin pillowy stuff. Features set. Hands folded on navel, rosary beads optional. Went to sleep in a suit or dress, wearing jewelry, sometimes glasses. As though to see on the other side.

His—Dad's—hand moved lightly on my upper arm. Skin to skin. Dad so deep under. Something invisible had settled over him. Had not died yet. But not alive either. Deep far sadness. Lead, under sand or water. Slow as soup, thick as syrup. Left life.

He said in a low quiet voice that was as much inside as outside of him. So you didn't know and couldn't tell. He was speaking. He seemed to say. You thought, remembered, recalled. Re— Collected. How—"They parade everyone past your body, to prove you're really dead and that it's not so bad because you look okay."

Then heard floorboards creak, and for a few minutes everything was still.

"You hate the old bastard, don't you?" he said.

I shook my head. Moved it so slightly, so slow and quietly—side to side.

"Lying on the couch like a corpse," he said. "A corpse couch. Couch corpse." He—Dad—began to giggle. Or sob, or both. Not quite one nor the other. Both and neither.

"I'll be dead," he said, "and you'll spend the rest of your life trying to bury me."

"No."

"Don't. Tell. Me." He breathed deep. Puff of breath with each syllable. "Be wandering through your life, and you'll be wanting to stick me in a hole and cover it with dirt." His breath was an alley, was the back of a building.

"Won't."

"Don't worry," he said, "because it won't work anyway."

We lay there so long that my eyes began to close, and I was drifting. Were all else near to me. Loved well the stately and rapid river.

"Even at night," he whispered, "when you think I'm lying here and you think I'm asleep, I'm doing other things you don't know about."

I drifted some more. Said or thought I said. As it was written. Said unto him: You alone know what it is.

"Don't be fooled," he said. And away and away.

And woke, awoke, in my own bed, and Ed was sleeping, making sounds like he was in a dream and eating ice cream or candy. Liminal. Limen. Threshold, border, between one state and another. Make urgent the appetites and needs which are smoldering below the. Of awareness.

Liminal light. Dawn, dusk. Not day, nor night. Liminal. Conscious, unconscious. Asleep, awake. Sleep or wake. Dream, memory. Dad and his brain. Slid.

·

The trees were still bare in March, and my mother began to get not heavier and fatter but thinner and thinner. Her eyes got bigger and darker, and at night Ed—who often didn't notice things— told me Dad was dying.

"Mom, too," I said, and he nodded. Had the whole time been watching.

"What'll happen to us?" I asked.

There were freckles on Ed's nose, and flecks of green in his blue eyes.

"They'll put us on a farm with horses and bikes," he said.

"No," I said. "I don't think so."

"They'll have ice cream and steak," he said. "We'll get adopted."

I shook my head. Maybe. Not sure. "We'll go to a court, and they'll make us stay there. It's made of bricks, and there are bars on the windows."

"Liar," he said.

"Fuck you," I told him, and after that I told him he sucked too.

．

The police came on a Sunday when it was raining out, raining as it had not rained in some time. Big buckets of rain. Sheets of rain fell on the street out front. In gutters, drainpipes, sidewalks, stairs. Washing the everything. Whole big. Washing dirt and slime from the world. There were two of them, and they both wore guns. Mom went out to the back hall to talk to them.

Dad called me and asked me to get him a cup of wine. I brought the wine to him in a Jetsons glass that used to have jelly in it from the grocery store, and he said he loved me. He said I was a good son.

They stood there in the living room. Mom. Big cop and the even bigger cop. Belts, guns, radios.

You wanna fuck with me?

Who you looking at?

Bigger cop looked away. Saw me. Eyes went over me. Saw Dad, eyes then on Mom.

"Considering the old man you have," Dad said and winked.

Mom came in—thin, hair part gray, and very tired I would guess. Told me to go to my room.

Ed was lying on his bed, and I closed the door and lay down. We could hear footsteps in the living room, and then voices. Mom and Dad's voices, and the low, unfamiliar voices of the policemen. Deep, close to us, though we had not known nor heard these voices before.

Mom said, "Honey," and one of the policemen said, "It doesn't have to be long."

Dad said some things, but he spoke in such a low, soft way that we couldn't tell what he said.

There were more footsteps, and more talking, and then the front door opened, and we heard a car start up out front.

Against thee. Thee only.

Ed looked over at me, and I looked at him, and neither of us said anything. But knew in our eyes, hearts, bones. That we would never be able to put our father in the ground, cover him with dirt and have him stay there. Always Dad, hovering, shadow. Never lose.

SIX

This was in the newspaper in Boston. I read this for sure. Black marks on white paper. Print. So knew it to be true. Published. Wide circulation. Fit to print. This happened. About a woman whose name was Dorothy.

She—Dorothy—was hiking along the Appalachian Trail in Pennsylvania. She was hiking with a friend named Kay.

Dorothy plus Kay. Both alike in dignity.

Dorothy and Kay had been friends in college. Dorothy lived in Boston, Kay lived near Atlanta. For over a decade, they got together each year. One year they spent a week in London, one year they went to Aspen. Here then there, year by year.

The last year, the year this happened, they were planning to hike a section of the Appalachian Trail in the mountains of Pennsylvania. The section was remote, it was mid-April, and they didn't expect to see many other hikers. Thought that.

This one I told to Joan. Couldn't stop thinking of this one. Said, Joan, these two women.

Stop. Stop. Put her hands over her ears, closed her eyes.

They had been on the trail for two days and had not seen another human being since the morning of the first day. All they saw were trees and deer, rabbits, chipmunks. Around noon of the second day they saw an airplane pass far overhead, and they felt a long way from their regular lives. Maybe that airplane was going. Who knows where.

There were wildflowers along parts of the trail, white and lavender and blue flowers, and Kay told Dorothy about her mother, who had been operated on for cervical cancer in February. Kay said her mother was doing well, was being given radiation treatment, and that the doctors were optimistic. No death here. Not yet. Aside from the nausea, Kay said, her mother now seemed fine.

That's when they first saw him, standing quietly by the side of the trail, about thirty yards ahead. Maybe ten feet off the trail, in woods. He was watching them, and smiling in a way that made both of them feel cold.

He. This individual.

He was in his twenties and had long hair and a beard. He wore jeans that were two or three inches too short and boots that were laced with baling twine. He wore a red T-shirt and a black nylon jacket with part of a sleeve torn away. His cheekbones stuck out, and his eyes were sunk so far back in his skull that Kay and Dorothy couldn't tell what color they were.

So bones in his face. Skin stretched over those craggy bones.

But the thing that scared them, the thing Dorothy talked about later, when she was able to talk, was how thin and wild the man looked, like someone who had barely survived a winter in the forest.

They almost turned, almost went back. Didn't, though. Kept walking, and when they passed him, his body didn't move and he didn't say anything. He kept smiling, and after they'd gone by, they felt his head pivot and his eyes staring, but he was more still than a deer.

You could read this in the newspaper. Then think. Pause and linger. Have your mind, such as it is or was, move in and around and on and through these facts. These things that did indeed happen. Could move not away from these facts, these events that did indeed happen. But toward them, in them. Porous. Interpenetration, interbeing. So you couldn't leave it alone even if you wanted to. It aroused, inflamed you. Earl Madden. Lit you up, you credulous fuck. Teacher of boys, lord of text. Dunce, dullard, dunderhead. Earl alone. Earl on his own at last. Earl in his own shadowy whispery head, in bed.

So that: When they—Dorothy, Kay—had gone a half mile, they began to walk faster, and Kay suggested they veer off the main trail to avoid running into the man again. There were smaller trails, trails that paralleled the main path, and trails that went to the north and south of a lake or mountain. This far in and away. Sylvan, untrammeled. In nature. Wilds.

They were more than nine miles from a road, but it was only twelve-forty, and the day was clear and dry. Both of them were in good shape. Dorothy was a runner, Kay swam and bicycled.

Rustic Pennsylvania. A glen, a glade. Babble brook. Pines and maples and aspens and oaks and. Hornbeam, hackberry, holly, beech, birch, chokecherry. And fucking insects too. You got ya. Had ya: cicada, spittlebug, ambush bug, chinch bug, promethea moth, polyphemus moth—giant size, eye-spots on wings—ladybird, firefly, glowworm, bluebottle and greenbottle flies, leafhoppers, stink bugs and shield bugs—which sucked plant juices. Common on blackberries. So well concealed.

By two o'clock they were feeling comfortable again. The sunlight fell through the pines and spotted the forest bed. They hiked on a trail that passed above a small lake, and then in a section that went through dense pines. Soft brown fallen needles under their bootsoles, cushioned each step.

When they—but—then rounded a bend in the trail, when Dorothy heard Kay gasp. She—Dorothy—looked up, and he was standing in the middle of the trail, about ten yards in front of them.

"You girls lost?" he asked. Voice high and nasal, slightly rural. Called them girls.

Kay approached first, and stopped a few feet in front of him. He was taller than she had at first thought, maybe two or three inches over six feet, and even thinner than he had at first looked—seemed—from a distance. The bones in his hands and wrists, in his neck and face, stuck out and made Dorothy think of someone with leukemia or anorexia.

"You all lost?" he asked again, and kept smiling, and the skin on his face looked like it was covered by dirt or ash.

"No," Kay said, and Dorothy stood just behind her friend, almost touching her.

"Why you over here?" he asked. Which meant? "Here" meaning? In the woods? On the trail? On earth? In daylight? His body oddly rigid, as though the only thing that moved when he talked was his mouth.

"We're just hiking," Kay said.

"We're meeting some friends soon," Dorothy said. Quick to think, lied.

The man smiled a little. Said, "Friends." As though to say?

What? Kay and Dorothy were friends? Kay and Dorothy had friends? Kay and Dorothy were not friends. But lovers? Which caught his attention. Possibly excited him. Angered, desired. Some flicker of something—just possibly—inside that skinny strange skull.

Then watched him turn and walk into the woods, like that, and within seconds they could neither see him nor hear him, as though he had instantly gone miles away. Or had not been. At all. Might imagine, you can imagine.

No? Are not these woods more free? From peril? Seeking the food he eats. Here shall he see. Garlands.

So: They began to walk faster, and twenty minutes down the trail, took a smaller side trail that went off to the left. They walked quickly and silently for over an hour, and then abruptly, Kay broke the silence. Said, "Who is he?" she asked, and by mentioning him, by speaking out loud and letting the memory of him exist between them, it was as though they were still on a trail in the mountains of Pennsylvania but not as afraid somehow, and as though nothing had ever before happened in their lives. This was new time.

"He had no pack or bag," Dorothy said. "Nothing in his pockets." So it seemed. She noticed. Did not miss much. Saw more than she wanted, intended, strictly needed to.

"Maybe, he's—maybe—just some mountain man," Kay said.

"A holy man—who—he lives on roots and berries." But almost as soon as Dorothy spoke, she knew she was lying, and knew too that she was lying so both of them would be able to keep walking. One foot, and such vast wilds. One wouldn't think, eastern Pennsylvania. Not Alaska, for God's sake.

And could see why someone who read this in the newspaper, say, in Boston, and who had trouble sleeping at night, and whose wife said he was no longer the person she fell in love with or married. And scary. How scary he had become. She knew it was not easy. But still, if he would just talk, just see someone. Seek help. Couldn't keep on. Would have to pack up and.

These boundaries and blank spaces on the tape. Couldn't stop thinking about, going over. And every fucking place you looked, saw, heard, noticed, remembered. Always out there just the other side of the lenses on his eyes or glasses or the window, the screen, glass, heavy wire mesh. Veils and fog.

So: By five-thirty they had not seen him again. The trail went downhill for half a mile, and the temperature was dropping. They paused long enough to put on windbreakers, and Kay asked how far they'd gone since they first saw him.

"Are we doing twenty-minute miles?" Dorothy asked, and Kay said, "Not quite."

"Maybe ten miles," Dorothy said.

They passed small gorges on the sides of the trail, gorges that looked like brown hammocks with trees growing in them, and sunlight spotting the branches of the trees. When they looked into the woods to the sides of the trail, they saw dozens of small trees for every full-grown maple and spruce. The trunks of the small trees were the size of the arms of children, and Dorothy thought that the smaller branches and twigs were like the arteries and veins running through the bodies of children. What an odd thought, she said to herself, and pictured the fine blue lines on the insides of her nephew's arms.

As to mammals, reptiles, amphibians. There were, though largely unseen—eastern and least chipmunks, gray and red squirrels, woodchuck, red fox, your spotted skunk, your river otter, your red-backed and meadow voles, your white-tailed and Virginia deer, skinks, wood turtle, spotted and bog turtles, snapping and musk turtles, plus your ringneck, green, and rough earth snakes, your hognose, black racer, and rat snakes, not to mention your true toads, chorus and tree frogs, your basic bullfrog and green frog.

They—Kay, Dorothy—passed an outcropping of white rock,

overgrown in spots by lichen, and as Dorothy stepped over a heavy root in the trail, Kay said, "You think we're overreacting?"

Dorothy looked at her, and she could see faint lines around Kay's eyes and mouth. She's thirty-two, Dorothy thought, and then she said, "Probably."

"I mean, he hasn't done anything. He's just a strange guy who maybe thinks we're strange too."

Dorothy said, "Maybe." And for a half hour they walked without talking. Though, of course, kept thinking. Thinking, spinning out, whirling.

Dorothy looked at her watch and it was five-forty, and almost as soon as she looked up, she saw Kay standing once again in the middle of the trail, staring into the woods. When Dorothy reached her, she followed Kay's gaze, and she saw him, standing in a small grove in the woods.

The grove was less densely grown, and he was looking at them, and looking in that same oddly stiff way. And then Dorothy saw the rifle, slung to his back with the strap, the same way she had seen folk musicians walk onstage at festivals, their banjos slung around to their backs so they could walk more easily.

At first she thought she might be mistaken, that the barrel might be a branch. But the longer she looked, the more certain she was that the stick was too black and straight and shiny to be a stick.

But once again he didn't move, he stayed in the grove, about twenty yards off the trail, and it suddenly occurred to Dorothy, a plunge into cold water, that this man knew the woods the way she knew her apartment in Boston, knew where each book, each piece of clothing, each plate and plant and pair of scissors was. He knew the trees and paths, knew thousands of acres of the forest, knew every mile of trail and patch of rock, and that if they were going to get away from him, it would only be because he grew bored with his weird game.

Kay began to walk, and so too did Dorothy, and after ten minutes said, "What now?"

Dorothy didn't know if Kay had seen the gun, but she wasn't going to ask. "Walk fast," she said.

"What's he gonna do?"

Dorothy looked at Kay, and her eyes were dilated as though it was almost dark. The black center of her eyes had grown larger to take in more light, more of what was around her, more of what was.

Dorothy shook her head. "Let's walk as far as we can before dark," she said, "and hope he doesn't follow."

"He could be listening right now," Kay said. "We wouldn't even know it."

"Just walk. C'mon."

For over two hours, they walked, and the sun moved closer to the edge of the sky, and as they walked, they began to feel calmer. There were still wildflowers on the sides of the trails, and they saw birds and heard them call to one another in the trees. And the trees, of course. Still there. Still high above them. Leaves and such. Sky, air.

Mr. Muir: Winds are advertisements of all they touch, however much or little we may be able to read them; telling their wanderings even by their scents alone. Wild places. Wild creatures. Glorious course as invincible and unstoppable as stars.

It was nearly seven when they stopped. Kay said that nobody would follow people this many miles.

"Should we camp?" Dorothy asked.

Kay nodded, and they went into the woods and zigzagged through the trees until they found a small clearing among spruce. They took off their packs and began to put up the two-man tent. The ground was covered with brown pine needles, and Dorothy wished for a moment that the tent was not red, and for a longer moment—and by far not for the first time—wished they had not come on this trip.

But when the tent was up, they spread their sleeping bags inside and then sat, leaning against the trunks of trees.

There was half-light by then, and the wind had picked up and was moving through the branches. Dorothy felt it on her face, almost as clean as a shower. Then her eyes were closed, and she heard the first loud crack. Kay began wailing and screaming.

Dorothy opened her eyes, and there was blood, a lot of blood, running down Kay's face, and Dorothy heard more cracks, and felt the sharp heat, the wet, in her arm, then on her cheek.

She saw blood on her arm and lap, saw a small piece of flesh lying on her thigh, and Kay was sobbing, "I'm blind, blind," and saying, "No, Jesus, no, no," over and over.

Dorothy watched—like this was something on television—as a—a spot on Kay's chest exploded red, and blood began to soak down into her shirt and pants, and she was no longer sobbing or screaming or saying anything. She was slumped against the tree, with blood running from her head and chest, and now—Dorothy noticed, knew—from her neck as well.

This isn't true, she said to herself, and when she looked down at all the blood, when she felt the burning, the bleeding—then another hot bolt in the back of her neck—she knew she wouldn't be able to watch all this happen—to herself or to Kay. Because the cracking sound. It had stopped when she wasn't paying attention, and now there was no sound or movement from Kay. Or. From anywhere in the world. There were no birds, there was no wind, and Dorothy knew she would be dead if this had really happened. She knew that even if she couldn't force herself to wake up, that she would feel pain if this was real, that she would be alert and scared, and not lying here with this warm, drowsy feeling, like someone ready to go to sleep. Shift blanket, pillow, adjust arm, hand, one leg then the other.

Then felt something sting her arm, where blood was coming from. Stood up, began to run. She ran with a slow fluid motion, because she wanted to run for a long time. Automatic, things in her brain. Flooding, chemicals.

Reached a trail, and kept running the way she ran around the reservoir in Boston near Cleveland Circle, the way she ran on Commonwealth Avenue, out past Boston College, into the hills of Newton. She ran and ran, this Dorothy, and the stinging—it came back, was there—in her arm got worse, and her neck and cheek began to sting, but everything else, all around and over her felt clean and washed and white. She could run for twenty or forty or a hundred miles. And did indeed. Go, kept going.

Reached a gravel road, kept running, and the gravel became paved.

In the newspaper, in your head. If you had read. Had time, lay awake, say, in bed and spun this out. Whirled and imagined with this. For it came to pass. It did indeed happen. These two women. Words on paper. Spoken. Item: page B9.

Ran until a car passed, and she began to scream even though she was out of breath and felt sweetly drowsy. And the car stopped a hundred feet beyond, and two men were running to her, and she was falling, and the pavement was rushing up to hit her, to smash her arm shoulder face—rush up so fucking sleekly fast—when she felt a hand on her arm, and a man said, one of the two, "Christ."

SEVEN

In September, almost a year after we were married—ten, twelve, fourteen months, I would say—Joan and I moved to an apartment in Watertown, the second and third floor of an old gray house, four—I'd say—blocks from Watertown Square. This place outside Boston. Near-in suburb, you might call it. What-a-town. Bordered by: Newton, Waltham, Belmont, Cambridge, and Boston proper—the Brighton, Allston sections of Boston. Bordered too by the Charles River.

Houses close together, no front yards to speak of. Two- and three-family houses, chain-link fences, telephone poles and power lines overhead. Trees here and there. Red-and-white checkered curtains in a kitchen window or two. Some patches of side yard, cement, grass, blacktop, aluminum lawn furniture. Madonna on the half shell in more than one yard. Part-buried bathtub. Mom-and-pop store. Everything crowded in, close together. The apartment was not insulated, and the closets were so shallow we had to turn the hangers at an angle for clothes to fit.

An old Italian woman, the aunt of our landlord, lived on the first floor. She was in her late seventies, maybe early eighties even, and she spoke no English. Often, when we were walking down the front stairs on our way out, we'd pass her door. She'd open the door and smile, and talk to us in Italian, her hands moving as she talked.

We'd say, "No *capisce*," and she'd repeat, "No *capisce*." Then she smiled some more, and took the sleeve of Joan's coat, and pulled her inside. I trailed in after her. More than once, now and then, when we were both standing in her front room, she—the old Italian woman—would take photographs from a desk drawer—old people on studio sets, mountains and streams and trees painted on a screen, and a mother and father, in black, sitting on chairs in front of the screen. And standing to the side and behind them, there were younger people—in their twenties and thirties—also in black.

Our neighbor pointed to a young man who stood on the left, and said a word in Italian. She looked from the man in the picture to Joan and me, and said the word again.

"Brother," I said. "Your brother."

She looked puzzled, then I pointed to the old man in the picture, a man with shiny dark eyes. I pointed to him, then to her. "*Padre*," I said. "Your *padre*."

"*Padre*," she repeated, and began to smile.

Father, priest, father.

She took Joan's sleeve again, and led us to the kitchen, and gestured for us to sit down. The walls were covered with pictures and maps, with calendars and pages torn from magazines. There was a picture of what looked like Italian wine country. There was a calendar from a funeral home—"Sensitive Service In A Time Of

Need." There was a picture of a white house with shrubs and green awning, a shiny hearse standing in the driveway. There was a map of Rome and a picture of a woman holding a breadstick and, underneath, some Italian words, red and white and green flag.

The old woman took a package of Oreos from a cabinet. She tapped my shoulder, pointed to the cookies, then pointed to her mouth. She had brown wrinkled skin, almost-black eyes. She smiled.

Wore a wine-red sweater over a housedress. Tissues stuffed in the left sleeve of the sweater at her wrist.

Gray hair. Smiled. Beautiful old Italian woman.

Joan took a cookie, and I watched her bite into it. Then we heard the stove, and the old lady was boiling water, was gesturing and smiling and saying things in a language we didn't understand.

Cookie, coffee. Son, daughter, father, aunt, niece, grandmother, nephew. Rome, Italy. Milan. Florence. Michelangelo. Coffee so strong it would take the paint off a car. Made the hands and fingers tremble. Hey, shaky.

Smiled. *Grazie. Bene. Molto bene. Grazie.* Blessing. *Graziosa.* Graceful. Pretty. *Bene, grazie. Ciao, bella.* So long, beautiful.

•

The weather was warm through most of September, and some nights we walked to Watertown Square and then walked on a path that went along the Charles River. In the distance—off to the left, kind of—we could see the Hancock and Prudential buildings in downtown Boston, and the river moved silently by in the dark.

Many cars, always, circled the circle in What-a-town Square. Stop. Go. Stop. Go.

In October the weather began to cool down, and we slept with blankets for the first time in months. That nip, that slight bite in the air. Window open an inch and cool clear clean. That air. Joan's period was late, and we thought she might be pregnant. Whoa. Ex-

Cuse me. We talked about what it would be like to have a baby, but Joan finally had a pregnancy test, and it turned out negative.

Fuck no. We ate breakfast at a place called Teresa's in Watertown Square. We'd go there at seven or eight on weekend mornings, and the waitress would bring coffee to our booth at the same time she brought menus. Everyone—the other people, the patrons, the employees—waitresses, cooks, counter guy, cash-register woman with yellow pencil behind ear, black hair, dishwasher guy, busboy, -man, maybe retarded—developmentally disabled—special needs—challenged—fucking moron, lunkhead, lout, goose, boob, ninny, dizzard—was quiet at Teresa's, and we'd watch the cook at the grill, breaking eggs with one hand, buttering toast, turning over home fries—then filling plates. And then: the plates on the table, steam rising—eggs, toast, home fries, sausage, coffee—and after the second cup of—joe, java—coffee we'd begin to talk.

.

Joan had brown hair that was cut short and that became less dark in the summer. She went jogging early in the morning—sometimes at five-thirty or six—and I'd wake up when she was peeling off her running clothes and getting ready for a shower. Her, there. Flushed skin. Hot and damp.

She'd say, "Morning, sweetheart."

"You went running," I said.

She nodded.

"What time is it?" I asked, and she said, "Almost seven," or "After seven." Flick. Time. Blink. Goes. An. Eye. By.

Then I closed my eyes, and I heard Joan in the shower, and later the water would be boiling on the stove. Steam, whistling. Coffee smell, morning. Oh.

She cleaned her face with cotton balls and alcohol, and her eyes watered from the fumes. Clean clear skin. Fresh soap washed pores. Warm water.

"Sleep well?" she asked.

I'd say. Mumble, report, assert, rejoin. "Yeah. You?"

"Okay," she said.

.

At night we cooked omelets and had sausage, and ate ice cream for dessert. Cholesterol special. I always washed the dishes, while Joan sat at the kitchen table afterward, reading the newspaper or magazines. She cooked, so Earl, the big guy, cleaned up.

One night, as we were getting ready for bed, I heard Joan in the bathroom, and she was crying. Sniffling, then sobbing, then blowing her nose, sobbing more.

Tears, then quiet, then sobbing some more, then a little more quiet. Wiped nose, dabbed at eyes, tears.

I knocked on the door, said, "Honey."

She grew quiet, silent, behind door.

"Joan, honey."

Still that no sound. Caught. Found out.

"What?" she asked, and her voice, tone—sounded like she had a cold.

"You crying?" Big Earl. I on the other side of the door. Not so totally stupid, dense, so as not to notice entirely. Asked.

She, Joan, unlocked the door, and when I opened it, she was sitting on the edge of the bathtub. The bathroom light was off, but I could see from the hall light that her cheeks were wet.

"What's wrong?" I asked. Went in. Slow, and sat next to her. Bathtub. Edge of.

She shook her head, and her hair swung limply back and forth.

Waited. Heard house sounds, outside sounds, clicks, taps, whirs, chitters, drip. Soft distant boom. Slip.

"You don't feel good," I said. Earl to Joan. And she kept shaking her head. Thin face, some faint freckles. Could picture her almost as a kid smiling. Lovely small child in her second-grade school picture. Cheeks, small teeth, lips. Smile that went all the way to her eyes. How could—who would—not love her, too?

"Why?"

"I'm hopeless," she said, and began to cry again. And that was the last thing she was—except of course in her mind at that moment.

I put my arm around her, and her shoulders were shaking. Whispered, "Sweetheart. Oh, sweetheart." Oh. Made oh sounds. Low. Where she was. With her.

·

When I finish brushing my teeth, I look in the mirror, and David Maxwell is standing behind me. In the bin, fast as that.

"Who's better?" he asks. "Rolling Stones or the Beatles?"

What the? What the?

"Beatles," I say.

"Nah," he tells me.

David is small and thin, and wears red running shorts with a white stripe on each side. Another one of us. In here. One of us. Not all that different, you stop to think. Consider this carefully. Don't slip, slide away. Stay with this now.

"No comparison," I say.

I turn and look directly at him. David Maxwell. Earl Madden. Both alike. He's twenty-four years old, but I always think of him as twelve or thirteen.

"Buddy Holly or Elvis?" he asks.

In dignity. Identify, don't compare and contrast. You think you're so fucking different? Better than? Worse than? Ha. Fucking ha.

David has a blue T-shirt on, and there's a pack of Camels in the breast pocket. I pat the pocket. "You shouldn't be smoking," I tell him.

He says, "Up yours."

Yours. Truly.

"Up my what?"

"Nose, ass. I don't give a shit." Little David. Short, thin. Tough guy, nervous. Jittery but silent.

"You'll get lung cancer," I say, and go past him, out the door, down the hall to my room. Can feel him behind me.

He's wearing black nylon socks and Hush Puppies. His footsteps are always silent. David can go in and out of rooms without anyone noticing. You'll look up and you'll be staring at a window or wall. A minute later you look again, and there's David, like an attendant at a funeral home, one of those pale men in dark suits who hold doors open. Indicate an empty chair or pew. Adjust flowers. Pallbear casket. Drive dark cars. Never smile. Sympathize. We care.

I put my toothbrush and toothpaste on the table next to the bed, then sit on the side of the bed and start to put on socks and sneakers. David stands in the doorway and watches me.

"Elvis or Buddy Holly?" he asks again.

"Close one," I say.

Fucking David.

"If you had to pick."

"Buddy died too young. Twenty-two, wasn't it?"

Maybe twenty-one. You believe that?

David nods.

I get the socks on and smoothed out, over toes, balls of feet, heels, ankles. Then loosen the laces on a sneaker. No blisters, corns. Foot is something. High arch. Bears the weight, so much weight, all the weight of your world.

"If Buddy had lived to even thirty, then Buddy Holly. Easy."

Buddy.

"But he died."

"He died," I say. Indeed. Plane crash. "So you have to go with Elvis."

An intercom scratches on, and a woman's voice says, "Dr. Stroud, line three-two-nine. Dr. Stroud, line three-two-nine, please." Then scratches off.

Scritch, scratch. Like Mr. McGregor's rake. End up in the pie. Like Peter's dad, you aren't careful. Better watch out, for fuck's sake.

Feeling poorly. Mr. McGregor! Indeed. Lippity, lippity. Trembled. He'll fucking kill you, eat you.

David shifts his weight from one leg to the other. Leans on the left side of the doorframe.

"Joe Louis or Muhammad Ali?" he asks.

"Never saw Joe Louis fight. Don't know."

"Ali," David says. "No sweat."

"Probably."

"Ted Williams or Joe DiMaggio?"

"The Kid."

"Jolting Joe," David says.

"The Splendid Splinter. Teddy Baseball."

"Yankee Clipper. Fifty-six straight games."

"Four-o-six."

"DiMaggio, easy," David says.

"Ted Williams. Purest hitter to ever play the game. Teddy fucking Baseball."

"No way."

"Yes."

"No fucking way, José."

"Earl," I say.

"I know who you are, asshole."

"Big mouth for a little shit," I say.

"Cause I'm smart."

"If you're smart, why're you here?"

"Why not?" he asks, and for the first time his voice—little bit of an opening—is less than certain.

"How much you weigh?" I ask. Apropos of nothing.

"One twenty-seven."

"How tall?"

"Five-three."

I finish the sneakers, just sit there. Not too loose. Not too tight. Socks smoothed out inside.

"No more smokes," I say. "That's why you're tiny."

"How come you're here?"

"No reason."

"You hurt your wife?" he asks.

"What?" The fuck.

"Did so. Why'd she leave?" The fuck?

"No I didn't."

"Big mean son of a bitch like yourself," he says. Such as yourself. I shake my head, both of us watch the floor.

Could take the little fuck out with a look, I had to. Just a look. Snap scrawny neck, chicken neck.

Nancy Kennedy, an aide, goes by in the hall, her sneakers going *squeak squeak* on the linoleum. *Scritch.*

"Boston or San Francisco?" David asks.

"I'm prejudiced."

"Mountains or ocean?"

"Ocean."

"Ted Bundy or Juan Corona?"

Juan Corona. Now there's a name you don't hear so much anymore. Forgotten, misremembered down the misty byways of time.

At first I don't hear. Ha. How's he know? Little twisted fuck. I'm looking in the drawers of my night table. Then it comes around again. My eyes, head, brain, thoughts, swing around behind the rest of it. Whole apparatus. Face to meet the faces. Etc. Look up, take in, apprehend. And David Maxwell is gone, little shit David Maxwell is vapor.

Juan Corona, West Coast, Imperial Valley. Early seventies. Killed. No play, no big news. Dead Mexicans. Nobody fucking cared.

•

"Tell me about Joan," Dr. Schumacher says.

Doctor Schumacher. Herr Doktor. German-American. Now it is time for mirth and frolic. Now it is time to dance.

Goose step. Rudolf Höss. Commandant of Auschwitz. "The Jew's way of living and of dying was a true riddle that I never managed to solve. I had to see everything. I had to look through the peep-hole of the gas chambers and watch the process of death itself, because the doctors wanted me to see it. I had to do this because I was the one to whom everyone looked." Höss said. Confessed.

So Herr Dr. Schumacher. Bach. Kant. We give you Dr. Krafft-Ebing.

Herr Höss clears his throat. Ahem. "The prisoners never missed an opportunity for doing some little act of kindness to my wife or children, and thus attracting their attention. No former prisoner can ever say that he was in any way or at any time badly treated in our house." Correct, Herr Höss.

"Today I deeply regret that I did not devote more time to my family. Yet what did my wife know about all that lay so heavily on my mind? She has never been told."

Earl. "What about her?"

Herr Doktor Schumacher. "Tell me about her."

"What do you want to know?"

Dr. Schumacher does not take his eyes from me. He is bald on top, with freckles where the hair used to be. He's wearing a short-sleeved white shirt, blue tie with red stripes. He watches, he notes.

"Anything you'd like me to know," he says, and I look for the edge—the shade—of a smile.

"You obviously have something in mind," I say. "Just ask it."

"Obviously?"

"Something," I say.

"Tell me."

"We were married."

"Were?"

"For five or six years," I say. "Months. Maybe seven."

I'm picking at a cuticle on one finger. I can feel a ragged edge. Dry skin, tiny sharp edge.

"Were you happy?"

As to—frolic, mirth. Now it is time. To dance. For mirth.

"What's happy?"

"Happy," Dr. Schumacher repeats, his face a frown and a question at the same time. Both together. Alike in dignity.

Oświęcim. In Galicia, Poland. Near confluence of two rivers. Vistula and.

"We laughed, we had some good times."

"Like?" Such as, for example.

"We went to movies. We used to go out driving."

"Did you enjoy lovemaking?"

Gulp. Look at bald fucking pate. Freckles. I beg your—fucking—no pun—pardon.

"Sure."

"Tell me."

"Yeah, it was fun. We liked it."

"No problems?"

I shake my head.

"Impotence?" I.D. Limp.

My head keeps going from side to side.

"Premature ejaculation? Loss of interest?"

"No."

"And Joan? Mrs.?"

"What about? Her?"

"She felt the same way?"

"Sure." You bet. Absolutely. Fuck yes.

"No problems for her?"

"I don't think so." To my knowledge. Recollection.

He writes things down on a yellow notepad. He writes without looking at the paper. Pen or pencil. Silver, fancy, fucking doctor. Fucking expensive writing instrument. No cheap yellow pencil. No Bic, fucking PaperMate, blue, med. pt. Acct. fine pt. Classy, stinks with class. Farting through silk.

"Where is she?" I ask.

"Where is who?"

Clever. Dr. "The Fox" Schumacher.

"Joan."

"Your wife?"

"Yes, damn it. My wife." Darn, damn. Smiling damned villain. Hah. Darn yarn, spin tale, tell tall tale. Spin spin.

"You tell me." Nazi fox. Rommel. Desert.

"If I knew," I begin, then look at him. He is not smiling, but looking at me with something like pity, the look you see for cripples. Or hint of: irony, contempt, boredom, skepticism.

"Do you know?" I ask, and he says, "You'll have to tell me."

After that I watch him, and even when he says things, I don't hear a word. Herr Höss. Family wanted, expected him, to become a Catholic priest. Career in church. Decided on SS. Better pension? Retirement package? Includes dental, chance to travel. No shit. Figures. Go figure. You can, could, look it up. He's—Schumacher is—just a face with eyes. Lips and tongue that move. Ho.

∎

Joan came home at five-thirty, evenings, because she coached the biology team at school and had started doing some administrative work as well. And she always had stories about the T, about the buses and trains. Everyone had a story. Few stories, at least. Each day she took a bus from Watertown to Harvard Square, and then a Red Line train to Park Street. She told me about the talkers, about the people who sang, about a man who collapsed in the aisle of a train, and how two passengers—both nurses—helped him. Drama in real life. The show, the big show. Education in real life. Got your nitty, got your gritty.

We ate dinner at the kitchen table, and then we'd watch Celtics games on television, or go out to movies. Joan liked Meryl Streep, said that she was the best thing to happen to movies since Katharine Hepburn. Or that lovely smart Brit. Thompson. Emma. Grit for a Brit. Stood up to fucking Hitler. Nation of shopkeepers. Wanna bet, Mr. Hitler mustache. Not like the Frogs. Give. Give. Fuck with their faces, fight with their feet. Brits. Plucky fucking Brits. Not to mention Mr. Will. Best ever. Central fucking figure in human race. Bigger, better than, Buddha, Jesus. No shit. What it means to be human. Define.

•

"With him," she told a reporter, "I was riding on the wind. Making love with him was guiltless, like a baby." Riding the wind, man. Hey. Guiltless like a baby. Hey.

I know these things. They happened.

Again, there are books. Evidence. Testimony, public record, transcripts. People talk. Like to talk. Need to. Be heard. Everyone. No matter what or where. That's the basic fucking human thing, you think about it.

Tell stories. In order to live. Ms. Didion. Basic as breathing. Eating, touch, taste, tell, say.

He was born in Ohio in 1934, to a sixteen-year-old prostitute.

The guy—him—to whom we refer. Name, identity to follow. She'd leave him for an hour or two with relatives, with neighbors, and she'd come back weeks later. She and her brother held up a gas station and clubbed the attendant with soda bottles. She was caught and sentenced to five years in prison. That is, the mother of Charlie. Our guy. Boyfriend of daughter said fucking was like riding wind, making love was guiltless, like a baby. Feature that. Innocent someone. Like a baby. Which in turn could, perhaps would—make a baby. Make love, as it were. Make life. Create human life. Begin again. Renew, start out. Poor bare forked animal, whereso'er thou are.

Charlie went to an aunt at first, a religious woman who prayed for hours each day and talked often of hell, of eternity and the fiery pit. But when his mother was paroled, he joined her once again, and they went to Kentucky, to West Virginia, to Ohio, to Indiana, to Illinois. They stayed in hotels and rented rooms, in places with water stains on the ceilings and walls, with chipped and cracking linoleum on the floors. When he turned a light on at night, he'd watch the cockroaches hurry for cover.

We think of him as a West Coast kind of guy. Beach Boys, Hollywood Hills. Cover of *Life* magazine. That stare, that glare. Little guy too. But this started, the all of it, in the East and Midwest. Heartland. Or started far earlier, say, with John Winthrop on ship *Arbella*. Poor frail boat on mighty ocean. Huddled, cold, sick. For we must consider that. Sermon on board. Scared three-quarters to death. Heaving, rising seas. Tossed boat like toy. 1630. Way the fuck back. We shall be as a city upon a hill. Mr. John W. The eyes of all people are upon us. In sermon. On board. Tiny storm-tossed.

There were "uncles," sometimes two or three new ones each week. For boy. *Life* cover boy. Loves the Beatles. Who didn't? Older uncles and younger uncles, uncles in business suits, in overalls, in uniforms. Some were gray, some barely shaved. But they all liked to drink with his mother, to stay up late, and to move him from the bed when they started to pant and whisper. Some uncles set him on the floor, some put him out in the hall with a coat for covers. Sometimes they did it while he was lying in the bed.

The little boy. For he too was a child once. He too would one day have a Family.

When he was twelve, she—loose mother—put him in a School for Boys in Terre Haute. He ran away and broke into a grocery store. He rented a room, and committed more burglaries. He was caught, sent to Boys Town, rising Xmas music, Pat O'., Mickey Fucking Rooney. Priest. Kindly, avuncular. Ha. And ran away after four days. Our boy.

Began to commit armed robberies, moved to Peoria, and was caught again. He was sent to another School for Boys, this one in Plainfield. In his three years there, he ran away eighteen times.

Moving steadily westward, toward freedom, wider places and spaces. Unclaimed land. Man could live, breathe free—un-fucking-trammeled. Govt. Etc.

Back on *Arbella:* Upon us. So that if we shall deal falsely with our God in this work we have undertaken.

He escaped one final time when he was sixteen, and worked his way west, stealing cars and breaking into grocery stores and gas stations.

He was caught, convicted of transporting stolen goods across a state line—a federal crime—and sentenced to another School for Boys, this one in Washington, D.C. About six months later, he was transferred to Natural Bridge Honor Camp, a minimum-security prison. A month before a parole hearing, when he was seventeen years old, he held a razor to the throat of another prisoner and fucked him in the ass.

He was sent to a federal prison in Virginia and then Ohio. When he was nineteen he was paroled. He moved to Wheeling, West

Virginia, married a seventeen-year-old woman, had jobs. He worked as a busboy, he pumped gas, he parked cars. He stole cars and committed burglaries. He drove a stolen car to California with his pregnant wife. He was arrested, tried, and sentenced once again. He violated parole, went to jail. McNeil Island in Washington State, Terminal Island in San Pedro, California.

And so cause Him to withdraw His present help from us, we shall be made a story and a byword though the world.

A story and byword.

So with time, doing time. He read the work of Dale Carnegie, he became interested in Scientology. According to a prison report, he was "active in softball, basketball and croquet," and was "a member of the Drama Club and the Self Improvement Group." He became interested in Buddhism. What did the Buddhist say to the hot-dog vendor? Make me one with everything. Ho. Ha. He. Boyfriend. Bad childhood, you could say. Moving here, moving there. Began to play the guitar, became a Beatles fan. Who wasn't? They too sought Buddha. George, John, Paul, Ringo. Sitar. White Album. Joan D. Fab Four. "We tell ourselves stories in order to live." A story, a byword. So cause Him. Withdraw. Shelter. Skelter.

Before he was released from prison in 1967, he asked to be allowed to stay. He said, wrote, public record. "This is my home," he said. "I can't adjust to the world outside."

Was released, and that spring, the spring of 1967, he went to Haight-Ashbury in San Francisco. He was thirty-two years old, and he had spent seventeen years in institutions. Slouched there. Summer of love, flowers in hair.

Five feet two inches tall, IQ measured at both 109 and 121.

PIG written on a door with one victim's blood. DEATH TO PIGS was written on a wall above paintings and photographs. Above another painting, RISE was written in blood.

The word WAR was carved on one victim's stomach. Another stabbed forty-one times.

.

On Commonwealth Avenue, in Newton, the houses had big lawns, and there were trees and bushes around every house. Even in the summer, when temperatures reached into the nineties, people kept their windows closed, their air-conditioning on.

We had moved. This was before or after Brookline? Watertown?

I wandered through the house, and late at night, while Joan slept deeply in the bedroom, I opened drawers in the kitchen, I looked in cabinets under the sink. Looked closely and carefully. Looked everywhere. Looked and looked and looked.

Phone sat on the counter, and as I looked, I thought how it ran to wires outside, and how those wires spread out to every spot in the world. To sands of Africa and Asia. Jungle of Siam. To side street, sleeping house, room on second floor, say, in Bath, UK, Bath, Maine. Bat Yam in Central Israel.

I picked up the receiver and listened to the dial tone. Pressed a few numbers, then hung up the phone.

It was 4:07, and Joan's breathing was deep, was even. I wondered what she was dreaming about.

Sometimes, she had told me, she dreamed in cartoons. Mickey Mouse and the Road Runner and Fred Flintstone would all appear. Sometimes Fred opened his mouth, and he had the voice of George Jetson or Donald Duck or Mr. Magoo. Bambi howled like a wild dog or sang a cowboy song. Sometimes Johnny Quest turned into Hercules, or Gumby danced with Bamm-Bamm or Pebbles.

Joan laughed when she told me. "You know what I mean?" she'd ask, and laugh more till her eyes grew wet.

She wanted to know what had become of me. What had happened. Where I had gone. Where was the man, the guy, who taught school, the hurt shy guy I loved so much? What love could.

Do. Does not envy, parade. Bears all, believes all, hopes all, endures. Ten thousand words in a tongue. Withdraw his present help. Shall be made.

I opened the bedroom door and looked in, and from the light of the alarm clock—faint blue on her side of the bed—I saw her sleeping on her back, one arm across her forehead, her neck long and white, the air going deep into her lungs. Looked, lingered, thought. A long time, the blue light flicking as the numbers changed, as time passed. And she was dreaming, my wife, I bet, about Snow White and Barney Rubble and Cinderella.

.

I won't talk about. My mom. What happened to my. Her. It's the one thing I won't talk. Discuss.

The call came through the office of the dean of students. I was a sophomore, and this was in October. All the trees outside were aflame, all the trees were red and yellow and orange. The leaves were hot, and fell like small fires to the earth. Abideth.

The dean told me. He said what happened to. Mother. He gave me the number of the policeman. The cop's name was Rourke.

Rourke got on the phone, and he did, he talked softer than a child. He told me how sorry he was, and asked how soon I could come to Boston. I'd moved away for college. Upstate New York a few years. He asked about Ed. Soft, gentle. This police officer. Finest.

And that's all I can say. Plus, can think about. My mother gone, been dead three days already, and I hadn't known. Gone to classes, read books and took notes, eaten in cafeteria, gone to sleep at night, sweet dreams, and all that ticking ticking time she'd. Mom, been dead and I had not known.

I wondered if Ed knew. Somewhere in the world. Did he pause? Look up?

Birds flew across sky. Sun popped up. Fell. Moon and ocean. Curve of earth. Sail *flap flap flap.* Harvest rice in paddy. Siam. Iceberg flowed along.

I thought of how quiet the rooms must have been as she lay there on the floor of the living room. The clocks ticking, the floors and walls and ceilings making small creaking sounds. The sinks would drip, the refrigerator and heat would click on and off, and noises from outside would come into the empty rooms. People walking by, cars and trucks and bicycles, dogs and cats barking and meowing, planes, trains, wind, rain, dead leaves rattling over the pavement, on the sidewalks and streets, in the gutters.

All of this. Imagine. Pause a moment, please. Drift in and around the rooms, would settle over the couch and chairs and rugs.

Maybe the phone rang. Maybe there were knocks on the door. Maybe, possibly. Someone selling magazines stood there, knocked a second time, frowned, went away. Story, byword. Each of us. You, me, nobody leaves alive.

So pause. Dignity, repose. Small thought.

And light moved through the rooms. Pale gray light at dawn, turning orange by midmorning, then flooding the rooms with yellow light at one or two. Then the slow lengthening shadows, motes of dust, shafts and streaks of light, then finally ghostly streetlights, and her eyes must have been open and staring while I walked along the hallways, the paths, into classes, down stairways. While light and sound, heat and cold moved in the empty rooms. You in your life. Somewhere too.

I didn't want the drawer pulled out, the sheet lifted from the face. They shouldn't have done that. They could have used photographs. They should never have brought me down there, where the pipes in the ceiling. They hissed. The smell like biology class was.

Formalin, alcohols, emulsifiers.

Skin marbles, skin grows shiny, paler, and underneath there are blue tints. They shouldn't have done any of this.

They kept calling from work, Mom's work, she didn't show, and then they called the police. The police went to the quiet rooms. Her peace, her repose. Then came with powder, with photographers, with tweezers and plastic bags and took hair and skin and fiber samples. They checked under her nails.

I didn't sleep before they rolled the drawer out. Felt the cold, saw the shape under the sheet, and they should not have moved the sheet.

What did it matter then?

The television gone, the radio next to her bed gone. Drawers opened and the things inside disturbed.

Poor bare forked animal. What did she have to steal?

"Who'd she associate with?" the police asked.

"Who'd want to do this?"

Looked at me.

Any enemies?

"Think," they told me. I do that all the time. But didn't of course say. "Think hard. Even the most insignificant detail can be important."

They wanted to know everything about Ed. They said, "Let us decide what's important."

They kept looking at me.

And I thought, if you could call this thought: After this, everything will get better. There will be nobody else to love.

I stayed four days. For the funeral home and for the Salvation Army to empty the rooms. We care, we are grateful. So sorry. Your trouble. Plot, urn, ashes, deceased, bereaved. Last wishes, desires, things. Finality.

Then went back to college. I wondered where Ed was. What he looked like, and if he thought of me. Where the fuck had Ed gone?

They said they'd do all. They could. They said, Let us know there's anything we can do. Rourke with his drinker's nose, with his soft voice and hard eyes. Cop. Guy from phone. Decent.

"Take care," he said to me. To Earl. Mr. the Pearl.

EIGHT

After they took my father away, Mrs. Maloney, next door, wouldn't talk to me or to any of us for over a week. We'd pass her outside, on the sidewalk, near the fence or in the backyard, and she'd look at us without seeing anything, would pass by with a stone face. Head up, wearing her heavy sweater, carrying a big black handbag, gold clasp on top, or walking once with Brandon. Not holding his—Brandon's—hand. Eyes up, straight ahead.

Don't you.

Dare.

You.

Eyes on the ground. Feet. Down, floor. Wipe that smile, that smirk.

The phone rang one night, alone, rang and, long after we were in bed, I got up. Ran. Went quickly to the phone, picked up the receiver. "Hello," I said, and all I could hear was the sound of breathing. Breath, her deep breath.

"Hello," I said again. A whisper. Just a.

"Little feces," Mrs. Maloney said in a low, soft voice.

I didn't say anything at first. There was an old and cold feeling in my neck and on the front of my head. Something from before. I did not want to think of or remember in any way shape.

"Little shit," she said in an even softer voice.

No lights on. Me, bare feet. Mom, Ed, asleep to all the world. Had no idea.

"Mrs. Maloney," I said.

"Who? Who did you say this was?"

"Mrs."

"You disgusting snot," she whispered. "There's no such person."

Linoleum, cracked, speckled underfoot. Curling at edges. Color, brown, tan, silver gold speckle.

"Who's this?" Earl. Boy of not very old. Asked.

"I'll smash your disgusting, snotty face."

Listened to her slow breathing. He, boy who was I. Pictured, thought of in his mind's eye—for there is such a thing, in a manner of speaking—her thick glasses, and the huge watery pupils behind the lenses.

"Who do you want?" I asked.

"Who," I said again. On phone, more courage possibly.

She breathed deeply. She sighed. Could picture the red spreading over her nose and cheeks and forehead, the lips thinning out. Big and angry. Knot, fist.

Was in the front hall. I was. And could see the linoleum on the living room floor from the light outside. A picture hung over the couch that was also a bed, and there was a pale square of light below and to its right.

"Do you have a penis?" she asked. "Do you know the thing that hangs down between your legs?"

I was. Said nothing. Silent, was invisible.

"In real boys, real men, that thing, that fleshy rubbery thing, stands up when it sees a woman." She breathed deeply again. "Do you understand?"

"Yes." Said. May have, think so. May misremember. But don't think so. Don't. A person, boy, kid, would not make such a thing up.

"You probably wouldn't know. Is that correct?"

"No." Pretty sure. But might not have said.

"So you know enough?"

"No."

"Then you're a know-nothing." You. You.

"No." Boy said. Did say very quietly no, though was sure she did not hear his low no. Too low, small, soft. Not there, almost not there.

"Which is it?"

The streetlight flickered outside. I stared at it for long, flickered so fast it seemed a steady light. Cars there were. Parked along curb, and lights on in some of houses across street—yellow rectangles, not squares, and orange and green squares because of some shades. Shadows moved across an orange shade. A man in shadow a dozen feet tall. Man not a woman. Not Dad. For he was taken unto. Taketh. The hour might pass from him.

"You know what they do with their things?" she asked.

Another shadow passed. A cat, I bet. Walked across the top of a parked car. Mrs.

Don't. And bound Jesus. Carried him away, delivered him to.

"They put them in women."

Ed turned over in bed. The refrigerator hummed, seemed for a moment to cough.

"You didn't know that, did you?" She seemed to breathe. Don't listen. Mrs. She. Shift the receiver.

"Am I right?" she asked.

"Yes." But did not say. She knew who I was. She knew. Looked up.

"Because you're a moronic son of a bitch then?"

"Yes."

"Well," she said, and made a sound that was something like laughter. "At least you know something then."

"No."

She said, "Nothing was like it is now because people were nice and went to church and didn't have deformed bastard children."

I could feel heat spreading through me.

"Not nitwits like you, stupid. Not white trash like yourself." She paused and breathed.

I didn't breathe. Taken captive of your brethren. Rage that reacheth up unto heaven.

"Well," she said, and her voice grew even lower. "We knew nice people when I was a girl. People with Ford cars and houses with porches." She sighed. The Irish in her now up. Would this be Mrs. M. talking again on the Great Famine? "Nothing to eat but milk and stirabout and potatoes. Gone lonesome. Bewildered. The stink. The poverty. Sods of turf. One putrid mass of family huddled in corner, darkest corner of cabin. Idle, lazy. Rags. Dead by wayside. Inarticulate noise in throat. Enraged weakened idiot. Gaped, rotted, dark and lowering."

A car went by on the street. The shine on the car's roof, its headlights, were so far away they were a movie. Then of course. Over there. Then: When potato failed. "So many perished. None to aid them. Coffin with movable bottom, mass graves. Skibbereen and Schull in Cork. Ribs skin. Wailings. Typhus sweeping. Fell in glens, roads, towns, hovels, seacoast, fell in fields. Brooding sky."

Then: When this happens it's like the sky opening and angels in white are singing and everything gets so huge it feels like the world will explode.

She put down the receiver and then picked it up again. Went away, came back. Had to check on Brandon.

The boy stood and felt how cool the glass of the window felt. Didn't know why he put up with this, did this. The pure love of darkness, of sin, of transgression. Plus a warm brownie, a scone, a chocolate chip cookie soft from the oven. Part of her was how a mother should be. She stayed home, always baked things, had a clean house, had moments of kindness.

"Would you like to hear what happens when people starve?" she asked. "What happens when a woman sees her boy grow up an idiot?"

My. His hand came away from the glass, and for a long time I didn't say anything. I'd heard before. My head ached, but with something that came from the other side of pain.

"You'd like to hear more, my boy. Wouldn't you?"

I didn't speak or say a word.

"You'd like to hear what a snot-faced moron you are?"

I made a sound in my throat that wasn't yes or no. Some sound, not speech.

"You ever seen a person starve?" she asked. "You ever seen a mother hold her dying child?"

"No." And I stood. Everyone asleep. Dad gone. Mom and Ed and Brandon asleep.

She began to breathe louder. Nothing moved outside the window. I touched the glass again. It was smooth and cool like the underside of a pillow. I moved my fingers on the glass.

She stopped, and I thought I heard something rustling. Squares of yellow light in houses outside. Not hers though. Her house dark. She was talking in the dark, under cover of night.

I looked out the window. Stood, held coiled cord. I was quiet, held my breath. It was empty outside. She was from somewhere. But right next door. And if you looked at her, most times she was normal, average. Looked like whoever. Nice as can be. Baked bread, muffins, cakes, cookies. Any kind. Corn, blueberry, raisins, chocolate chips, white icing, orange-peel frosting, lemon frosting with tiny shreds and slips of lemon peel.

There was more rustling. Her end of phone.

I heard a match strike, heard her inhale. Thought I heard her blow her nose. Her voice got lower still. She was breathing heavily.

Wanted to do something.

Couldn't speak, did not.

She shifted the phone. Sounded like tissues rustling. Not anything.

I listened to her breath.

My head ached. Eyes down, eyes on floor. Don't you dare look up. Think to speak. Whisper, whimper, whine.

Maeve Maloney. Mrs. M.

I pressed the button on the phone. Thumb down on the thing. Her voice. Went dead.

●

In the morning my mother hummed to herself. Moved around the kitchen and said, "Don't forget your lunch, Eddie."

"Mom," he said. "I hate school."

"Edward," she said, and he and I both looked at her.

She was tall and had dark hair that fell to her collarbone. She wore glasses that came to a point, that were sideways teardrops. Her eyes were brown, and when she laughed the sound came from deep within her chest. All the way. Such laughter. That lightness could emanate.

"Why can't we have ice cream for breakfast?" Ed said.

"Because," Mom said.

"Because why?"

"Because I said so."

"That doesn't count," he told her. He was standing in the doorway to the pantry. There was a hanging white curtain instead of a door. Film, veil.

"Edward," she said.

"Mom," I said. Erased, as it were.

Her neck and ears were getting red. Oatmeal was bubbling on the stove. I turned the gas off, heard the flame sputter out. *Sput, sput.* Oatmeal starting to smell burned.

"Why do I have to eat shit every morning?" he said. Ed. The curtain hid the side of his face.

"What'd you say?" Mom asked. She, Mom. Standing near the refrigerator.

"I hate oatmeal. It tastes like shit." Speak to your mother like that.

"You little ingrate," she said.

"I want Froot Loops," he said. "Cocoa Puffs, Lucky Charms."

"Why don't you eat a bowl of sugar?" she said. Voice like. Curled voice, not friendly. "Rot your teeth. See if I care."

"I want cookies and chocolate." His face getting red like her face.

"You can't have any," she said, and her voice curled more and rose. She sounded almost happy, set free.

"You're ugly," my brother said. "I hate you."

I. Not a word, a peep. Looked at the oatmeal.

"Get out of this house," Mom said in a soft, level, even voice. "Get out of this house this instant."

"I'm not coming back. You're so fucking cunt-ugly you make me sick," he said. Gulped air. He. Ed. Me. "You suck. Dad hates you too."

He went out the back door. Blam, shake. And down porch stairs. Splinters. Peeling paint. We heard the outer door slam, blam. Twice. He ran fast, shadowlike, moving, along side of house.

I got a bowl and spoon, went to the stove. Boy who was left.

Mom stood near—at side of—the refrigerator. Red mark like slapped on her cheek. She stood and looked at the pantry curtain. Brown stain the size of an apple near the bottom of the curtain.

I. The smell was. Spooned oatmeal into my bowl. The sides and bottom of pan were black, awful smell. Sat at the kitchen table and ate. Chewed, moved jaws, tongue. Glue, and bits of black. Burned.

Mom left the kitchen, and I heard her close her bedroom door. Didn't hear anything else. Just clock ticking, water dripping on the inside of toilet. Swallow and shut the fuck up.

·

Carla was tall, and had short blond hair. She sat in front of me in an art-appreciation class, and when the lights went down and the teacher began to show slides, there was a halo of light around her head. Her neck was long, and the collar of her shirt framed her neck against the light on the screen. This Mr. Madden. Pressure packing tighter inside, in college.

"Abstract expressionism," the teacher said, "was, in a way, a response to the chaos of our century. To war and mass extermination and fragmentation."

On the screen there was a painting—long swirls of drips, black and white and tan drips. The longer I looked, the more I followed a single drip, under and through and into the white mass of canvas.

Carla was twirling a piece of her hair around her index finger. Her fingers were long like her body, were thin as wire.

·

She's sitting in the front dayroom when I get back from lunch, only it's a different young woman from outside this time. Several have been here. Appear a moment, then go. She looks even more like Joan than some others. Hair's real short, wearing a black sweater, black jeans, gold necklace. Joan never owned.

Joan had to go. Who the fuck could stand it? Swoop way up to ceiling to top of house trees. To fucking stars. Doing voices, high low. Whisper, rant. Learned young Mr. Earl Madden. So quiet sometimes. Then read book and book. Take his medicine. All over the fucking map. Teach his students, talk to people on street. In bank, supermarket, on line at ticket counter for bus or plane to where the fuck you going now, Mr. Earl the Pearl. Throng of bearded men, sad-colored garments, you got your gray steeple-crowned hats. Mr. Hawthorne.

You got that, fucking lugheads. Wake the fuck up. You think my class is television. Slouch smirk. Mouth breathers. Slouch on the couch. Eat Cheetos, hand in pants. How many of you read the assignment? Read the assigned reading? Tell the truth for once in your life. Get your thumbs out of your mouths. Hands out of your pants. Put the remote down. Close your mouth, open your eyes. Ever heard of reading? A fucking book?

With women some wearing hoods others bareheaded assembled wooden edifice door of which heavily timbered with oak studded with iron spikes. Scarlet Letter.

Get it? Spikes, you numbnuts.

Slide back. Cycle down. Rapid rushing thoughts confused rapid, flash fast *clickclickclick.* She, in dayroom. Just sits there, even after I come in, like she's been told not to say anything, like she's been told what happened last time. Like I'm supposed to notice her, and pretend I'm stupid and think she's Joan, and start talking to her.

Not Joan of course. She sits there and looks in front of her, and I know for sure the differences. Joan doesn't wear black, and she wouldn't cut her hair so short, and she wouldn't just sit there. My wife knew I wasn't stupid. Whatever the fuck else in the short time we had together. This charming even handsome and articulate and sometimes brilliant young man. Knew—Bible, you got your King James, you got your New King James, you got your Revised Standard, your New English Bible, your Jerusalem, favored by your scholars. Hey, you ever notice you take your Jeru from Jerusalem you got Salem. You got your witches, switch channel change text, set of fucking stories.

Now your Bible. Back to your Bible. You got your basic sacred text. You see what I'm saying. You fucking listening, or do I have to yell? Talk louder faster more dazzle brilliance. You got your Aramaic, your Greek Hebrew Sanskrit. Yr fucking Septuagint—(Gk version of OT), yr Peshitta (simple, no shit) Version. Who slew? Flew? Who flung doo? Spotted Walls by Who Flung Doo? Who? Huh? Slew, begat, therein, wherein. You got your revisers, translators, transcribers. Fucking Christians hate Jews hate Palestinians. Irish hate English, white black, yellow red. You got your sand nigger, you got your basic fucking hater. Isolationist and superior. I hurt more. Longer. Better. My God, yr god. Who fucks who? Will that be with or without Vaseline, K-Y, Astroglide? You got yr mick, polack, dago, kike, nigger, limey—each and all greedy, lazy, stupid, cruel—A-rab, slope, kraut, sneaky, sex- power- money-crazed. Cunt. Cock. Anus. Orifice. Opening.

■

Mom drove, Ed was in the passenger seat, and I was behind him, next to a warm tin of cookies Mrs. Maloney and Brandon had baked. We passed a doughnut shop, a hardware store, a gas station, a florist shop, and then we stopped at a traffic light. A fat woman pushed a baby carriage in the crosswalk, and Ed said, "Look."

There was a small gray poodle in the baby carriage. The dog wore a white bonnet and was covered by a pink blanket. God's honest truth.

"My God," Mom said.

"Why's she do that?" Ed asked.

Mom said, "I don't know. Maybe she wanted a baby. Poor dumb beast."

The fat woman was wearing a long yellow raincoat, even though the sky was blue. When she reached the other side of the crosswalk, she went around a corner and out of sight, like that.

Light changed, stores turned to houses with squares of lawn and chain-link fence in front of them. Then lawns grew larger, and there was a median strip separating the traffic.

Then there were no traffic lights, and there were long curves in the road, and we went faster and faster.

Mom said, "I don't want you two to pay attention to any people you see or hear."

"Why not?" I asked.

"Cause it's a mental ward," Ed said.

"Honey," Mom said to Ed, and she put her hand on his arm.

She turned, for a moment, to look at me, then looked back at the road.

"It's a hospital," Mom said. "And you might see people who aren't feeling so well." Ha.

"They're nuts," Ed said. "This is a psycho ward."

"Earl, honey," Mom said. "Your brother's just trying to scare you."

"It's a nuthouse, Mom," Ed said. "I'm just trying to tell the truth." Nothing but.

"It's people, Earl, who are having problems, people who drink too much or who, you know, can't take care of themselves and such."

A man in a pickup truck passed us. He wore a blue watch cap. He just went by. Kind of old. Maybe yellow pee stains on underwear.

"They need to be in a safe place," Mom said.

"When people are too crazy to go to jail," Ed said, told me. "When they can't be held responsible for what they do, they get sent here." Mr. Information.

"Edward," Mom said.

"Sorry, Mom," he told her. "But it's sort of the truth."

None of us said—a word, peep—anything for a long time. Mom and Ed both looked in front of them at the curves of the road. We passed a blue sign that said HOSPITAL, and Mom put the right blinker on. We turned in and went for a few hundred yards along a driveway. The grass was still brown, and there were tall, bare trees lining the driveway. Very—long slow lens—graceful shot. Sense of space, calm, repose.

We stopped at a big Victorian house where a sign said VISITORS STOP.

Mom parked, told us to wait, went inside. Behind the house we could see a long hill, winding roads and paths, small brick buildings. A man in pajamas and slippers stood in the middle of a path and stared at the sky.

"I wanna go home," I said to Ed.

"Too late now," he told me. He-me. Ed-head.

We both looked at the man.

"You chicken?" he finally asked.

"No. Just wish I was home."

Saw Mom come down front steps with yellow paper in hand.

"Okay," she said when she got in the car.

Drove past brick buildings, past a rusting shed. Black grates on all the windows, but we didn't see any more people in pajamas. Eyes on sky.

Near the back of the hospital grounds, we parked next to a two-story, redbrick building. Got out of car, Mom said, "Lock it."

Went to front steps. Two white pillars supporting an overhang above porch. Paint cracked and chipping off pillars and underside of overhang.

Mom knocked on gray metal door. Heard keys, then door opened, big man in white stood in hallway.

"Hello," he said, smiled. Bottom tooth missing. "We been expecting you."

Walked in, he locked door behind us, keys attached to belt with black nylon strap.

"I hope you had a good drive," he said, and Mom said, "Yes."

Someone moaning behind a second door.

"Fucka ducka," someone said.

Man unlocked that door, sounds and smells strong.

"Fucka ducka," woman in a gray smock said. "Fucka ducka, fucka ducka," she kept saying. She stood near window in big room.

Three people sitting in front of television set that was turned off. One man's mouth hanging open. Mouth breather.

"Norman," someone shouted.

"This way," man in white said. Locked second door, and we followed him through the big room, then down a long—dim light—hallway. Took a right at the end, to smaller hallway.

Man squatting underneath fire extinguisher that hung behind cage on wall. Wore pajama bottoms, but no pajama top, no slippers, unshaven. Few long strands of pale hair on chest. Useless nipples. Couple of few brown moles on white shoulders and bony chest. Sprinkle pattern. Sea salt. Star spray, only brown.

"Dad," Ed said in a soft voice, but the man didn't turn or say anything. No peep.

"Honey," Mom said. Ed and I—both—together, turned to her.

NINE

The soon-to-be famous man. *Life* magazine, *Look* magazine. Front page in London, Saigon, Times Square, Cape Town, Moscow, even Red Square. Pure products of America. Shit. A nice-looking fellow. Real manners. Kept his feet off the furniture. Said, Yes, sir. No, ma'am. Six feet tall, blond hair and blue eyes. Seen pictures and am clearly not mistaken. I know a thing or two about this one. Heir to Walt, been a marksman in the Marine Corps.

This is what he brought: a 9-millimeter pistol, a .357 Magnum revolver. A .35-caliber pump-action Remington rifle, a .30-caliber M-1 carbine, a hunting knife, a sawed-off 12-gauge shotgun, a 6-millimeter bolt-action rifle. He brought a telescopic lens. On his big day he brought water, candy, peanuts, raisins, sandwiches, and fruit cocktail. He brought a transistor radio, toilet paper, spray deodorant.

Deodorant. Feature that.

He was locked and loaded, he was prepared.

He wrote: "I don't quite understand what is compelling me to type this note. I have been to a psychiatrist. I have been having fears and violent impulses. I've had some tremendous headaches in the past.

"I am prepared to die. After my death, I wish an autopsy on me be performed to see if there's any mental disorder.

"I've decided to kill Kathy tonight. I love her very much.

"I intend to kill my wife after I pick her up from work. I don't want her to face the embarrassment my actions will surely cause her."

He was twenty-five years old, he had been an Eagle Scout. There was a picture of him from when he was in his mid-twenties, sleeping on his side on a couch. A small black dog was asleep near his feet. A book was leaning against his lap, one of his hands cupped the side of his face. His hair was short, his features were regular and handsome.

What is it that draws me so to these people? That they do what we fear to dream about? Why do they always make the covers of magazines? And we read so greedily. In the newspaper business they say, If it bleeds it leads.

A few months earlier, after years of physical and emotional abuse, his mother had finally left his father in Florida and moved to Texas to be near her son. Enough was enough. Think of that. How hard that must have been for her, in 1966, the middle of the Johnson years. U.S. troops moving more and more steadily into Vietnam.

That night, the eve of the big day, he picked up his wife at work, dropped her off at home, and around midnight he went to visit his mother. He stabbed his mother in the chest, then shot her in the back of the head.

"To Whom It May Concern," he wrote. "I have just killed my

mother. If there's a heaven, she's going there. If there's not a heaven, she's out of her pain and misery.

"I love my mother with all my heart."

He returned to his own apartment, where his wife was sleeping. He stabbed her three times in the chest. He wrapped her body in a sheet, then sat down at his typewriter.

"Twelve AM—Mother already dead. Three o'clock—both dead."

He wrote about his father. He said he hated him with a "mortal passion."

At the bottom of the page he wrote, "Life is not worth living."

The next morning he went to the observation tower of the university where he was a student. Longhorns, was not a fucking pussy. The tower was three hundred feet high. A few days earlier, he had visited the tower with his brother, had noticed the heavy stone wall around the observation deck, had noticed the view of the surrounding campus.

On this day, the day that would make him famous, put him on page one and lead every news report everywhere, a receptionist asked him what he was doing, and he smashed her skull with the butt of a rifle.

On the twenty-seventh floor of the tower, he shot a man and his aunt who had come to the tower for the view.

Then he went to the tower's observation deck. The people walking below were tiny, they were smaller than insects. Traffic moved in the measured way it moves from such large distances.

He looked through the telescopic lens, noted the crosshairs, and began to fire. Went *pop* and *pop* and *pop*. Was in a zone. Went pull and pull and pull. He shot six students, then he hit a pregnant woman in the abdomen. She lived, but her baby's skull was smashed.

Went *pop, pop, pop. Crack. Pop. Crack crack crack.* Was deep in it. Was all the way in and on this thing. Just kept going like all the electricity in his eyes and hands, his arms and legs were on and in him and working like magic. Just flowing together. So far up there above just about everything.

An eyrie. Aerie: nest of a predatory bird, as an eagle, built on a high place. House or stronghold built on a high place. Unassailable: not capable of being disputed or disproven; not capable of being attacked or seized successfully. For a time at least.

He shot forty-six people, killed eighteen. One man was five hundred yards away and was shot in the stomach. One man was training for the Peace Corps, one boy was delivering newspapers.

The police used snipers to try to shoot him. They sent an airplane with marksmen to the tower, but he drove the plane off with rifle fire. Finally the police stormed the tower and killed him.

This was August first. Summer, shimmery Texas heat. A Monday, midday, Texas sun.

.

Mom was at the kitchen table drinking beer, and Ed and I were in the living room watching television. An unshaven man held a gun on a man and a woman. Windows open, traffic passing outside like always. "Don't move," he said on TV, and the woman said, "Steady there now, Luke."

The man with the gun licked his lips. He looked from the woman to the man to the woman again.

"You think he'll ever come home?" Ed asked, and I kept watching the screen, mouth open.

"Who?"

"The pope, numbnuts."

"Dad?"

"Yeah."

"Don't know," I said.

A commercial came on, and I got up and went to the kitchen.

Mom was smoking a cigarette, and there was a glass of beer and a brown quart bottle on the table. There were dishes piled in the sink, and two pots on the stove from dinner from the night before. One had greasy water with a hot dog still floating in it, and the other had cold creamed corn. Mom was reading the newspaper. Radio on low, all news always. She looked up when I came into the room.

"How you doing?" she said.

A stream of smoke came out of her mouth, and I watched it rise and surround the light that hung on the wall above the table.

"Good," I said. "Can I've a taste?"

I stood next to her, and she held the glass while I took a sip. It was bitter, and I could barely swallow.

"Yuck," I said, and Mom laughed. Then she coughed, wiped her mouth.

We heard the outside hall door open.

"Earl," Mrs. Maloney yelled from outside, then we heard her in the small hall. "Maureen," she yelled, which was my mother's name. "You there?" We could smell warm cookies.

I opened the door to the back hall. Mrs. M. The cookies—I could tell—were cinnamon and oatmeal and raisin.

"What?"

"Come out here," Mrs. M. said.

Mom said, "Go ahead."

I went out to the back hall where it was dark, and Mrs. Maloney handed me the paper towel filled with warm cookies. "For Ed and your mother," she whispered, and poked her head though the kitchen doorway. I came in from behind her and handed the cookies to Mom, and Mrs. M. said, "I'm wanting to show the boy something next door, Maureen, if it isn't a bother."

"Course not," Mom said. She was already eating a cookie and sipping on her beer.

Ed was still one room over, eyes on the tube, mouth agape.

"Look in the den next door," she said to me, and I went to the hall and out the door with her. Down steps, through gate, past peeling paint, her steps and door and dark hallway. Mrs. M. behind me the whole time. Brandon was asleep in his chair, his mouth open.

"He's hoping to catch flies with that mouth," Mrs. Maloney whispered to me, full of mirth, and something sad, too.

Brandon made a rasping, snorting sound in his nose and throat. I went back to the kitchen. Mrs. Maloney was at the stove. "See what I have," she said, smiling and nodding at the same time. "It's like living with a corpse."

I didn't say anything.

She was putting more warm cookies on a plate. They were slightly brown, and I could see the air waver from the stove.

"These are some more for your mother and brother," she said. "You think you could bring these over, then come back?"

"Sure," I said.

I took the plate over, and my mother smiled when she saw me, and Ed was eating cookies in front of the TV. "For you and Ed," I told her. "I have to go back."

When I was in Mrs. M.'s kitchen again, she told me to sit down. She poured me a glass of milk and set cookies in front of me.

"Go ahead," she said. "What's the matter with you?" Paused. "Okay then, sweetheart."

She ran her hand lightly through my hair. Fingers moving gently around on my scalp. I felt the heat from the stove on my back.

"C'mon," she said.

I took a cookie, and bit into it, and chewed. I sipped milk, and behind me, Mrs. M. said, "Is it good?"

"Delicious," I told her.

I sipped, and ate more cookies, and she stood behind me, keeping up with the fingers in my hair, which felt so good. Saying, "That's a boy. That's a fine boy I know."

.

Joan said, "C'mon." She took my hand, and we heard water lapping the sides of the lake, the lake where she had gone as a child.

Everyone was asleep, and we were barefoot. We had on shorts and T-shirts, and Joan said, "Earl, honey, c'mon," in a loud whisper.

She pulled me down the hall, through the living room and kitchen, and I could smell her shampoo, her skin, her long thin arms and legs. I could hear people breathing, people turning in sleep. Her beautiful sisters and brother and their friends and her lovely mom. Their freckles and smiles and loose sleeping limbs.

"What're you doing?" I whispered. "You're crazy," I said.

She unlocked the kitchen door, and I followed her outside. Moon, stars, real tall pines and maples and oaks. Pine scent, deep earth smell. Sweet dark air. Made you feel amazing to be alive. More stars than I'd ever imagined there could be. Everything else dark and shadowed and looming. Silvery.

"We're going swimming," she whispered.

I followed her around the house, then down a series of steps. We passed a stone wall, then we were on sand and pebbles. Sheen of night.

The lake was huge and shining. Its surface glowed almost, and there were stars on the water. Small lights on far shores.

"Hurry," Joan said, and she pulled her T-shirt over her head. Her nipples were dark, were hard.

She unbuttoned her shorts. Pushed down shorts and underwear, and I could see the dark patch. Long pale limbs. Lovely breasts, curve at hip, shoulder. Neck, sweet hair. She. Shined as water.

"Hurry, Earl," she said, and I felt her shiver. Felt myself growing down there, getting hard.

Took off my clothes and felt air moving between my legs. My thing, unembarrassed. My. Shy.

Joan took my hand again, and we began to step into the water. Her hair was short like a boy's. Waist narrow, hips swelled. Pale round behind.

"Stop," I whispered, then I put my arms around her. She was cool and warm. I cupped her breasts in my hands, felt nipples.

The water was cold. The water could not have been more than fifty, sixty degrees. Who knew?

"Farther out," she said, and began to walk deeper into the lake. Sand underfoot in water.

When the water hit my crotch, I held my breath. Oh. Her shoulders white, hair dark in starlight.

When the water was up to her neck, she turned to me. Kissed, her mouth to my mouth, but light, and put her arms around my neck. Pushed off the bottom of the lake, and her legs snaked around me, wrapped my waist.

"Earl," she said. "Earl the Pearl," she whispered. "Jewel of the sea."

Grew warmer and warmer.

"Come inside," she said. "Hurry. Please hurry."

.

"Fuck yes," he says. This punk. Tattoos. Dagger, rose, long scar on side of neck, skinny. "Way easier than you'd think," Jerry Wright is telling me. "Even with the shit, with the fuck-fucks out there. Still easy."

I look at him and nod. He keeps talking. Jerry. Doesn't need encouragement, likes to talk. Everybody wants to talk talk talk.

We're in the community room in back, with all the chairs, the couch that has stuffing falling out. People pass by in the hall. Now and then someone will lean in, say hello, maybe ask for a cigarette. "Got a smoke?" Give them a smoke if you can. Outside windows, through the mesh, are fields, trees, power lines, dead gray sky.

Jerry's small and skinny, a bald chicken, but has muscles like a boxer—a bantamweight or lightweight. Tics. Keeps blinking his eyes. Nerve on cheek, left side, jumps under skin. But a white boxer, would cut around eyes and nose. Bleeder.

Fucking jumpy.

"I mean, at Concord this wasn't something I'd talk about, you know." He stops and looks. Blinks. Blinks. Blinks some more. Looks quick left, quick right, quick leftright. Tic, nerve.

I nod, make myself go slow. Breathe, slow, deep.

Let Jerry whirl. Full of shit. Punk. Still, I like the man. Fucking Jerry. Mean as a snake. No mother love. Wire tough, little prick. Is what he is.

"Cause everyone's locked up there with the long bids, and you got fucking guys falling in love with other fucking guys, you got the usual shit like jealousy and hurt feelings, you got chocolates and valentines from one ripped dude to another." Pulls on his cigarette, squinches up his face. " 'You didn't notice my hair. Didn't kiss me when the cop was looking.' " Jerry does girly voice. Blows smoke.

"I mean, normal guys," he says. Looks at me, looks to each side. Flick tic. Flick flick. "Only they're down fifteen, twenty, twenty-five to fucking life, and there's no pussy for a real long time, and they fall in love with other guys. You know—the fuck—what the."

He draws in more smoke. "Shit," he says and laughs.

"How long were you in?"

"Two years, then here."

I nod more. Breathe. Don't go fast. Don't speed up. Take your time, big fella. Let the Jerry go spin spin spin.

"These guys don't want to know what you'd do to pussy on the outside, so I don't say anything. But I'm telling you, you got eyes to hear, it's so fucking easy you wouldn't know it."

I light a cigarette. Go. Slow.

"You ring the doorbell, they look through the peephole, you tell them you're from the landlord's office. You're from a modeling agency, you're from the board of health. You're a painter, exterminator, plumber—doesn't matter."

He takes another drag, and smoke clouds his face.

"Some of them say, 'Go away. I'll call the cops.' They'll say, 'Why didn't anyone call first?' They'll want to see ID, and you flash your bank card. Sometimes you can get a badge at a joke shop, at a junk place. Show them your grocery-store card, fucking credit card that you charged to the max. Nobody gives a shit. Who looks? You know."

"When was this?" I ask. "Before Concord?" When, Jerry? Place it, dude.

"Before here," he says. Straightens the crease on his pants. Jerry's got a thin boy's face. Hollows and slants and bones. Big dark eyes, and it looks like he doesn't shave yet. He's skinny like a teenager, even though he's over thirty. He has a smile that makes me smile, it's so broad and open.

"You show them your driver's license, you got nothing else. At a time like that, who's counting the numbers?" Looks down, to the side, the other side. "The fuck," the Jerry adds.

"So they let you in?"

"Two, three, four times they'll say, 'Sorry. I'll call the cops. I don't know you. I can't let you in.' But then you'll hit one who opens the door. She'll open up and stand there smiling, and you walk in like you belong."

Carole Mitchell goes by in the hall. One of us. Artichoke. It's midafternoon, she's still wearing her bathrobe and an orange shower cap.

"Hi, Jerry," she says, and he waves to her.

"Crazy bitch," he says, shakes his head.

Tic, twitch. "Everyone wants somebody to talk to, listen to. Basic human fucking rule." Looks left, right, behind. Nerve on cheek jumps. "Nobody'll stay in their own room. Too fucking boring, too lonely."

"What do you do then?" I ask.

"When?"

"You get in?"

"You know the joke about the gorilla?" he asks.

Shake my head.

"Where's an eight-hundred-pound gorilla sleep when he gets to your cage?"

"Dunno."

"Anywhere he wants."

"I don't get it."

"You're in, you do anything you fucking want. Front, back, top, bottom. A.M. P.M. Chocolate. Strawberry." Smiles big, smiles warm. Large as nervous life, sitting here.

Very tough to match this individual smiling man. Tattoos included. With.

The Jerry Meister.

•

Smiling Jack Kennedy was still president, and Endicott Peabody was governor of the Commonwealth of Massachusetts. After the discovery of the fifth strangled body in late August, nothing happened for three months. You had your calm at the center of your storm, if you will. Quiet, too quiet, if you get my drift, snowstorm. Waiting for the other fucking shoe to drop. Hammer to hit. Bomb to blow up. Blow to strike. Bullet to fire, leaf to fall. This, that, whatever.

The police and medical examiners and psychiatrists met to talk over the case. All serious as a heart attack. You bet. Serious as cancer. They all agreed that because nothing was ever missing from the apartments of the victims, robbery could be ruled out as a motive. Real shrewd, top-flight forensic work.

And because there was no sign of forced entry, and nobody— no neighbors, no deliveryman or repairman—had seen anyone or anything unusual, the police speculated that the Strangler would look and act normal. He was someone who probably had a job, who might be married, who could be the father of children. No horns or tail. Probably didn't drool or stutter or talk too loud, or break out in show tunes while asking if he could check the gas meter or the furnace. No fucking high jinks.

In early December a woman returned home to the apartment she shared with two friends. The apartment was on the fourth floor of a building on Huntington Avenue, about three blocks from where the first woman had been killed. She found her roommate. Who:

She had been strangled with her own nylon stockings, a slip and belt were also twisted around her neck. She was lying on the living room floor, wearing shoes and stockings. But the rest of her clothes, her underwear, her robe, were torn away, and her legs were widely spread. So brutally exposed. Where—so obviously, but always undisclosed, so many came from.

This time different, though. She was twenty years old, about a third the age of the first five victims. She was also black, and she lived with roommates.

Three and a half weeks later, on the last day of the year, a seventh woman was found on her bed, in her apartment on Park Drive. There were three nylon stockings tied around her neck. Her pajama top had been pushed above her breasts, and she was otherwise naked.

This woman was twenty-three years old. Her apartment was

less than a mile from the twenty-year-old's apartment. Again there were differences.

This woman had been in bed, a spread covering her to the neck. Her eyes had been closed, her arms were at her sides, and her legs were together. She had been raped and then put to bed as though she was sleeping.

An autopsy showed that at the time of her death she had been pregnant a month.

These were facts. This happened in Boston. While President Kennedy was in the White House. I knew these details to be true. Could easily imagine the silence in the rooms before the body was discovered but after the murderer had gone. Could hear water drip in pipes, and feel how light would shift and change in the room where the body was left. Go from light to dark. But in very slow, very tiny increments. And if there was a watch or clock in the room, there would be the faint sounds of the hands of the watch or clock, still moving, still going about its measured business. Lending a trace of something—maybe dignity, or forgiveness, or mercy, or release—to an otherwise gruesome scene.

·

This is what it sounded like in my apartment, in my house, at any place I ever stayed, at three in the morning. A long and deep and endless nothing, punctuated every hour or two by small sounds—by hums and ticks, by creaks, by dim whines, by thin clanks, by a rustle, a shift, by taps and pings. Whirs, chirs. *Chit chit chit chit. Sheshesheshesheshe.* But mostly the silence that, after a long time, seemed like a hum. So faint that it was hard to tell if it was any sound at all. If it was something deep in my ear or brain, molecules whirling, atoms spinning, or just the sound of the earth moving around the sun. It was like the moment when you couldn't tell if something was very hot or very cold. Inside or outside. Very close or very far. Real loud or soft and somewhere between.

After a long time, after I listened and listened and still didn't know, I went into the bedroom and lay down next to Joan. If Joan was there then.

Just lying there, I'd feel the heat from her body and hear the sound of air going into her nose and mouth, then down her throat to her lungs, then into her blood. I'd picture the oxygen moving down her arms and legs. Then to her brain. I guessed. Thought about it there in the dark. Pictured neurons and synapses, and her eyes moving rapidly in sleep, and dreams like movies, like every memory and image and sensation of a lifetime—from an extra blanket to the girl in nursery school who cried when her mother left.

.

This is what might have happened, I will try to tell Dr. Schumacher. Herr Doktor Schumacher, for he seems to want to play out this thing with me. If for no other reason than for the needs, the parameters and guidelines of the *DSM,* the *Diagnostic and Statistical Manual of Mental Disorders,* the big thumping red book published by the American Psychiatric Association. Factitious Disorder by Proxy, and so on.

He has a pen and a yellow legal pad and he looks at me over the tops of his glasses and makes the murmuring, urging, encouraging noises. "Mmmmmm, ahhhhhhh, yessssssss. I see. Of course. Sure."

I am not sure, even though I get four shots of Prolixin every day, and Jerry has told me they use Prolixin at Concord and Walpole and Bridgewater, because it is stronger than Thorazine and Mellaril and Stelazine and even Haldol, even vitamin H, as they call it. Prolixin lasts a long long time and makes you feel inside like your very atoms are covered with wool, with something heavy. But I will try this one, will say, "Maybe something like this happened, because why else am I here?" We have rushing, racing thoughts. Derealization, depersonalization, dissociative amnesia.

"Whatever we did or didn't do, we were what? Loyal, loved each other. Cared deep. Kind. Meant not to hurt, not to offend in any way. Jesus. Jesus." I say this out loud to him. To Schumacher. Think it first, then say it. Then he writes it down. Saying, "Hmmmm. Yesssss. I see. Indeed."

Schumacher. Taps teeth with pen. Looks evenly. "Hmmms," some more.

"It starts. Maybe it starts with a drink, with me lying on the couch at three A.M., at three-twenty, maybe at three-fifty. Every half hour a clock somewhere—a clock at a church somewhere—will sound, a single bong on the half hour, a bong for each hour on the hour.

"Ka-bong, ka-bong, ka-bong. Gloom and doom all flocking night.

"So then. Fuck what? I will? Options? Choices? Get up and go to the kitchen, and every moment these bad feelings are going through me. Feelings so bad, so violent and scary, that I think I should do something to stop them. I should use a knife or a razor on myself, should turn the gas in the oven on, should open the door, seal the windows, should breathe deep. Maybe I should find rope and go to the cellar. Get the fuck get the fuck get the fuck.

"Things pick up a little. Things move along maybe faster. Quicker quicker. Snap snap. Click click. Fucking move it fucking move it fucking move it."

"You dumb fuckwipe." This is one of the voices. "I know you, you asshole. I know what you're thinking."

But I find bottles in a cabinet above the refrigerator, and I find a glass and ice cubes, find tonic water, find the frosted bottle of gin. And in the story, in the version that I will try to remember, will try to tell Dr. Schumacher even though he has me on Prolixin, I will make a drink in the kitchen, in the dark. Hands fucking shaking. Spilling shit. Knocking over, spilling this or that. One ice cube, two ice cubes, hit floor. "You clumsy fuck," the voice says. "Know you. Never could tell your ass from a hole in the ground."

I will not put a light on, and if Dr. S. asks me why, I will not be sure what to tell him.

"Scared," I'll say. "Jumpy. Could be. Maybe was afraid what I'd see with the light on."

"Maybe the electric bill was too high," I'll tell him, and he might smile, might adjust the knot on his tie, might brush something from the sleeve of his coat. Keeps writing, saying, "Hmmmm."

"You make a drink," he'll say, a simple statement of fact, a cue to continue the story, the version of what happened that night. That night, I think, in spring, while my wife slept, while the woman I love dreamed about cartoon characters, or her sister Dede.

"I make a drink," I say, "and I'm having these thoughts."

"What thoughts?" he might ask.

"Bad thoughts, violent thoughts. Thoughts about bulging eyeballs and a rope so embedded in the skin around the neck that it's sunk into the flesh, has disappeared."

"Where do these thoughts come from?" he'll ask, and I'll tell him, "I don't know." I'll say, "I wish I did know."

"So you make a drink," he says, and I say, "And I go back to the living room. I lie on the couch, and I sip, and the feelings keep coming at me. So I drink fast, and the gin is cool like menthol, like Salems and Kools, but warm when it's in my stomach and moving in my chest and head." And though I don't say it, that's a good feeling.

"What night is it?" he'll want to know, and at first I frown. I won't have thought of that.

"Sunday night, maybe Monday night. Early in the week," I'll say.

"And what does the gin do?"

"It changes the thoughts. Makes me less afraid of them, makes me mad, really angry, at what made me afraid of them."

"What made you afraid?"

"Joan," I say quickly, and I'm surprised by this. I didn't know this. Had no hint, no idea at all. She's asleep, and she hardly makes a sound.

"So what do you do?"

"I get up, and I go to the bedroom door, and I open the door and look in, and she's just lying there asleep. Just dreaming away."

"So what else do you do?"

"Nothing at first. I just watch her, and she still doesn't move."

"So," I say, and stop.

"So," he says.

"I make another drink, still in the dark. And standing there at the kitchen counter, standing there and pouring, I start to feel the gin, start to get a nice buzz."

"And?" He's looking at me over the tops of his glasses.

"And I make the next drink, in the dark, and I go to the couch again, and I lie there and think about her making me feel ashamed for my thoughts. She dreams about Goofy and Tinker Bell, and I don't, and there's supposed to be something wrong with me."

"What then?"

"You dipshit," the voice says.

"I keep drinking, and these waves come over me, and I think of her sleeping. I try not to, but when I finish the second drink, I go to the bedroom door again. Only this time I open it, and it swings around and bangs into the wall, and she doesn't move.

"I'm mad now," I say, "madder than I've been in a long time. Seeing red, pumped. Hearing the voice say, 'Shitheel. Pussy.' It does and doesn't make sense, but I'm angry as hell at her, I'm really fucking enraged, and I feel huge, and all she's done is sleep."

"So?" So, sly German fuck.

"So I hit her, and she wakes up and just stares at me."

"What do you hit her with?"

"A book," I say. "There was a book, a big hardcover, on the table by the bed."

"Then what?"

"She keeps staring at me like she's trying to remember something. Maybe who I am, or how I got here. Like I'm someone who came in a window or hid behind a door. I'm someone she doesn't know, someone who doesn't belong."

"Belong where?"

"Anywhere."

"Then what?"

"She's staring, and I can see her eyes even now. Real wide. Taking this in maximum. I swing again at her, only with my hand this time, my open hand, and she swings back at me."

I stop talking. Dr. Schumacher has a look on his face. Different color, new light. Like he's seeing something he's never seen before, blinking behind his glasses.

"That's when I'd probably do it," I'll tell him.

"Do what?"

"It."

"What's it?"

"That's when I would have killed her."

"How do you kill her?"

"With my hands."

"With your hands how?"

"I put them around her neck, press my thumbs down in the front, and I push all my weight down on her."

"She struggle?"

"Legs kick for a while, then they just twitch, and I keep pressing harder and harder because I keep thinking I'll only half kill her. I keep thinking if I stop she'll start looking at me, and I'll have to do it all over again. And I hate the way she looks at me."

"How long's it take?"

"Don't know. Lose track of time, but then I realize what I've done, that I've killed her, and that I have to do something with her body."

"What do you do?"

"I don't know."

"You don't remember?"

"I don't know if I remember."

"So," he'll say, and tap a pen on the desktop. Dr. S. Smooth.

"I must have done something with her body."

"How come?"

"I wouldn't just leave it."

"So what'd you do?"

"Wrapped it up, maybe, wrapped it in a blanket or a rug, wrapped it up so nobody would see me carrying it out to the car."

"So that's what you did?"

"I think."

"Took it to the car."

"To the trunk, then drove around."

Looked up. Pen in hand.

"Newton, Boston, all over the place, trying to figure out where to drop it."

"She's in the trunk?"

"Yes."

"Not the backseat?"

I'd shake my head.

"What'd you wrap her in?"

"Sheets."

"No weapons?"

"Huh?"

"Knives? No guns? No blunt instruments such as a tire iron or a telephone or even a boot?"

"No."

"You're sure of this?"

I nod.

"Was it raining out?"

"I don't know."

"Moonlight?"

I shake my head.

"How cold?" he'll ask, and I'll keep shaking my head.

"You know she's gone?"

I'll watch him, and I'll picture her eyes. I'll know and recall, which is to say, I'll remember, particular things about the texture of her skin. Say at the shoulder, at the nape of her neck.

I'll nod.

"What about rope? Wire?"

I'll shake my head.

"What was she wearing? Were there any sounds?"

I'll watch him carefully and closely as he watches—observes—me. I'll look for clues in his face. I won't say a word.

TEN

She was twenty-one years old, and she was a senior at the University of Washington. She had blue eyes, and brown hair that came to her shoulders, and she was a good singer. She worked at a Seattle radio station as a ski-report announcer. This was the mid-1970s.

I'm sure of these things. There are, of course, photographs, reports, depositions, investigations, files, articles, books, memories, dozens and dozens of artifacts, keepsakes, bits of paper, ribbon, cloth, hair and bone and teeth and blood samples. Threads of thought and near memories. Of hundreds of people in hundreds of places in dozens of months and years. Many states and countries even, two different centuries now.

She lived with four roommates in a basement apartment in the University District. On a Friday morning, her boss—the station manager—called her apartment. She hadn't come to work.

Her bedroom was empty. There were small bloodstains on her pillow and on a sheet, there was another small bloodstain on her nightgown. A pillowcase and top sheet were missing, and the bed had been made, hospital style, with tight, almost military corners. She never made her bed that way, her roommate told police.

Six weeks later, at Evergreen State College, about sixty miles south of Seattle, a nineteen-year-old woman was reported missing. On her way to a concert at 7:00 P.M. when she was last seen.

In mid-April, at Central Washington State University in Ellensburg, about 120 miles from Seattle, a twenty-one-year-old woman was approached as she left the library at around 9:00 P.M. The man had a cast and a metal splint on his left arm, and he carried an armful of books that he kept dropping.

"Please help me," he said to the woman.

He was thin, about five-ten, and had a dark watch cap pulled down almost to his eyebrows.

She helped him carry his books to his car, and when they reached the dark and empty parking lot, he stopped next to a VW Bug. He looked at her in a "weird" way, she said later, and asked her to unlock his car.

She refused. He unlocked the car, and when the interior light came on she saw that there was no passenger seat.

"Get in the car," he said, and she began to shake. She ran, and he did not follow her.

A few days later, another young woman, a freshman biology major, disappeared from the Central Washington State campus. She was last seen at 10:00 P.M., as she left a meeting for prospective dorm counselors.

In early May, at Oregon State University, 250 miles south of Seattle, a twenty-two-year-old religion major was reported missing.

On the first day of June, a twenty-two-year-old woman left a bar called The Flame. The bar was near Seattle, and she left around two in the morning to find a ride to a party.

Less than two weeks later, an eighteen-year-old University of Washington student disappeared around 1:00 A.M. on the way to her sorority.

She had been visiting her boyfriend and was going home to study for a final examination. She had about a hundred-yard walk from her boyfriend's fraternity to her sorority.

Later, witnesses told the police that around that time— between midnight and 1:00 A.M.—they had seen a man who was on crutches. One of his legs was in a cast, and he carried a briefcase that he kept dropping.

A fraternity housemother would later tell police that she thought she heard a scream late that night, but she wasn't sure.

On Sunday, in mid-July, almost fifty thousand people crowded Lake Sammamish State Park, about twelve miles east of Seattle. The temperature was in the eighties, and along with thousands of other people, members of the Seattle Police Department were holding a picnic on one side of the park.

A man in his twenties, wearing a white T-shirt and blue jeans, his left arm in a sling, approached a young woman near the park bandstand.

He was supposed to meet some friends, he said, but they had not shown up. He'd hurt his arm playing racquetball, and needed help loading his sailboat onto his car. Could she, would she, help?

When they reached his car, there was no boat.

"Where is it?" the woman asked, and he said smoothly that it was at his parents' house.

"I can't leave," the woman said. "I have to meet some people."

She described the man as tall and thin, handsome, as "very polite at all times," as "very sincere. Easy to talk to." The man, she told police, "had a nice smile."

He approached other women. This time he wore white sneakers and socks, white shorts, a white T-shirt. He seems to have changed clothes.

A twenty-three-year-old woman wearing cutoffs and a white blouse over a black bikini top was seen leaving with the man.

Later that afternoon, around four, a sixteen-year-old girl was approached by a young man whose left arm was in a sling. Could she help him launch a sailboat? he asked. She couldn't, she said. There were people waiting for her.

Near the restrooms, he asked a nineteen-year-old woman for help, but she wasn't feeling well and said no.

At around four-thirty, a different nineteen-year-old woman agreed to help him. Like the twenty-three-year-old earlier in the day, she would never be seen alive again.

Two months later, near an abandoned logging road in Issaquah, about twenty miles east of Seattle, a hunter found a human skeleton, the bones still partly connected by decaying sinews. In the overgrown weeds, a few yards away, he saw a human skull.

The police arrived with a medical examiner and a forensic anthropologist. They found no clothes, no jewelry, but in an area the size of a basketball court, they found twenty-six human bones, eight clumps of hair, brown, and red-blond. They found two spines, one skull, and two lower jaws.

Using dental charts, they identified the bones as the remains of the two women who had disappeared in July from the state park. Teeth marks on the bones indicated that animals—coyotes, maybe rats and raccoons, maybe bears—had eaten the flesh, had dragged pieces of bone into the underbrush on the side of a hill.

In mid-October, in a heavily wooded area a hundred miles south of Seattle, a hunter found two more sets of bones. One set was the remains of a twenty-year-old woman who had disappeared from Vancouver, Washington, in August. The second set of bones could not be identified. This victim had been a woman who had long brown hair, who had been white, who had been about five-six and 120 pounds. She had been between sixteen and twenty-four years old.

There are hundreds and thousands and tens of thousands and hundreds of thousands of facts concerning these cases. Millions of facts and details and pieces of evidence on record. So many things to know. Nothing to know. One thing only to know. One thing, no thing.

The following March, near the town of North Bend, thirty miles east of Seattle, two forestry students found a human skull on the side of Taylor Mountain. The mountainside was sealed, and a search began.

The remains of four women were found. Skulls, pieces of hair, a tooth, a femur, an ulna, bones and fragments of bones.

The remains of the woman from The Flame were the first to be identified. Then the eighteen-year-old biology major. The next was the woman from Oregon State University, and the fourth was the woman who had disappeared the previous February from her basement apartment in the University District. Whose sheet was tucked in so tightly, military style.

Again no clothes or jewelry were found, and again the flesh had been consumed by animals.

The police continued to search for the man with the cast and crutches and sling, for the man with the VW Bug, for the man from the park, the "polite" man with the "nice smile." The well-spoken man.

Years later, after being caught, then escaping, maybe thirty-five victims later, he was caught again, convicted, and finally executed in Starke, Florida.

∎

They let Dad out of the hospital that summer, in July, but he did not live with us again. He moved to a furnished room in Brighton, with a hot plate. Three- and four-decker houses shoved close together. Cars parked everywhere, trash barrels and Dumpsters instead of lawns. PALM READER, $10, in a second-floor window. Dad now had a social worker and disability and official status as a ward of the commonwealth.

Mom said he needed to be by himself for a while. When Ed asked when he'd move back with us, Mom said she didn't know. Might be never. She shrugged.

His room was on the first floor and had a window that looked out on a driveway and on the house next door. There was a single bed and a dresser that had cigarette burns along the top edge. There was a bathroom the size of a closet, with a rusting shower stall and no window, and a fan that went *clank clank clank* when the bathroom light was turned on.

The woman who owned the house was named Mrs. Ronald Porter. Her husband was dead, and she watched television in a room across the hall from Dad. Wore nylon stockings that were rolled halfway up her calves, and she talked to the TV, answering questions on the game shows, telling women on the soap operas to "dump the bum. He's up to no good. He's like the rest of them. Why buy the cow when he's getting the milk free?" Milk sounded like melk.

Dad had gained weight in the hospital. His face had become round and pale. There were amber bottles of pills lined up on his dresser. He kept telling me and Ed that we had grown so much he hardly recognized us. He talked slow, from underwater somehow, and when he laughed he sounded like television.

Mom sat on the edge of the bed with him, and he whispered that his check was coming Thursday, that he got plenty to eat. Then none of us said anything for a while. We heard house and street sounds.

Mom leaned and whispered something in his ear, something we couldn't hear, and Dad began to rock and cry softly. "Hopeless," he said, and his voice was thick and deep and slow. "Afraid no hope for me," he whispered.

"No, honey," Mom said. She put her arm around his waist, and he covered his face with his hands.

.

In school, Alex Moore, a fat kid who was in the grade ahead of me, said during recess outside that my father was a lunatic, a crazy, a nutcase. I tackled him on the blacktop and pinned him down, the fat fuck, his head between my knees.

"You're crazy!" he screamed, spit and snot flying from his nose and fat red lips. Bam. Right on his fat fucking nose. Bam on his fat fucking lips. Bam bam bam. Left right. I hit him in the face again and again.

"Crazy, crazy, crazy!" he kept yelling, and I kept punching his face. His nose and mouth began to bleed, and there was blood in his hair and eyebrows, on his lips and teeth and neck.

Huge fucking hands and arms, grown-up hands and arms pulled me off the fat fuck.

Mr. Gottlieb and Mrs. Boyle pulled me off him. Huffed, puffed. Said, "What the?" "What the?"

Arms at sides. March. Sit in room. Talk to bearded man, then to smiling warm sympathetic woman. Nodded, asked questions, wrote things down. And they brought me to the principal's office, and then I went home.

I had to see a counselor from the school district or they would not let me return to school. Each week I met with a man named Charley who took me out to diners and bought me Cokes and asked questions about my father.

"What's it feel like when you see him?" Charley asked. "Sad?"

I said it was, and he told stories from when he was a kid.

He grew up in Norfolk, Virginia, and his mother never knew who his father was. She had boyfriends, and he'd hear his mother late at night, laughing and talking to men in a low voice in the next room. He'd hear ice cubes clinking against glass, and he'd hear the springs of the bed. He'd try to go to sleep, but he never could. And some nights there were sounds that alarmed him, but he was too scared to get up and go into the bedroom. Most days when he left for school, his mother was still sleeping.

"I was about your age," he said, "so I guess it's okay that I tell you."

We were in a diner near Watertown Square, between Mount Auburn Street and the Charles River. Cars kept passing on the street outside. We'd hear the door to the diner squeak open and close with a hiss.

"I came home from school one day, and I found my mother's body on the floor of the bedroom. She'd been beaten to death with a flashlight. A day later a sailor from a navy ship confessed."

He went to live with an aunt and uncle in St. Louis, and he always had the feeling, he said, that the sailor had been his father.

"I don't know why," he told me, "but I was sure the killer was my old man. He'd come back to stop her."

I sipped from my Coke, and he swallowed some coffee.

"I guess what I'm trying to tell you," he said, "is that no matter how bad it gets, you can always do okay."

.

Mom began to work as a waitress at a doughnut shop in Newton Corner. Ed and I would visit her sometimes, and she'd serve us coffee and doughnuts, and we wouldn't have to pay. We'd sit at the counter and she'd serve us like we were anybody else.

She wore a pink uniform to work, and white nylons and white shoes like a nurse. She'd bring home doughnuts almost every night—honey dip, jelly, powdered, chocolate, coconut, and Ed and I would eat them for breakfast.

Around that time Ed was caught stealing tampons from a drug-store, and Mom had to go to the store manager and say she was sorry and pay for the tampons.

"Are you sick?" Mom asked him at home, and he said no.

"Why tampons?" she asked.

Ed told her that a friend of his had dared him to do it.

"What friend?" Mom asked, but he wouldn't say.

That night, when Mom was at work, I asked him why he'd stolen tampons.

"Cause that's what chicks put in their holes," he said, and smirked. Then he put on his coat, went out, and didn't come back home until long after Mom had come back from work at ten-thirty. So he must have been out until at least midnight. Maybe beyond. And it seemed as though we would see less and less of him. Me and Mom. From around that time. Pretty sure.

•

He climbed over the fences in backyards, I imagine. I am somehow compelled to imagine. A man, some man. Not Ed. Not my father. Some he in darkness.

Picture him: He moved quietly behind trees and bushes, this in-dividual, he stood on back lawns.

He always wore dark clothes and sneakers, and some nights he almost felt like he was invisible, that somebody could look out a back window or door, and he would be standing with his face against the glass, and they wouldn't see him because he had be-come a part of the darkness, a part of the night.

He drove his car to a neighborhood and parked on a busy street, on a street where a strange car wouldn't be noticed. In the hot weather he would begin around nine-thirty or ten, and he was always careful of dogs, and of people sitting on their lawns in the dark.

He liked the rich neighborhoods best, the neighborhoods with big lawns, and houses with lots of trees and shrubs, and plenty of glass. He thought that by seeing them, by looking in their windows and watching them, he somehow was in control of their lives, even though they didn't know it. And by being in control of their lives, of course, by extension, by a flawed flick of logic, as it were, he was—therefore—in some sense—in control of his own life.

Because he had this potentially angry thing about money and class. About inclusion and exclusion. Within and without. Interiors, exteriors, liminality.

So on a night in July, say, a Tuesday night during a heat wave, perhaps. Say he began at ten in a neighborhood near the West Newton hills. The temperature had been in the mid-nineties during the past few days, and at night it didn't go much below seventy.

People were hot and tired and lazy, he thought. The heat was like alcohol and pills, he thought, because it got inside people and loosened them up and made them do things they wouldn't ordinarily do. They'd leave windows open, and shades up, and some of them didn't bother to lock doors. The summer and the heat created a kind of dream-time, an other-time, a time just outside the ordinary occurrence of things.

He stood in the bushes behind a two-story white house, and looked in the window of a den, and saw the flickering light of a television. A woman in her fifties was sitting in a lounge chair. She sipped something from a glass and watched the screen. Ice cubes clinked. There were photographs on a mantelpiece, books on shelves, magazines, drawings and sketches in frames on the wall.

She wore dark shorts and a white sleeveless top, and her hair was gray. There was a light on in a room on the second floor; he'd seen it when he approached the house. But he wasn't sure if anyone else was home.

Wasn't sure, but at the same time thought there was not. Not anybody else at home, anyone else who lived in the house. This woman had once been married but was now no longer married. She had raised a family. Had once been married, but the children were grown and gone. And the husband was gone as well. Had died. Or there had been a separation or divorce.

He, the man. Didn't know how he knew. But did know. Somehow. Was fairly sure of it. Was usually right about these kinds of things. He had an instinct for it. Odd, uncanny even. Scared him sometimes. Knew somebody was sad, or had lost something. Was thinking of a particular person from a long time ago. Weird.

But standing there.

As he watched her. She frowned at something on the TV, and he wondered where she got her money, and how much she had. If she had worked for it herself or inherited it. That made a difference to him. He wondered about if she had a job, and what kind of job it was. A lawyer, or some sort of administrator job for the artistic set. Giving money to starving artists. The autistic set, he thought, and smiled to himself. He was a member of the fucking starving autistic set. Don't fucking touch me. Don't fucking get near me or I'll scream. Then he wondered if she had ever worked at all, in the have-a-job sense of the word.

He pictured himself going around to the other side of the house, to the front, to the garage that was connected to the house, and trying the door there, and finding it unlocked. Going in real quietly. All that stillness, the hush.

A small utility light would be burning above a counter in the kitchen, and he'd take a cutting board from a peg on the wall, a wood cutting board with a handle, and he'd take it with him. The stove and counters were clean. There was a spoon and cup in the sink, water filled to the brim of the cup.

The table in the dining room was polished and shining, the

chairs neatly in place, and above the buffet there'd be a mirror, a mirror with blue gilt on the sides, and he'd see himself for a moment, a partly crouching, shadowy figure, a big man who hadn't shaved in days, a man wearing glasses with heavy black frames and thick lenses, a man holding a cutting board.

Underfoot, the carpet was thick. Everything about the place was tasteful and confident and well appointed. At least that's how it seemed to him. Not a single thing—a candlestick, a light fixture, a piece of molding on a doorframe, the glass in the windows, the locks on the doors, the paint on the walls—seemed out of place, seemed to doubt for even a moment that it belonged there, that it was perfectly and appropriately appointed. This man had such a very deep sense of this.

He'd step down into the living room, and though it was dark, he'd see the couch and chairs, the fireplace, the small tables and the built-in bookshelves. And he'd hear the television more clearly, a comedy, a man and a woman talking, and laughter after every line.

The doorway to the den would be lit with wavering light, and he'd stop just outside the door, and she still wouldn't hear him, and there'd be no sound from the second floor.

"Why do you say that, George?" a woman asked on TV, and there was laughter.

"Because your mother told me," a man said, and there was more laughter, louder laughter.

He smelled something faint, something clean like lemon and polish and old wood, and he thought how it must be to live there, to wake up and see the couch, the pictures on the walls, the trees and bushes outside. To both see and not see them—in the sense that you were a part of them and they of you—that these worlds were integrated.

Then he, large man, black-framed glasses, thick lenses. He

stepped into the room. She gasped. Kept her mouth open. He put his finger in front of his lips.

"Shhh," he said to her, and her hand covered her mouth.

"I won't hurt you," he told her, and raised the cutting board, swung it.

Heard something in the bushes, something like a cat or squirrel. The woman turned to the window, and he was looking in her eyes. He didn't move or blink or breathe. She turned back to the television.

He saw a cat on the lawn staring at him, the eyes glowing green for an instant, and he moved away from the window, across the lawn, through bushes, then over a five-foot chain-link fence.

There was a dog barking somewhere nearby, but it didn't sound like a German shepherd or Doberman or even a Lab. It had a high bark, was probably a terrier or poodle.

He passed behind a big Victorian house that had a porch swing, and no lights, and passed through a dense row of hedges to a house that was lit like the Fourth of July.

It was a dark ranch house, with a big picture window in back, and on the side there were bedrooms, and he saw a woman standing at a sink behind the picture window, and he heard her say, "Kate," and a voice from somewhere in the house said, "I'm changing."

On the side of the house, he saw her room. The blind was down but half open. She. He stopped. Was seventeen or eighteen, and she had dark hair that went partway down her back. There was acne on her forehead and chin, but she was pretty. She's a cheerleader, he thought, and he pictured her in the short skirt, the ribbon tying back her hair, doing splits and cartwheels, all the boys staring at her panties.

She was wearing cutoff jeans, and a red T-shirt, and he watched her close the door. Then in a movement so swift that he had to catch his breath, she pulled the T-shirt over her head, was standing in a pink bra. She unbuttoned her shorts, dropped them. He, the man I imagine. Could see the shape of her ass through the white panties. Then she unhooked the bra in another swift motion, and her breasts were free, were small half-moons with brown tips, and she took her panties off even more quickly, and he saw triangle, the, of dark hair.

It happened so quickly, so, that he wanted it to happen again. He watched her walk to a closet, open it, and pull a short nightgown over her head. But as he watched her, he almost—what he almost—wanted to cry, to punch himself—laugh—sing—hoot—joyfully—because she wouldn't—didn't—had no idea—know what she did to him. How lovely. Speechless. Ah-ness.

She walked to the door, opened it, then flicked a switch, and the room was a dark window. And he stood in the hot and itchy bushes, listening to the hum of fans and air conditioners, to the tick and twitch of insects. Thought of her standing there for a perfect instant—shorts and red T-shirt—and he wished almost that he had turned away, that he had seen nothing. Not seen such unbearable. Ahness. Such aching longing now.

ELEVEN

In my basement apartment, during graduate school, I was lying in bed. It was 1:00 A.M., Saturday night, Sunday morning, and I was reading a magazine, waiting to fall asleep. Typical. Usual thing for me. How many seconds and minutes and hours like that? If I had a dime for each, I'd be, he'd be. Earl Madden, why, he would be some kind of. Would much later that I had not told Joan these stories. Not said what was on my, his, mind. What are you? Fucking? Crazy? Nuts? Sick? Twisted? Psycho? Disturbed? Delusional? Hypomaniacal? Or something?

Jesus, I wouldn't have stayed with me. But this, earlier.

The lamp next to my bed was on, but the rest of the apartment was dark. In grad school. Could hear the usual quiet sounds—cars and trucks in the distance, pipes, boards creaking in the ceiling and walls, wind pushing paper over the pavement outside, insects ticking against the glass and screens on the windows.

I wanted to, was trying to finish reading an article about an exploding star before I went to sleep. The star exploded 170,000 years ago, and scientists were only now able to see it, had known about it—the star—for a week.

At the time of the explosion, human beings weren't quite human yet. There were hominids, creatures with small brains who were beginning to walk upright and to use crude tools.

An astronomer—our people—had been taking photographs from an observatory—our space. It was early morning—in our time, and he was ready to go home but then decided to develop the last set of pictures. When he saw one photograph, he thought there was a flaw in the plate or film. Then he stepped outside and looked up, and there it was in the sky itself. A light so bright it could have been a spaceship, only the light came from millions and millions of miles away, and happened before humans existed. Holy holy holy, he thought. Could have got down on his knees in praise and wonder. Awe, miracle, pure freaking beauty and unexpectedness.

The article said that the astronomer didn't sleep for days. Nobody had seen anything like this in four hundred years.

I shut off the light, and lay in bed, and tried to go to sleep. There was light coming in through the small window near the ceiling, and it made a rectangle on the far wall, the wall near the dresser.

Sometime later—ten minutes, a half hour, an hour, maybe two hours later—the phone began to ring. It was at least two or three in the morning, and the rings seemed loud and distant at the same time. I counted, counted until they reached seventeen, and then the ringing stopped.

Nobody I knew would call at that hour, but I still tried to imagine who it might have been. And for a long time after the rings, I heard each peal the way you see light after you've closed your eyes—as something clear and singular and lost. As something from before. But only moments, only moments before. Near before as opposed to far before.

·

The shots come—in here, in the hospital, on the ward—four times a day. Maura or Stephanie, Andrea or Priscilla, whoever the nurse on duty is. She will tell me.

"Earl," she will say. "Time for your shot."

I'll roll up my sleeve, and the nurse on duty will rub the spot with alcohol. It stings, it makes my eyes tear, it reminds me of vaccines and tetanus shots, of shots of Novocain and boosters and shots for sleep and vitamins, of shots for nerves, for peace.

"All set," they say, and I nod, and feel the needle pinch, and then the heat spreading again, the heat going all the way in and around, and the air is watery and wavy, sort of, and I'm heavier than death in a way, I'm older than stones, I'm gentler than down.

Prolixin is a kind of death without burial, it's falling on a bathroom floor, but the bump not really hurting. Prolixin is red eyes and a dry mouth, and not having many of those thoughts. Prolixin is shaking all over, but especially in the hands and arms and feet. Prolixin is spilling glasses of milk and water, missing your mouth with the plastic spoon or fork, and not tying your shoes very well. Or taking a very long time to tie them. But it is also a good deal better than some other things too. The rushing, quickening, racing thoughts. The voices that say, that try to say, C'mon, c'mon, c'mon. I know you. Hey hey hey hey. I know you, Mr. Big Shot. Mr. Big Shit. C'mon c'mon c'mon.

Prolixin is getting a little pee on your shorts sometimes, but that can happen to the best of us. It just goes to show you it does. Now just zip up, and try not to get your undershorts caught in the zipper.

C'mon.

Shhh.

At eight in the morning, at one in the afternoon, at six in the evening, at eleven at night. They give you, give him, vitamin P, keep you steady.

"Okay, Earl," they say. "There you go," they tell me.

And I thank them. For an hour, at least, I'm safe. I'm as easy as they go. Mr. Nice Guy, Mr. Personality. You hear the one about the duck goes into the bar, says to the bartender, Can I've a beer? Bartender says, Will that be cash or charge? Duck says, Just put that on my bill. Ho ho ho. You are right, sir. Fucking A.

·

They went into the houses at night, when the owners were sleeping. These are all facts, these are things that happened. They went into anonymous houses, houses where it was easy to get in. Houses where they could force a screen or lock. Out west, in the hills, in California. The Golden State.

There were two or three or four of them. They wore black, and they crept and crawled through the dark rooms, moving so quietly that nobody ever woke up. He never went himself. He was the father. They were family. In depositions, in testimony, to police. In newspapers they later told how. Everyone needs to tell.

They carried knives in their hands. There was something amazing about being in a house, one of them said later. That every tongue should confess. Late at night, with people asleep, and moving from room to room without sound, afraid and excited to find out what would happen if anyone woke up.

This was in the spring. This was in the hills, at big houses with the lawns and pools. Pools outside shimmering in the dark like you wouldn't believe the fucking lights at night. The dead of night.

This is what he, Earl, and I, told her, told Joan. And before long, began to tell students too. And they all listened. Loved it, hated it. Thrilled them, chilled them.

They began to bring wire cutters, and they learned where the phone lines were connected outside. This was in April and May, when the flowers were out, and leaving the houses they'd smell lilac and loam, they'd smell the dense lawns. Even if they couldn't see, they'd know they were there—the sleeping people, the perfumed flowers.

My students, in their ties and white-and-blue-striped shirts, the button-down collars, the good teeth, the beautiful shining eyes. They looked up at me and took this all in. They were all eyes and ears. That ye may approve all things, are manifest in all the palace, and in all other places.

"Eros-thanatos," I almost whispered. " 'Death is the mother of beauty.' Wallace Stevens," I said. "Listen. Listen very very carefully." And I walked slowly up and down the aisles, their eyes riveted. " 'It was evening all afternoon. / It was snowing / and it was going to snow. / The blackbird sat / In the cedar-limbs.' "

I paused and turned and I had them then. All of them. Beautiful languid boys. Raised my arm, smiled. "Mr. LeBrun," I said. "How can it be evening all afternoon? How can it be snowing if it is going to snow?"

"It's Buddhist, Mr. Madden," Mr. LeBrun said. "That's just the point."

"My creature lives," I said. "I'm very proud of you, Mr. LeBrun."

.

It's March, in here. The second or ninth of the month. And a Wednesday, I believe. Wednesday, I think, because there was meat loaf for dinner, and Willy Davidson, this big scary lifer from some chronic ward screamed at dinner that he wouldn't eat meat loaf, that they could all go fuck themselves, that he'd sooner eat warm fucking shit with blood in it. This was in the big dining room over near the chronic building, and he threw his plate. Peas, meat loaf, gravy, applesauce, plastic spoon, fork, knife, paper napkin—all flew in a fast arc at the back wall where they hit. Then fell. No drama.

So it's Wednesday, the second or ninth. Not entirely sure why. Snowing a little outside. White flakes, cold, few flakes. Black sky. Stephanie said, "When's spring coming?" and George said, "Not for another month, honey."

So it's the first or second Wednesday of March because spring is almost here, and not too long ago there were pictures on the bulletin board in the nurses' station of George Washington and Abraham Lincoln, and right around then—right before or right after—there were hearts and cupids with bows and arrows, and Mrs. Goldstein, who smiles all the time even though they took away her upper teeth, asked me to dance around the dayroom with her.

"I'd like to," I said, "but I hurt my foot." A lie. And she winked at me. Mrs. Goldstein's a sweet old lady. Why's she in here? What happened?

The green clovers haven't come yet, so it's early March, and I know it's Boston because almost nobody uses Rs when they talk.

"How ah ya?" people ask. "How's ya mothah?"

•

They found the first girl on the Strip in Los Angeles, where hookers and pimps and winos and druggies hung out. She was fifteen years old, weighed about ninety pounds, and she had brown hair.

I know more than I want to know. I wish this hadn't happened. Supposing to add afflictions to my bonds.

One of them stayed in the car, the second one approached her on foot, showed her the badge he kept in his wallet, and told her she was under arrest.

Inside the car he handcuffed her arms behind her back and drove to the older man's house. They brought her inside in the dark, and when she saw the aquarium in the living room, she knew this wasn't a police station, she knew she wasn't under arrest.

"Who are you?" she asked. "Who?" she repeated.

They made her sit down in a chair. One of them left the room and came back with a rag, two pieces of foam rubber, and a roll of tape that was two or three inches wide. The younger man got behind her, held her shoulders, and the older one stuffed the balled rag in her mouth, covered her mouth with tape, and wound the tape three times around her head.

He pressed the foam patches to her eyes and taped them to her face, again wrapping the tape two or three times around her head.

They told her to stand up, and she tried, and fell down. They helped her up, and then unlocked the handcuffs. They took off her jacket and blouse. They unhooked her bra, they took off her shoes and socks, her jeans and underwear.

"Don't worry, honey," the younger man said. "We're not gonna hurt you. You'll be okay."

It was eighty degrees in the house, but she shivered like she was standing in snow. They handcuffed her again, and the older one held her elbow so she wouldn't fall.

They brought her to a small spare bedroom off the hall. They laid her down on her back.

How art thou fallen from heaven; their faces shall be as flame; will shake the heavens and the earth will remove out of her place.

Her clothes were in a neat pile in the dining room. The younger one looked through the pockets of the clothes. The older man went first in the room. The younger man heard grunts and squeals from the bedroom.

After a few minutes, the older man came out, wearing only socks. He got his camera and took a picture of her before the other man went in.

They watched the photo develop, and then the younger man went into the room. He was done in a few minutes.

They found a spool of nylon rope in the kitchen. The older man measured out four arm-lengths of rope and then cut the piece with scissors. They took a plastic garbage bag from a drawer.

In the spare bedroom, they sat her on the floor. The older man got behind her, the younger man sat on her legs. She was shaking violently. She writhed from side to side, she squirmed, she made moaning sounds through the rag and tape.

The older man put the bag quickly over her head and sealed it at her neck with the rope. He tightened the rope, and pulled and pulled, and the plastic bag puffed out like a sail, and was then sucked in.

She squirmed and shook, she tried to butt them with her head. Her back was sharply arched, but the older man pulled the rope even tighter.

"The little cunt," he said. "The little bitch."

In their streets they shall gird themselves with sackcloth: on the tops of their houses and in their streets, every one will howl, weeping abundantly.

She stopped struggling, was still, and he let go of the rope. He listened at her chest, but there was nothing there—no movement, no life.

They put her clothes in a trash bag. They checked the living room and dining room and bedroom. They took off the rag, the tape, the patches of foam, and put them in the bag. They took off the handcuffs.

Then they carried her to the car. They put her in the trunk, the trash bag in the backseat. They stopped at a Dumpster and got rid of the bag with clothes. Then they drove for a few miles. They went up into the hills, into the neighborhoods with big houses.

The older man drove. He turned off the lights on a quiet street. Then they stopped at the side of a hill.

They got out quickly, opened the trunk, carried her to a flower bed just past the curb.

A neighborhood man found the body at six the next morning. When the police arrived, they saw her naked body, legs spread, one hand underneath her back. Brown ants were crawling on her shoulders and arms and legs.

There was a red indentation around her neck, with rims of purple bruise on the sides of the red line. There were marks on her wrists and face, a little crusted blood on her upper lip.

It was Halloween morning.

.

There's a young woman sitting on a bench on the lawn in front of the ward, just sitting there with a book on the bench next to her. She looks a lot like the woman I saw weeks earlier. It could be the same woman or someone who looks similar. This woman on this day is wearing a gray skirt, a blue coat, and she's sitting here like it's a bench on Boston Common.

I don't know.

Maybe, maybe not.

Possibly I'm not supposed to notice anything unusual about this. This has nothing whatsoever to do with me. Why should it? There are a hell of a lot of people in the world.

.

I drove sometimes for hours, late at night. I drove with the windows partway down and the doors locked. In Watertown I drove along the river, past the boats that were tied up, past the Metropolitan District Commission pool, the IHOP—the International House of Pancakes. I drove past the place where there had been a bowling alley, and where a cleanup crew had been shot early one morning when they came to work. Three or four or five of them had been killed, shot point-blank, taped up, one winter morning.

It had been on television. The reporter standing outside, the bodies carried out on stretchers, covered by sheets—the modesty, the shyness of death.

Late at night, driving, there were still cars out. Once in a while I'd see couples, sometimes three or four people on their way home. From bars, from parties, from places I only guessed about.

Mostly people were alone in their cars, and at stoplights, maybe in a passing lane, our eyes would meet—we'd glance, glare—and then look fast away.

In Newton, I always drove on Commonwealth Avenue, from the hills in Auburndale, past the fire station at the corner of Washington Street, its red lights burning, and then on toward the ponds near Newtonville, at City Hall.

Heartbreak Hill from the Boston Marathon began at Walnut Street, near where we lived for a time, and my car went smoothly up the hills there, past the big houses, past the lawns and trees and bushes.

There was a traffic light at Center Street, and a phone booth on the strip of grass between Commonwealth and the service road. Occasionally I'd see someone hunched over the receiver in the booth, and I'd think of who people would call at one or two or three in the morning. What was going on in that life? Some crazy-ass thing or another. You had to wonder.

A mile or so after that I passed Boston College, where the trolleys on the Green Line began, and I'd cross the line from Newton to Boston, and the streets became dirtier, and there were fewer trees and bushes. The trolleys were no longer running at two or three in the morning, and on a Sunday night in July, when the bricks of buildings were moist with sweat, I drove the length of

Commonwealth to the Public Garden at Arlington Street down-town. I rolled up the windows. I guess because of the potential of crime. And what the fuck was with that? You stop to think about it.

I went right on Arlington, took another right, a left, and there was the bus station, still lit up, and the kids sitting inside, standing around on the sidewalk, whispering and laughing in small groups like this was recess.

I double-parked about fifty feet down and saw other men in cars, their lights off, sitting and watching.

The kids were almost all boys, with two or three girls who were so skinny they could have been boys. They wore mostly black, and they had on jeans, and jeans jackets despite the heat, and T-shirts. Their hair was colored and spiked and shaved in places. A few of them had hair that was long like 1968, and most of them smoked. Platform shoes and boots and some sneakers. Lots of tattoos and body piercings. One girl had a baby.

A thin boy with blond hair knocked on the passenger window. He looked fourteen.

I rolled down the window, and he said, "How you doing?"

His voice was low and high at the same time, was changing.

"Good," I said. "How you doing?"

"Can I get in?" he asked.

I leaned and unlocked the door. He got in, and I could smell cologne—Old Spice or Brut or English Leather.

"So, ah," he said.

"You hustling?" I asked.

He looked at me. His features were small and clean. He didn't shave. He was pretty.

"No, dude," he said.

"I'm not a cop."

"I know."

"Just curious," I told him.

"You want something? Drugs? A blow job? You wanna fuck me, you can."

"How much?"

"Fifty a blow job. Seventy-five to screw."

"How old are you?"

"Nineteen," he said.

"Right."

He looked at me again. "Sixteen," he said.

"Where you from?"

"New York."

"City?"

"Upstate," he said. He lit a cigarette with a Bic lighter. He pulled smoke deep into his lungs.

"How long you been here?"

"Couple of months."

"You make good money?"

"Okay."

He pulled again on the cigarette. "You writing a fucking book?"

"No," I told him.

"You want me to suck you or what?"

I shook my head. I took a twenty from my wallet, gave it to him. Mr. Big. "Be careful," I said, and he got out, and I watched him walk over to his friends. Slouching boy, thin boy. Boy walking with shoulders held back. Boy near bus station. Say thirteen, say 3:00 A.M. And that was probably a nice gig—compared to where he'd left, the last place called home.

It was three-thirty when I got home, and Joan was up, sitting at the kitchen table, sipping a drink.

"Where do you go, Earl?" she asked, and she looked like she was ready to be hurt, like she knew she'd be hit.

"Just driving," I said. "Nothing and nowhere in particular."

"You okay?" she asked.

I leaned down and kissed her. I nodded.

She was wearing one of my T-shirts for a nightgown.

"You hungry?" she asked. Her hair was short, was pushed back behind her ears.

"I am."

She stood up, patted my side with her hand.

"Sit down, pal," she said, and I did. She'd never called me that. Like this was a regular feature of our wedded life.

She took out a bowl and some milk and a half dozen eggs. She cleared a small space at the table, pushed aside napkins and place mats.

I listened for sounds in the house but couldn't hear a thing. I almost thought the blond kid was hiding somewhere. I almost got up to look around, but I held back. I sat and was silent, and watched Joan.

She got ham and mushrooms and an onion. She cut the ham into small squares, made a pink pile, then started the mushrooms. She laid them on the board and made thin slices.

She took some cheese from the refrigerator. She looked at me for a moment, and didn't smile. She cut long strips of cheese, so thin that I could see light through them.

"Hi, Earl," she said, and I said, "Hi, Joan." As though we did this every day.

She sliced the edge of an onion and pulled off the skin. Underneath, it was white.

Then she cracked the eggs into the bowl. I thought I heard something, maybe in the living room, and I almost got up to look. But there were no footsteps. Just the wind maybe, then Joan lifted her drink and the ice cubes clicked. I didn't know what she was drinking.

She splashed milk in with the eggs, then beat them with a fork.

She put in salt and pepper, basil, then she turned on the stove. She put butter in the pan, and I heard it sizzle.

"Joan," I said. "Is everything all right?"

"You tell me, honey."

Her eyes were dark.

I nodded.

She poured the mixture into the pan, and there was a hissing noise. She lowered the flame and began to clear the table. She took a spatula and lifted at the edge of the eggs. She tilted the pan and let the liquid part slide to the edge. Then she started to lay slices of cheese on half the eggs.

The cheese began to bubble, and she lowered the flame. She laid the mushrooms and ham and onion on the cheese. She lifted the edge again, and it was brown underneath. She slid the spatula under and flipped half the eggs on top.

She took two glasses and poured orange juice. Which again, I didn't even know we had in the house. Like where did this come from? A stealth trip to the grocery store? She took two plates, shut off the stove, and sliced the omelet in half with the spatula. She slid the halves to the plates and got forks and napkins.

"Earl," she said. "I don't care what you do or where you go." She looked at me. "I love you, and I'll love you tomorrow and next week and two years from now." She put her hand on the back of my head. "Everything else is shit," she said. "You know what I'm saying."

This was in July, when we lived in an apartment in Watertown. An old Italian woman lived downstairs.

"God, Joan," I said, and she smiled.

"Eat, pal," she said. The "pal" word again. Just dropped in there, big as life. As though it happened every day. As though my coming in at this hour, and her being awake, and eating together—well, this was our life. This is what we did.

She put the plates on the table and sat down.

"Okay," she said. By then of course it wasn't. Anywhere. Home, school, before, after. Love, work. Within or without. We made believe. Picked up our forks and ate as though everything was normal.

TWELVE

I don't know when the idea came up at first—during one of our arguments, right after it—but all at once Joan was going to Quebec City alone, and I was staying home. I'd been talking too much about the sickos, keeping even weirder hours. She was scared.

The condo there was rented and paid for. Through her father. Neither of us thought of that as strange. Her going alone, me home. Even though we'd been planning the trip since December. Then it was April, rain and fog outside, and Joan was going by herself, to Quebec City, during April teaching break.

I got up early on Sunday morning with her. It was light out, but so gray and quiet that it seemed earlier than seven. Joan was getting dressed on the other side of the room, and I stayed in bed and watched her. She had long legs, and white skin like paper. Without the light on, her skin was shiny, and I started thinking of her driving all the way to Quebec alone. I pictured the highways and tollbooths, and Joan stopping for gas in strange towns. Then I started thinking of her getting dressed in a room in Canada.

She went out of the room, so I got up, put my robe on, and went out to the hall.

It felt like four in the morning—no cars or voices anywhere— only the gray light outside. Even the old Italian woman downstairs didn't seem to be awake. There were no sounds from her place. I couldn't remember the last time I'd been up at this hour on a Sunday.

Joan's stuff was near the front door—a suitcase, a paper bag, boots, a pale green shoulder bag. She'd packed the night before.

She put her coat on and went to the front hallway. I heard the outside door open and close, and I started to bring her bags down the front steps to the sidewalk. It was cold out, no more than forty. The ground was wet from rain.

The car started up in the driveway, and Joan backed out and pulled up to the front walk. She got out, came around, unlocked the trunk.

"I'll do this," she said. "Go inside. I'll come in to say good-bye."

Inside, me, I rinsed off a bowl and spoon in the kitchen sink. Then leaned against the refrigerator.

She came in and kissed me. Cheek, kissed me. Shoulder to shoulder. "You'll be okay?" she asked.

I nodded. "You?"

"Course."

She kissed me again, cheek, said, "Bye-bye," and went through the hallway. Departing figure. Capable woman, short hair pulled back in ponytail, dark wool coat on, keys and coffee in one hand, glasses on end of nose, attractive young woman going somewhere. But not leaving for good. Not this time.

I locked the door behind her and heard the car start up out front. Sat in a chair in the living room and thought about what I'd do in the next seven days. I had the time off from work. From teaching. I thought about seeing movies or calling people. Ha, big fucking joke. Who would you call, Mr. Personality? Marilyn Fucking Monroe? Frank Fucking Sinatra?

I know you, ya fuckwipe, shitheel.

Then I. He started to feel how quiet everything was. Sat in the chair and listened to the silence all around.

Maybe only sat for a few minutes, but when I got up, felt stiff, as though I'd been sitting for hours. Went to the bathroom and stood in front of the sink, looking—examined—myself in the mirror. I needed a shave, and my hair was sticking up in back. Then I felt at my throat, and it was sore. Something was starting up, maybe a cold.

Then I began to think it was from too many cigarettes and not enough sleep. I noticed something funny in the mirror. There was a design of leaves in frosted glass, almost like a crown for the mirror. I'd been looking in the mirror for over a year, but couldn't remember—recall, spot, place, identify, call to mind—ever seeing the leaves. Then I swallowed, and my throat really hurt. And I started to wonder about myself—noticing leaves and sitting in silence.

I went upstairs to the bedroom. Got into bed and smoked a cigarette. Then I, me, pulled covers to neck. Looked at smoke curling near ceiling. Not sure when, but fell asleep. I didn't notice, remember or recall any dreams.

·

Sometime during sleep thought I heard the phone in the hall ring. Seemed to ring a long time, but I wasn't getting up. Didn't. Turned instead in bed, pulled pillow over head. Went under again.

Somewhere, far away and for a long time. Though once more, no recall, no memory. No sense of that. Dark ships, empty castles, deep forests, long oceans.

When I woke up, it seemed like I'd been asleep a long time, that the phone had been ringing hours ago. The light from outside was still gray, but a darker shade of gray. It felt like two or three in the afternoon.

I swallowed, and I knew for sure that I had a cold. It hurt to swallow, like someone had punched me in the throat. Big, swollen, throbbing pain in the throat.

I wondered who had called, because we almost never got calls except from credit-card companies trying to sell. Then I swallowed again, and this time it hurt more. Felt under jaw with hand, then around Adam's apple. All swollen, and a tight, stuffed feeling at top of nose.

Clock said 5:38. Lit cigarette, looked at clock again. Been asleep almost nine hours, on top of what I'd slept during the night. Must be sick, I thought. Shit, fuck. But didn't matter either, didn't have to be anywhere, do anything.

After the cigarette I stayed in bed awhile. Wondered if Joan had gotten there yet. Boston to Quebec City was eight-hour drive. Even with stops for food and gas, she was there. Had to be. Assuming no crash. No fiery collision, no charred remains. Et cetera. She had driven to a city in a different country, all during the time I slept.

Swung my vacationing legs around to the floor, sat up, and felt at neck again. Still hurt, head was beginning to ache. Had to get some aspirin, check the cabinets for cold capsules.

Stood up, put robe on, went out to hall. Everything still quiet. Strange to be there, not only because Joan gone. But because I was supposed to be gone too. That had been the plan. I thought, This is how place would feel if we had both gone away. Empty rooms, sounds outside magnified because it was so silent inside. No lights on, nobody coming to visit. Not that anyone came to visit. Fuck no.

Everyone I knew thought I was in Quebec. We didn't tell anyone about my not going. Who would care anyway?

Then I started to feel like a visitor, or like someone who wasn't supposed to be there. Nobody but Joan Millis even knew I was in the apartment.

I wondered who called earlier. Someone who didn't know I was supposed to be gone. Or someone selling magazines, or wanting donations for Little League.

I sat down at the kitchen table. My head and throat hurt bad. Put my fingers to temples and started to press. Did that a few minutes, then started the same on top of nose. Felt that if there were extra holes in forehead and nose, pressure would stop. Thinking that probably isn't normal, I thought, so sat awhile, and then got up and went to bathroom.

The leaves were still on the top of the mirror. Opened mirror door, got three aspirin, and swallowed them. There was no cup by the sink, so I turned on the cold water and lapped water from tap.

Sat on the edge of tub. Don't know why. Felt tired, probably. I looked around the bathroom, at the toilet and sink and shampoo. I noticed things like cracks in the paint below the sink, and the way the tiles on the floor were cut. I sat there a half hour. Felt slow and stupid, felt like an old man.

Heard voices. Said. Said, "I know you, old man. You old fucking geezer. You're ready for the home, you're ready for the Jell-O cubes, now aren't you? Will that be lime or peach today, Mr. Madden? You got your drool towel? You old fuck you."

It was dark when I got up. I went slow.

Made cup of coffee, drank it upstairs in bedroom. Smoked cigarettes, put fresh clothes over the back of a chair. Socks and underwear, shirt and jeans. Then took off the stuff been sleeping in, put robe back on, went to bathroom for shower.

"Move it, ya fucking dimwit. You fucking drooler. You tuck your fucking undershirt inside your underpants, ya dweeb. Pants pisser. Bed wetter, fire starter, wife beater, shit licker. C'mon. C'mon. Move it, ya fem fuck!"

When he—Earl—the guy finished and dried off, he got into fresh clothes. Then started looking through some of Joan's books. If I—he—was sick, I—he—could at least read. Expand the mind. Food for thought.

There was one huge book in paperback—it must have been two and a half inches thick—and I pulled it out. It was better than a thousand pages long, but I figured I had all week. Then I realized. Oh boy, my stuff. My kind of guy. Joan must have bought it because the author was famous. Was on TV.

I settled on the bed. I got up at one point for the bathroom, and another time to make a sandwich. But I kept going back to read. I couldn't stop reading. I forgot about my throat.

Much later my eyes started to hurt. I was on page 246. This was great. It was getting light out. Birds were making noise. The guy in the book had just killed two men. One man on the floor of a bathroom at a gas station, the other on the floor at the front desk of a motel. Both men were married and had young children. This was a true story.

Looked at the clock: 6:22, Monday morning. People everywhere were getting ready to go to work. Coffee brewing, showers being turned on, cars starting up. I tore a piece of cardboard from a matchbook and put it in my place in the book. Then I shut off the light.

Kept thinking of the guy in the book. Had spent most of his adult life in prisons. When he got out, he didn't know how to go into a store to buy a pair of pants.

Thought of man shot in bathroom at gas station where he worked. Had wife, children, went to school. Wanted better life.

Son, daughter. Tiles on floor of bathroom. Sink, pipes underneath the sink. Other man behind front desk of motel. Wife and children. Going to college days. Working hard, trying to make ends meet. Ends meet. Sagged back on carpet. Headlights of passing cars on ceiling of motel office.

Wife at home with children. Hoping the little one, the baby, would sleep through the night. For a change. Back then.

Later, in Watertown, I, Earl, lit a cigarette and watched the tip glow in the gray light. Took some drags, then stamped it out in the ashtray. Felt my throat, and it still hurt. Right after that, fell asleep.

·

This went on all week. I'd sleep for twelve hours, read, go to the kitchen, open a can of soup. I'd heat the soup, then eat it from the pot at the kitchen table, staring at the wall. I didn't change my clothes.

Sometimes I'd get up after sleeping from six in the morning until six at night. I'd read for two hours, eat something, take aspirin, smoke cigarettes, and go back to sleep.

The phone would ring once or twice a day. I started to be afraid of who it might be. I never answered. I'd think of people who didn't like me. Though I couldn't name very many. Maybe some of the kids, the students, were going home and telling their parents about the crazy stories their crazy teacher was telling them. About boys in crawl spaces and whatnot. And what have you, and now the parents were angry and trying to phone me.

Then one morning the phone started to ring. I was on page 721, and there were legal battles about executing the killer. He was waiting on death row. The international press corps was gathered in Utah, ready for the first execution in the United States in years.

The phone didn't stop after ten or twelve rings. It kept going and going. I counted for a while, but I stopped counting after forty-two rings. Then I got mad, then scared. I started thinking it was Joan, calling to say she'd thought it over and decided she'd had enough of me.

Then I was sure it was her, and I knew she was right to feel like that. The phone kept ringing, and I looked at the floor next to the bed. There must have been a hundred crumpled tissues lying there, almost a week of blowing my nose. There were empty cigarette packs, Kools and Kools and Kools and Kools, and cups, and Milky Way and Mounds and Almond Joy candy wrappers.

I must have smelled like a goat. I hadn't been near water since Sunday. I felt my chin. I had a five- or six-day wino beard.

Then the phone stopped, and I stared down at the book. I hadn't read anything but newspapers in months, and here I was reading the biggest book of my life. And I was looking forward to the execution. I kept picturing the firing squad, and wondering if they'd shoot for his head or his heart.

Then I got up and went to the phone. I almost expected it to ring again. I picked up the receiver, pushed seven numbers, and waited. I cleared my throat.

"The time at the tone will be eight twenty-seven and forty seconds," the woman said.

I listened until the time was exactly 8:30, then I hung up.

I went back to bed and smoked a few more cigarettes, and thought of my carton running low. Then I just sat there. This was Friday morning, this was when Joan went to Quebec City and I stayed home.

After a while I heard a siren outside somewhere. It got closer and closer. It became real loud. I didn't feel scared when the noise stopped out front. I heard doors slam, and I waited there quietly. I felt calm. I waited for the feet on the stairs. I kept waiting.

Then I heard voices in Italian out front. I got up, moved the curtain aside, and looked down. There was a white ambulance, with orange and blue stripes. Two guys went to the back doors of the ambulance, pulled out a stretcher, and carried it around to the side entrance, where the old Italian woman lived.

Two neighbors stood on the sidewalk. They were old and spoke Italian. A few minutes passed. Then the stretcher was wheeled out. The old woman was covered to the neck with a blue blanket. Her face was like a prune. She said things in Italian to the neighbors. She looked small from where I was. The two men lifted her into the back of the ambulance. Doors slammed, and they drove off.

I got into bed and went to sleep.

∙

Pretty soon it would be the parents of the kids at school on the phone. And then the principal. I'd answer, and I'd say the same crazy shit I'd been saying in the classroom. About the pure fucking products of America gone crazy. About the poor. And the boys and girls, and the light in their eyes. The promise, the fear and anguish and the betrayal. And so it was written and so it shall be and he smote them. For we shall be as a city upon a hill. And you take Jeru from Jerusalem you have Salem. And Nathaniel Fucking Hawthorne himself, Mr. American Fiction, boys and girls, he changed his name because his great-grandfather was the hanging judge in the Salem witch trials. So that if we shall deal falsely with our God in this work we have undertaken and so cause Him to withdraw His present help from us, we shall be made a story and a byword through the world. Mr. Winthrop on the creaking decks of the storm-tossed *Arbella*, on its way to the New World—1630, boys and girls. And so Hester Prynne, my friends, years later, my friends, she sins, and she bears the mark. But she says. She avers. Claims. Evokes. Resonates. Says. What we did had a sanctity of its own. So Mr. H.'s great-grandfather, when he sent those girls to be burned or drowned or crushed by stones. His judgment, as it were. Sin. His great-grandson, took that sin, made a story, byword, transformed his old crime. Sanctified as it were. Murder to gold.

.

The sleep didn't last long, and what there was of it wasn't deep. It was more like being three-quarters asleep. All the time I was aware of sounds from the street and light seeping in through the curtains. I dreamed about phones ringing, and me trying to answer, but not being able to move. Then there was a firing squad, and I woke up with the explosions of guns.

The room was quiet. There was a sliver of sunlight on the floor from the edge of the curtains. I swallowed, and my throat didn't hurt.

Today's Friday, I told myself again.

I made coffee and went to the bedroom with the cup. I began to read again. There were appeals and stays. The killer gave interviews, he wrote letters to his girlfriend. Christmas passed. The execution was set for a Monday morning in January.

After a few hours, I went to the kitchen for a second cup of coffee. It was one in the afternoon. Outside, clouds had moved into the sky, and I couldn't see the sun. I got coffee and hurried back to bed.

By page 950 the execution was proceeding. The killer wore white pants and a black shirt. They pinned a white circle on the shirt. They'd shoot for the heart.

He was strapped into a chair. A priest made the sign of the cross over him. Then everyone stepped back. They put cotton in their ears. There were four explosions. Blood started to drip onto the white pants.

I kept reading. There were only sixty more pages, I had to go to the end.

First there was an autopsy, then cremation, then funeral rites. Finally there was the killer's mother, alone in a trailer, crippled by arthritis. She no longer went outside.

Still children without fathers, wives without husbands. Two decent men. And with thee will I break in pieces.

I closed the book, weighed it in my hand.

The clock read 5:11. I put the book on the table next to the bed. Then got up. Took fresh clothes out, laid them on the bottom of the bed. Then started to gather the junk from the floor. Put the tissues and wrappers in the wastebasket, collected the dirty cups, even emptied the ashtrays.

When I got to the bathroom, took everything off. Then looked in the mirror. Had the face of someone who slept on Boston Common.

Rubbed water into beard for a few minutes, put on the shaving cream. Got razor, started shaving cheek on left. Took time. There were small cuts, but I rinsed off the blood.

Then got in the shower. Lathered up all over, then rinsed off, did it again. Got shampoo going in my hair. All the white suds, my hands in piles of cream. Rinsed off, and did that a second time.

When I got out of the shower, the room was a cloud. Could hear rain outside, little feet in the gutter.

Kept thinking the phone might ring, that I might answer it. Kept thinking maybe it would be Joan.

But it didn't ring. I didn't answer. She was already. Long ago. Long time. Far away, gone.

THIRTEEN

He was five foot two, had dark eyes and red hair, and worked as a garbageman. He was eighteen years old, and his girlfriend was fourteen. He came from a family that had seven children. He dropped out of school, was nicknamed Little Red, and lived in Nebraska.

The weather in Nebraska in late January is harsh, and the landscape barren. This happened too, I know, though if it were sunny and seventy degrees, if there were palm trees, it might not have happened.

Later, after everything, to police, to court officials, he said, "The more I looked at people the more I hated them because I knowed they wasn't any place for me with the kind of people I knowed. I used to wonder why they was here anyhow. A bunch of goddamned sons of bitches looking for somebody to make fun of some poor fellow who ain't done nothing but feed chickens."

In December he robbed a gas station and took the twenty-one-year-old attendant away from the gas station, in the city of Lincoln, to the Nebraska plains. He shot him four times in the head and left his body in a ditch.

In late January he was at his girlfriend's house when her mother and stepfather began to yell at him. His girlfriend watched. "They said they were tired of me hanging around. I told her off and she got so mad that she slapped me. When I hit her back, her husband started to come at me, so I had to let both of them have it with my rifle."

He went to the baby sister's room and shoved the barrel of his rifle down the two-year-old's throat. She choked to death.

Then he and his girlfriend turned on the television and made sandwiches. They ate, then dragged the stepfather's body to a chicken coop in the backyard, covered it with newspapers, and dragged the mother's body to an old outhouse. They put the little sister's body in a box, then watched more TV.

"Don't know why it was," he said, "but being alone with her was like owning a little world all our own. Lying there with our arms around each other and not talking much, just kind of tightening up and listening to the wind blow or looking at the same star and moving our hands over each other's face. I forgot about my bow legs when we was having excitement. When I'd hold her in my arms and do the things we done together, I didn't think about being a red-headed peckerwood then. We knowed that the world had give us to each other. We was going to make it leave us alone. If we'd a been let alone we wouldn't hurt nobody."

Almost like Huck Finn: We had the sky up there, all speckled with stars. . . . Or, the river was a whole mile broad and awful still and grand.

He wrote a note that said, "Stay a Way. Every Body is Sick With the Flu," and tacked it to the front door of the house.

The girlfriend's sister came to visit, but the girlfriend wouldn't let her in. The police came and were turned away. Her grandmother was turned away.

After two days the police came back and went inside, but Little Red and his girlfriend had left. They took a .22 rifle, a shotgun, and stopped at a store for ammunition. They fixed a flat tire and bought gas.

They stopped at a farm, and he blew off the farmer's head with a shotgun. A few miles away, they shot a seventeen-year-old boy and his sixteen-year-old girlfriend and left their bodies in a storm cellar.

He said, "I began to wonder what kind of life I did live in this world. Even to this day I'm wondering about it, but it don't matter how much I used to think about it. I don't believe I ever would have found a personal world or live in a worthwhile world maybe, because I don't know life, or for what it was. They say this is a wonderful world to live in, but I don't believe I ever did really live in a wonderful world." There is none to comfort me. For my sighs are many, and my heart is faint.

They forced their way into the home of an industrialist and shot him in the head. They tied up and gagged the businessman's wife and maid, and Little Red stabbed them both over and over.

"Nobody knowed better than to say nothing to me when I was aheaving their goddamn garbage," he said.

They crossed into Wyoming, and on the side of a highway they saw a salesman sleeping in his car. They shot him nine times. He poured out his fury like fire.

"People will remember that last shot," he said. "I hope they'll read my story. They'll know why then. They'll know that the salesman just happened to be there. I didn't put him there, and he didn't know I was coming. I had hated and been hated. I had my little world to keep alive as long as possible, and my gun. That was my answer." They hunt our steps. For our end has come.

.

By the time I was in the ninth grade, I was taller and heavier than my mother, and almost as big as my father.

Ed and I didn't like to stay in the same room anymore, so I moved my bed to the hall. There was a dresser at the foot of the bed and a closet at the end of the hall. I put a blanket over a window to keep the light out, and my mother didn't say anything. She didn't notice.

Mom had left the doughnut shop and worked as a cashier at a department store called King's. She worked from three in the afternoon until eleven at night, and sometimes on my way home from school I'd see her walking to work, her red smock over her arm. One time, when I was with some friends from school, I pretended I didn't see her, walking on the far side of the street.

She had gray hair by then, and was forty or fifty pounds overweight. She took pills to help her lose weight, but late at night I'd see her in the living room, in front of the TV, eating Twinkies and Devil Dogs and Yodels.

Mom had a friend named Irene whose husband had died of a heart attack. Irene had red hair, smoked Salems, and wore red lipstick. She called me "doll" whenever I saw her, and she was missing a tooth on the top, in front.

She'd say, "Get me a beer, doll," and Mom would say, "Irene, you're a scream."

When I handed Irene a can of Miller, she'd say, "Wait," would look in her enormous purse, and hand me a dollar bill.

"You're lucky," she said to my mother.

.

One night in January, Ed and I got in a fight. He'd worn one of my shirts, had ripped it, and then denied wearing it in the first place. Much less ripping it. Saying he hadn't worn it, that made me mad. That was the part that made me feel I could kill him.

He punched me in the face, and I began to make guttural

sounds. I grabbed his hair with one hand, his throat with the other hand, and began to bang his head against the wall. Again and again. Everything was white. I was huge.

His fucking skull made a dull, almost hollow sound. After a minute. Five or six bangs or so and he wasn't fighting anymore. His eyes rolled up in his head, goofy white space, and a gurgling noise came from his chest.

I slapped his face and said, "Ed. Ed."

He slumped to the floor and breathed like he was asleep, and then his eyes blinked open, and he was okay.

He and I were about the same size, even though he was a year and a half older.

I told him I was sorry, and he said, "You better be careful, you, fuck, you. You'll kill someone."

.

Dad stayed in his room in Brighton, and every few months I'd take the Kenmore bus to Oak Square, and I'd visit him.

Dad got thinner every year, and his eyes were yellow at the edges, and watery.

"You're a good boy, Earl," he'd tell me, and he'd feel the muscles in my arms. He'd say, "You get any bigger, you'll be beating up the old man."

He'd take a pint of whiskey from a drawer in the night table next to his bed. He'd get two small juice glasses from the medicine cabinet in the bathroom, then he'd pour. He'd put water in mine, would hand it to me, and we'd sit on the side of the bed and sip. Dad always got drunk on one glass, and he'd cry and tell me he loved me.

Dad would say, "Don't be an asshole loser like me."

He always had a few books next to his bed. *The Story of Babe Ruth.* *The Autobiography of John Muir.* I sipped and read. I read the first paragraph of Muir. "When I was a boy in Scotland I was fond of everything that was wild. With red-blooded playmates, wild as myself, I loved to wander in the fields to hear the birds sing, and along the seashore to gaze and wonder at the shells and seaweeds, eels and crabs in the pools among the rocks when the tide was low; and best of all to watch the storms thundering on the black headlands and craggy ruins of the old Dunbar Castle when the sea, the sky, the waves and the clouds, were mingled together as one. Though solemnly warned that I must play at home in the garden and back yard, lest I should learn to think bad thoughts and say bad words. All in vain. In spite of the sure sore punishments that followed like shadows, the natural inherited wildness in our blood ran true on its glorious course as invincible and unstoppable as stars." Whiskey and words. I swooned.

I began to smoke in the spring of the ninth grade. First Larks that I stole from Mom. She always had a carton. Then Kools when I had money to buy my own.

I washed dishes at a small restaurant in Newtonville Square, and I caddied at a country club near Route 128. When I lost a ball, or walked through the line of a putt, or gave a golfer the wrong club—a three iron instead of a four iron—some of them were nasty. They'd begin to call me "fucking caddie." They'd say, "Where's the ball, fucking caddie?" Or, "Will a seven iron get me to the green, fucking caddie?" It was as though "fucking" was my first name. Though not all of them were like that. Rich motherfucks. Jackass pants, red asshole pants. Plaid-wearing, Town Car–driving lickshits. Mutual asswipe funds. Thank you, Mommy, for the inheritance. Dicklick. Boarding take-it-up-the-ass fucking school in rural Connecticut. Pardon fucking me.

·

In the spring of ninth grade, our junior high school had a farewell dance. Our last week of junior high before high school.

I went to the dance with Melissa Silber, a girl from my social-studies class who had dark eyes and braces on her teeth. Nice girl.

Would have good teeth when it counted. When I walked to her house to pick her up for the dance, corsage in box, her mother invited me inside and sat me on a couch in the living room. I was tall skinny boy. Freckles, wide shoulders, hair parted, tie. Poor boy. Troubled parents. Hard worker. Known to be smart. Poor but honest. Got good grades. Kept feet off furniture. Decent manners. Evoked sympathy, not fear.

"It's nice to meet you," Melissa's mother said, and introduced me to Melissa's younger brother and sister. The brother had Down's syndrome like Brandon, and when he spoke, I couldn't understand much of what he said. The sister's name was Karen, and she said, "Melissa's getting ready," and winked at me.

"You like school?" Mrs. Silber asked, and I told her I did.

A dog that looked half German shepherd and half collie came into the room. The dog jumped so that its front paws were on my thigh, and licked my face.

"Mason, down," Mrs. Silber said.

The brother said, "Mason," and slapped the dog's rump. Mason, as in Mason-Dixon?

I pushed the dog off me, and it lunged at my crotch, sniffing loudly.

"Do you play basketball or baseball?" Mrs. Silber asked, and I shook my head.

I pushed Mason away, but he kept trying to sniff between my legs.

Then the brother said something that sounded like "Melissa," and when we looked up she was standing in the hallway, in a pink dress that made her look like cotton candy.

·

Jackie, the caseworker, says, "Dr. Schumacher wants to know if the Prolixin is helping."

"It is," I tell her.

"He's wondering if he should take you off."

"No, he shouldn't."

"Why not?"

"Cause it helps. Keeps me steady."

"Helps what?"

"Everything," I say.

"You're not remembering anything," Jackie tells me.

"Yes I am."

"How long you been here?"

I shake my head.

"Where's Joan?"

"Decomposing," I say.

"That's funny?" she asks.

"Turning into dust, Jackie. She's fucking rotting in the ground."

I get up and stand over Jackie. I weighed 227 when they put me on the scale this morning. I'm six-one.

Jackie stands up too. The top of her head is at my chin.

"Think about it, Earl," she tells me. "Something has to happen here."

We're in the back dayroom, next to the porch that's covered with the same wire mesh that's on the windows. It's still too cold to go out there, to the porch.

"You tell me, Jackie. Where's my wife?"

"You're supposed to tell us," she says. "You're supposed to find out how you got here. Make contact with reality."

She starts for the door.

"That's the point," she adds.

After she leaves, I sit down again and stare at the cracks in the paint. I think about how I slept till three or four some afternoons.

Claire Hite, fellow patient, goes by in the hall. Singing "The Impossible Dream," only with customized lyrics. "To fuck the unfuckable man," she sings.

Joan's mother and father live outside Lexington, Kentucky, now. I can't think of the last time I saw them.

Joan has four sisters, I think. At least one is married and has two boys. Maybe a Beth. She has a sister Karen. There's a Dede. One brother, Todd. One other sister.

Where's Ed? Where are Mom and Dad and Mrs. M. and Brandon?

People disappear every day. Men with families, with wives and children and jobs. They don't come home from work.

One woman left after dinner to get milk at a convenience store. Her husband and four kids were washing the dishes. This was in Weston, just outside Boston.

Four months later a hunter found her naked body floating on a pond in upstate New York. There were no knife or gunshot wounds, no blows to the head or body, no evidence of strangulation, no foul play. She died by drowning. Her clothes and car were never found. This was true.

She was forty-one years old. No history of mental illness, a Catholic who went to confession twice a month.

If Schumacher asked, I'd say I didn't know. Need to arrive at the truth myself. Lost job, lost wife, no family.

"But how'd she get to the pond?" he'd ask. Speaking of the missing forty-one-year-old woman. He'd be wearing a tie, and one of his V-neck sweaters instead of a suit coat.

"She went crazy," I'd say. "Couldn't take it anymore."

"Take what?"

"The kids, her life."

"There's no evidence whatsoever. This is a woman who sang when she ironed her husband's shirts."

"That proves she's nuts," I'd say, and Schumacher would smile.

I'd say, "Anything happen recently? Her mother or father die? An old roommate have a heart attack? Get cancer?"

He'd shake his head.

"Ask God," I'd say.

"And you," he'd say.

"What about me?"

"What about you, Earl?" he'd say, and his voice would get low, like we were whispering secrets.

I'd watch his eyes behind his glasses. Oddly light eyes.

"I shot the bitch," I'd say.

"What bitch?"

"Joan."

"Joan's a bitch?"

"No, but I shot her anyway."

"Where'd you get the gun?"

"From a guy in the Combat Zone."

"What'd he look like?"

"It was dark. It was in a strip joint."

"How much?"

"Fifty."

"What'd you pay him with?"

"Two twenties and a ten."

"What kind of gun?"

"Thirty-eight. It was heavy in my pocket."

"And you shot Joan?"

"Right."

"Where?"

"What do you mean 'where'? In the stomach where? Or in the car or cellar where?"

"In the car where first."

"We went for a ride," I'd say, and he'd settle back, would fold his hands on his chest. He'd be watching my face, and I'd hear people in the hall, beyond the door. People saying hello, people singing. People's footsteps.

"So you went for a ride," he'd say. "What kind of car?"

"Honda Civic."

"What year?"

" 'Ninety-four. Had eighty-six thousand miles on it."

"Good. So you go for a ride."

It was Sunday, it was late January, but one of those sunny days after a cold front when the temperature gets up in the thirties. It'd been cold for at least a week, and we hardly left the house except for work or groceries. This is speculation, only now I'm really in his office, and I'm Earl, and I'm talking. But both of us are agreeing that this is figurative. This is a what if. What might have happened had he killed my wife.

·

Earl. The Fucking Pearl. Is in here because of the confusion, the rushing thoughts, the hypomania, followed by the cycle of deep depression, the crying episodes. The call to the police reporting the probable murder of a wife. They arrive, find babbling, disheveled man, unshaven. Bleeding from hesitation cuts on hands and wrists and arms. Boxes, books, clothes, bags, torn from closets and shelves. Subject is disoriented as to all three spheres: as to time, place, and person. So where's the fucking body if you killed your wife?

·

"So you went for a ride," Schumacher says.

"Right."

"Whose idea?" Ask them to repeat questions. To gain time for thought. Reflection. Don't let the fucks rush you.

"Hers."

He nods.

"She came in while I was watching TV."

"What were you watching?"

"I don't know, you asshole. How'm I supposed to know everything?" He notes interjection. Hostility.

I look at him. I'm surprised how mad I get. How quickly. He's surprised, too.

"Football? An old movie? A show about wildlife? Maybe bears or otters?"

"Old movie."

"What?"

"*Grand Hotel.*"

"Good," he says. "Wonderful movie." Could see the genuine pleasure in his eyes. Almost like this man enjoys life.

I nod.

"Who's in it?"

"John Barrymore, Greta Garbo, Lionel Barrymore, Wallace Beery."

"I vant to be alone," he says, smiles. Wistful.

"Right."

"So you're lying on the couch? Sitting in a chair?"

"Couch," I say. "Lying down. And Joan comes in. Says, 'It's beautiful out. Let's go for a ride.' And I say, 'Sure.' "

"Because you don't like the movie, or you want to kill her?"

"The movie," I say. "I've seen it twice before. I know the lines better than the actors."

He nods, touches the side of his nose with his index finger.

"So I say, 'Yeah, let's go for a ride,' get up, get my shoes on, put on a sweater, get my coat. And my hands start to shake when I'm zipping my coat.

"Joan had gone out to warm up the car, and I went to the cellar, to where I'd left the gun under some rags in the storage room. I did it fast so Joan wouldn't think I was taking too long, and when I was down there that scary shit was happening."

"Like?"

"Like voices. 'I know you, you shitwipe.' Like I wanted to put the barrel in my mouth and press the trigger."

"But you didn't?"

"Obviously," I say, and he smiles.

Exactly, he might think.

"It felt heavy. The gun. And it had this oily feel to it, and I put it inside my belt. And just having it there, just feeling it press into my stomach made me feel better, like there was help on the way."

"Help for . . . ?"

I'd shake my head.

"So I went upstairs, and I took a pint of whiskey from the cabinet over the refrigerator, for the cold, and I put it in my coat pocket, and went outside.

"Joan smiled when I got in, and I remember seeing the freckles on her nose and cheeks, and her eyes, and I remember feeling how much I loved her, and felt scared, felt sorry for her. But also relieved, because she might be dead soon."

"Might?" Schumacher would ask.

"I don't think I was sure. But I almost felt like giggling, too. Everything was hot and cold, and outside, as we drove, there was this sharpness, this clarity to the world, probably because of the cold.

"We went out Route 16, through Wellesley, out where the houses thin out, and we saw a few horses, and there was a sanctuary for birds and wildlife with trails where you could walk.

"We pulled in and parked, and I leaned over and kissed her on the mouth, and I remember she looked at me. She said, 'Earl,' and then laughed. She said, 'Later,' and I felt sorry for her because she didn't know.

"We got out, and I was surprised how cold it was. We could see our breath, it was so cold, but the good thing was, there were only two other cars there. Hardly any people."

"What time was this?" Schumacher asked. He looked at his watch.

"About three."

"So you had two hours of daylight?"

I'd nod.

"And?"

"We started walking, and in the first half mile we passed a woman with two teenage kids, and then a man with binoculars. We nodded and said hello."

"And Joan didn't notice anything?"

I shook my head.

"You didn't act funny? She didn't sense anything?"

I said, "No.

"There were miles and miles of paths, and no roads or cars, and after the binoculars man, no people. After about two miles, I got Joan to leave the trail. I got her to come up the side of a hill, through the trees, with all the leaves crackling underfoot. We walked up and up, for maybe ten minutes, and then there was this grove of pines, and a ravine behind it, and no paths anywhere that we could see."

I pushed my hair back. Behind my ears. I looked at him, but he'd be looking down at his hands, still folded on his chest.

"There wasn't anyone around, anyone for miles. And this was January, this was when it was cold as hell, and people wouldn't be tramping around in the woods."

"What was the ground like?"

"No ice or snow," I said. "Frozen pretty solid."

"And you took out the gun?"

"Told her I loved her, said I was sorry. Said I wished everything had been different. Said I wished I wasn't such a fuckwipe.

"She was standing and looking at me. I thought she'd start crying. Her eyes started to fill up.

"I turned around so my back was to her, and I took out the gun, and then I faced her, and she had that look on her face. She was surprised for a second, her mouth open, and just staring, and then she seemed to understand.

"So I pointed the gun, and fired, and there was this spurt of blood on her forehead, a dark hole the size of a nickel. And she fell down, and I just stood there and kept hearing the noise of the gun echo and echo and echo."

He looked up for a second, and then he looked at his hands, at the top of the desk.

"And then I took her clothes off. I took off her coat and boots, her socks and jeans. Everything. Even her watch and ring, and this gold chain that was around her neck.

"Her skin was so white, and I kept thinking and worrying about her being cold. And her skin shined, maybe because the light was so weird, and it was like this was a chapel with the pine trees, and Joan lying there like it was an altar. Aside from her forehead, she looked peaceful, like she was sleeping and dreaming about cartoons and fairy tales and stuff."

"You left her there?"

I nodded.

"What'd you do with her clothes?"

"Brought them with me."

"And left her body there?"

"I dragged it into the pine trees."

"How'd you drag it?"

"By the feet."

"And that was it?"

"Yes, sir," I told him.

"So why no body? And why aren't you in jail?"

.

Late at night, when I was driving, I picked up a woman who was hitchhiking on Beacon Street in Brookline. She had blond hair that came to her shoulders, and she wore a dark suit coat.

As soon as she got into the car I could smell the alcohol on her breath.

"Thank you so much," she said. "Thank you. You're so sweet," she said.

She put a hand on my arm and said, "Thank God. I thought I'd be out there all night."

"Where you going?" I asked.

"Newton Center."

I passed Cleveland Circle, and around the long curve by the reservoir, I went sixty, and she leaned back in the seat, and the air from the window blew her hair.

Her eyes were closed, and in Newton Center I had to shake her shoulder, had to wake her up.

"C'mon," I said. "We're here. You're home," I almost shouted.

Her eyes opened, and she smiled. She kissed me on the lips, then got out. I watched her walk across a parking lot, then disappear in shadows near the back of some stores.

She had blond hair, and a suit coat that was probably black, maybe dark brown. She was about twenty. She wore sneakers and blue jeans. It was 2:17 in the morning. She was five-five, about 120 pounds.

.

Earl, that fuckwipe. He can bear any thought. Any cruel image, idea. That shitlick cannot bear, cannot endure certain flicks, flecks, specks, sparks of memory. Which is to say: facts. Dad. Worthless. Useless. Old man. Going. To room. Fuck. Fuck. Brandon to home. Mrs. Fucking M. Crying crying, lost her only. Fuckface Earl. Little Feces. Cannot bear. Joan packing boxes. Sisters helping, brother Todd. Sister Karen plus Dede. Nice family, Millis. Loving, helping Joan pack up apartment. Fucking madman curled up in a blanket in the bathtub crying, saying, muttering darkly, "The last scud of day holds back for me, / It flings my likeness after the rest and true as any on the shadowed wilds, / It coaxes me to the vapor and the dusk. / I depart as air. / I shake my white locks at the runaway sun, / I effuse my flesh in eddies, and drift it in lacy jags." Father Walt. Bear all, endure all, hope all. Cannot bear to think of that. Her being gone.

·

School was always easy for me. School made me think I'd do well in the army or prison. Bells rang to tell you to do things, be someplace to do something. Homeroom at eight, math at eight-thirty, gym at ten, biology at eleven-fifteen, and so on through the day.

Teachers liked me because I was quiet, because I caught on to things fast. Did the work, showed up on time. Was never a liar or weasel. They'd explain about the Second Great Awakening in American history, and I'd know instinctively what had happened and why. I knew about the restlessness in Americans, the need to move and redefine and seek again and again. I'd know why wars occurred, and how they were inevitable. Loved the big sweeps of time.

I didn't even work that hard, not really even in college and graduate school. I found out what teachers wanted, what each course required. Show up for lectures, for seminars, read ten or twelve books, give an oral presentation, and do one short (ten pages) and one long (twenty pages) paper. Never expected anything to be given to me. Entitled to nothing. Big difference there.

In school the floors were clean, the radiators hissed and hummed in the winter, there was warm food in the cafeteria at lunch, and most people, most of the time, were polite. Teachers were always good to me. They touched my shoulder, patted my arm, told me to keep it up. I said, Yes, sir, No, sir.

They wore pretty dresses, comfortable sweaters, and had voices that were warm and strong. They knew things I did not know. They knew that Faulkner had written as he did in response to the defeat of the South in the Civil War. Had the South won, his books would be very different, they said. Hemingway was hurt in World War I. Badly injured, physically and mentally.

Jefferson owned slaves, and Lincoln suffered from deep and recurring melancholia. If Trotsky had won the power struggle with Stalin, the world might be a different place. The Golden Age of Pericles was founded on a vast slave state, and Henry Ford was the backwoodsman who tamed technology. "History is bunk," he famously or infamously said. FDR and Kennedy were rich kids. Johnson and Truman were not. That made all the difference. But fell out in each in crucially and fascinatingly different ways.

All I had to do was show up, do the work, and I'd pass my way up through the grades. From eighth grade to ninth grade, to high school, and then freshman, sophomore, junior, senior years, and college was over too. Graduate school counted years and landmarks. First year, second year, pre— or post—Q exams. Working on a thesis, defending a thesis, on to the job market.

All of it swirls and swims now. Everything swirls and swims. I used to know the great geological ages, from Pliocene to Pleistocene to Paleocene, and all those millions of years. Paleocene was part of the Tertiary period, lasted from 60 million to 70 million years ago. The first birds and early mammals appeared during the Paleocene, but now all those zeroes, those great sweeps of time swirl like water in a storm.

Continents moved, huge masses of ice and rock and earth heaved, fires erupted, planets collided, and enormous, strange beasts crossed the earth on webbed feet. This was long before the Sun King, before Hannibal or Attila or Christ. Great maws opened in the crust of the earth, and things fell in, things disappeared in the ice and fire.

I used to know these things. I took a test and listed the geological times, I spelled them right, said something about each. Later there were ages—Bronze and Stone and Iron—but I can't remember them either, though Stone must have come first.

There was Genus, Order, Phylum, Species, Class, and more, but those swim too. There's an ocean of swirling water in my head, and I could retrieve things if it were different. There was Kingdom too.

There was Australopithecus and Ramapithecus. There were hominids and knuckle walkers, and there were pictures, re-creations, of creatures in animal skins, with clubs, with hair over most of their bodies. They had long arms, and their brains were growing larger and larger. One creature held a baby in its arms and looked with its deep-set eyes over the landscape. It had a long sad face, an enormous jaw, a small forehead. But already the eyes knew. As they knuckle-walked through the days, foraging, hunting, living in caves, living under the rain and wind and snow.

Neanderthals were the first to bury their dead, with clothes and other artifacts on and around the corpses. It seems to indicate that they had formed some notion of an afterlife, some place beyond, where there would be more life of some kind. The dead would need things on the other side, would need clothes, stone tools, a few beads, a pretty rock with streaks of red and blue.

Archaeologists found a Neanderthal mother's grave, and she had her arms around her baby. Both had died, probably in childbirth, and those who buried them had some notion of a link, a bond, that would extend beyond mere life. Something that could reach the other side.

At night, when everything swims, and I can't, don't want to, tell Phylum from Precambrian, when the alimentary canal merges with the ulna, and Hotspur and Hector and Joe Christmas and Mrs. Ramsay and Isabel Archer move across the storm inside, I start thinking of the Neanderthals in their cave, standing or squatting over their dead. There could be a fire (did they have fire?), and there are beads and stone tools on the body.

People are moaning, are weeping, for the dead, for the lost and gone, and I lie here. Breathe. Try to slow down. To stop. And picture tears of grief coursing down the hairy Neanderthal faces, hundreds of thousands of years ago.

FOURTEEN

When he was a junior in high school, Ed was caught shoplifting three times and had to go to court. The first time he was put on probation, the second time he was supposed to see a psychiatrist. The third time—because he was failing high school anyway—he agreed to join the army. He was a high school fuck-up but scored very high in standardized tests.

Mom signed papers, and he left after Christmas, first for basic training in North Carolina, then for Germany.

Mrs. Maloney still lived next door, and by the time Ed joined the army, I was in high school and Mrs. M. was getting old and bent over and thin. Brandon had gone away to live in a home for retards. Excuse me. Developmentally disabled people. Special-needs individuals. Because Mrs. M. could no longer care for him at home.

Dad went back in the hospital that winter, one of the winters.

Mrs. M. told me it was Mom's fault, but I knew she was full of shit to her eyeballs. I almost never argued with Mrs. M. because she'd begin screaming and crying.

One time Mrs. M. fell down while we were yelling at each other, and she began to gasp for breath and tell me she had pains in her chest.

She'd call next door on the phone sometimes, at midnight or one or two in the morning, and she'd start talking about the colored people, as she called them, and the Jews and Gypsies and Japs. She said that when she was a girl there was a colored family named Jackson that lived down the street, and everyone thought the world of them, "colored or no color," she said.

"They were like you or me," she said. "Now the Japs," she went on. "That's another story."

"What about the Irish?" I asked one time.

"Shanty Irish or lace-curtain Irish? You have pigs and thoroughbreds," she said.

I saw Dad when he came out of the hospital, and he had gained a little weight. He said he had cancer and wouldn't live long, but he said that was okay, he said it was time. Everyone had a time. He knew it, God knew it. The pope in fucking Rome knew it too.

When I asked Mom, she wanted to know if he'd been drinking.

I nodded that yes he had, and she said, "His time won't come soon enough."

·

Jerry on the ward calls David Maxwell a "cocksucker," and David tells Jerry to "fuck off." The usual dumb shit. Same high level of discourse.

They're about the same height, but Jerry has twenty, thirty pounds on David. We're in the front dayroom, and Claire walks through and says, "Hello, boys," and smiles like she's on a boardwalk.

"A motherfucking cocksucker," Jerry says.

"Where'd you learn to talk?" David asks. "Some slum?"

"D Street, South Boston, U.S. of A., pal." Jerry stands up.

"Gimme a smoke," I say, and Jerry hands me a Marlboro.

I put the cigarette behind my ear.

"I don't believe you associate with this slime," David says to me. "He's a short-eyes."

Jerry swings, and David screams, "He rapes babies!"

David shouts something incomprehensible, and Jerry starts hollering and keeps swinging at David.

Jackie and Stephanie and Walter run in, and I watch them pull Jerry from David.

Blood is dripping from David's forehead.

.

I can say for sure that the vent blows air and my father is dead. I remember how skinny he got. His eyes were like coals and seemed to burn deeper and deeper in his head. Clothes hung on him, flapped like there was wind when he moved.

Mrs. M. stayed next door and grew older and older and smaller each year, and Mom cooked dinner for her once in a while.

There was a time when she was in a wheelchair, and on the phone she cried.

I could do things, I remember thinking.

If I lit the house on fire, she could not move. She'd be in bed, and I could pour the gasoline on her and drop the match, and her screams would rise with the flames. But sometime along there, I can't remember when, the welfare people came, and she went to a home like Brandon. Not exactly like Brandon, but similar.

Her head sank into her shoulders, and her walk slowed, but her hands grew bigger, were like the roots of a tree.

Out in the hall, here, on the ward, Alicia Powers, the night aide, she goes by with her flashlight. She leans into the room, says, "Earl," and I say, "Yeah?"

"You okay?"

"Sure."

"Roger called in sick, so I'm on alone tonight."

"Okay," I say, though I don't know why she's telling me.

It's after midnight, and the vents come on only for a minute or two, and the ceiling has long strips of moonlight and outside security light slipping through the curtains.

"Sleep well," she says, and I hear her move down the hall from room to room.

Michael Williams is gone, but only because he is never here anymore. Nobody saw him leave. Not Jerry, not Claire, not David, not me. He could be on the streets, walking somewhere right now, or sitting in a bar with his Elvis looks, waiting for someone to move on him.

My brother Ed is gone. He sent a letter from Germany his first year there, but since then he is wandering.

He might be in the army, and he might be shoplifting. He stole tampons, women's underwear, perfume, and a cigarette lighter even though he didn't smoke. He talked about lighting fires. He was not there when Dad died. Ed did not see how skinny and yellow Dad got.

When I cleaned out his room in Brighton, I found books and books, and some naturist magazines under his mattress. Magazines with pictures. Mom had gone to the store for Lysol, and I looked at the pictures.

Men and women and little boys and girls at nudist camps. Playing volleyball and sitting around a swimming pool on deck chairs. Eating lunch or breakfast or dinner. Families together. Except most of them wore socks and sneakers. And some of the women wore bathing-suit bottoms, maybe when they were having their periods.

I heard the front door, and I put the magazines in the green trash bags. I put them underneath the clothes we were throwing out, the yellowing underwear, the frayed shirts. I didn't want my mother to see, and feel sad and lonely and guilty the way I did.

Claire goes by in the hall. Her slippers scrape the linoleum, and I can see the flowers on her robe.

.

When I first taught at the school. Those first days of seeing, knowing her. She must have seen him. Did see Earl.

A tall person who loved to teach. Was very free and alive somehow in the classroom. With youth. With boys of adolescent. Age group. Puberty.

He loved his books. He had read so much. Misters Parkman, Thoreau, Whitman, Winthrop, Faulkner, James, both William and Henry. Edwards, Mather, etc., etc. Plus the later stuff, of course. The women too. Wharton, Cather, Hurston.

Loved his books, loved his boys.

She saw this. Ms. Joan did. Saw too. How desperately lonely. Cut off. Utterly friendless. Awkward, shy, very sad, woeful family. His. Story.

.

He. I. Turn pillow over. Count how long been here.

The police must have brought me. I wonder if they know about Joan.

I wiped the blood from the knife and threw it into the Charles River from the Mass. Ave. bridge. The blood wouldn't come out of her clothes or my clothes, so he would have put all of them— shoes and coats, too—in a plastic bag, left the bag in a Dumpster, behind a restaurant in Newton Corner.

Her body in the cellar, behind the furnace, under boxes in the storage room, in the closet with old newspapers next to the water heater.

Wiped prints off gun, threw it far out in Crystal Lake in Newton Center. Threw it at least a hundred feet out. Must be at least ten feet deep there, on side by the Green Line tracks.

The bottom's full of weeds, of silt, of mud and broken bottles. Maybe old tires, maybe bones of humans.

.

Have pictures of Joan. School pictures. Wallet size, first through fourth grades. Can almost not bear to look. All black and white. First-grade photo she has blouse on, pattern of small flowers, dark jumper over blouse. Short shining hair, light brown. Short, shining, smiling baby teeth. Small eyes, nose, lovely sweet smile. A little shy. But happy with the world.

.

At the funeral home there was Mom and me. A priest came from Sacred Heart Church, and two men were there who worked for the funeral home.

The casket was made of gray metal, and Dad wore a coat and tie that Mom had bought at King's two days before. The coat was gray and the tie red.

We sat on folding chairs, and the priest said prayers. He said, "Hail Mary, full of grace, the Lord is with thee." Mom knew the words and prayed out loud with the priest.

There was white powder on Dad's face and red tints on his cheeks. Underneath, his skin was yellow and blue like a bruise. They had put cotton in his cheeks so they'd puff out, but it looked more like he'd been chewing tobacco when he died.

When the prayers were finished, one of the funeral men touched my elbow, and nodded, and motioned for me to stand up. Mom leaned into the casket and kissed Dad on the cheek.

I thought about Ed, and where he was. I thought of him on a boat on the Pacific Ocean, or sitting in a bar in a city in Germany. I thought of him walking on a street somewhere. Then I followed Mom out of the room.

I wondered if Ed knew that Dad was dead, the way dogs were supposed to howl when their owners died, even if they were thousands of miles away. I wondered if Ed paused on the street or boat, or in the bar, and felt a tug and knew. And I wondered if he looked up at the sky, or spit, or ordered another drink. Like this day was different, like something important had happened.

.

Joan's sisters and brothers, her mother and father, could not have been nicer to me. They were all tall and had long arms and legs and good teeth. They had the kind of manners that put even someone like me at his ease. Even some fuckwipe like me. I tried not to smoke in front of them or say "fuck" or "shit." I tried not to tell stories—out of my intense awkwardness and nervousness— about Native Americans torturing their adolescent boys in rite-of-passage ceremonies, or quote erotic passages from Walt Whitman or the Song of Solomon.

After I had met my first member of Joan's family, Joan asked Dede on the phone what she thought of me. "Well, I like him very much," she said. "Plus he has good hair, and that's not to be overlooked."

Good hair for a useless fucking dicklick.

.

This man: He was six-one, had blond hair and blue eyes. He too had worked as a garbageman, and as a seaman on freighters on the Great Lakes. He was one of eight children, and he left school after the eighth grade. He married a fifteen-year-old girl, and they had a child, a daughter. The daughter is alive, and I try not to know about him. But he is real too. Real as air and wind, real as blood and water.

There was a tattoo on his left arm that said BORN TO RAISE HELL. He was an alcoholic and drug addict.

He knocked on the door of a town house on One Hundredth Street in Chicago. It was 11:00 P.M., and as he waited outside the front door, he took a knife and a gun from his pockets.

Three young women answered the door, and he pointed the gun at them.

"I won't hurt you," he said. "I just want money."

He herded the three women to a bedroom on the second floor. There were three more women on the second floor, so he ordered all six to the bedroom, told them to sit on the floor.

At eleven-thirty a seventh woman came home, and just after that, two more returned. There were nine of them now, and he tore sheets into strips and tied the women up, one by one.

When they were all tied up, he sat on the floor and talked to them. He said, "Don't be afraid. I won't hurt you."

"I won't kill you," he told them.

He brought one woman to a different bedroom. He stabbed her once in the chest and then strangled her with a strip of sheet.

He began to get hard as he strangled her.

He went back to the first bedroom and took two more women out of the room, this time to a third bedroom. He stabbed one woman in the chest and neck and face. The other woman tried to resist.

He stabbed her eighteen times. He stabbed her in the back and in the chest. He stabbed her in the neck and face, and though she was probably dead already, he began to strangle her with his hands. He ripped the underwear from her body and began to tear the cloth into small pieces.

He went to the bathroom and washed his hands. Then he took another woman, the fourth one, brought her to a bedroom, and stabbed and strangled her.

He stabbed and strangled each woman, until there were only two left. One wedged herself in a corner, under a bed.

Why would some dumb fuck insist on telling these stories to his wife, and thus drive her away?

The nurse heard him come for what he thought was the last woman. She heard the rustling of clothes, she heard a zipper. The bedsprings squeaked rhythmically, and she heard him say, "Wrap your legs around my back."

The bedsprings squeaked for twenty or thirty minutes and then stopped, and she heard the two of them leave the room. She heard a groan downstairs, and she made herself smaller and smaller in the corner, in her corner under the bed.

Bring down my gray hairs with sorrows to the grave. Thou hast laid me in the lowest pit, in darkness, in the deep.

For a long time she stayed there, long after the house was silent.

At five in the morning, alarm clocks in the house began to go off. She kept waiting. She heard movement out on the street.

She finally crawled out from under the bed. She saw bodies everywhere. She reached a window that looked out onto the street and crawled to a ledge. She began to scream.

Everybody is dead, she screamed. I am the only one alive.

FIFTEEN

Stephanie sits in the staff office. Smokes, sits, talks. I could be here, I could be in bed. But I can't sleep as usual. No fucking sleep for the big guy. So I sit and listen. And boy, she needs to talk tonight. Needs an ear, shoulder, eyes on her face and hands. Taking her in.

This is her, Stephanie talking. Her turn. Stephanie has the talking stick. "Earl, baby. Hey, buddy. No sleep. Time's moving slow tonight. Does that sometimes on me too, especially when something's wrong with one of the kids and I feel like I should be home.

"It's nothing too bad, nothing too serious. John has a cold, and it's at the stage where he's coughing so hard that you can feel it in your own chest, like you'll cough part of your lungs up. Not that I'd be able to do anything if I was there anyway. But still, still and all. Walter said to go home. Walter. He said it was no problem for him to cover for me, but I can't leave. That new one, the little one, that one named Wright, in restraints in Isolation yesterday, and Schumacher's got him on thirty milligrams of Haldol. I doubt he'll move, and I know Walter could handle him easy, but I shouldn't leave. You can't tell.

"I shouldn't say this. You won't repeat this. But they say Wright's the one was maybe doing those rapes around the arboretum back in the fall. He was at Bridgewater, and I don't know why they don't keep him there. He's got those rape eyes. Maybe it's my imagination, and maybe I'm just flattering myself, but I can feel his eyes, even when my back's turned, even when he's on the other side of the dayroom. The little, the little pervert.

"A few of them still up, still watching the eleven-o'clock news. You can take that one. Wright. You can have him. He misses hearing about himself on the news, looking at his police sketch.

"I don't know how John got the cold. Maybe doing his paper route so early mornings. Still so cold, so damp then, and the moisture got in his lungs.

"When he was small, it was awful. We thought he had scarlet fever or lung disease or something. He'd get a little cold in his chest, and he'd have trouble breathing. It was like a knife scraped over stone. I'd sit there next to his bed and wish I could breathe for him. Please, God, give him my air, I'd say.

"Doug would get up and lean in the doorway and say, 'Honey, c'mon, he'll be okay.' But I had to stay. As though if I wasn't there wishing on every breath, willing the air in and out, he'd stop breathing. He'd die, and it'd be my fault.

"It's crazy, but you think that way, and I don't think it hurts anybody. You just fear for them, and there's so little you can do."

·

Some things you see on TV, you read in the papers. Whole town in Minnesota sexually abusing their kids. Not just two or three incidents. Twenty or thirty adults, sex parties where they passed around kids like candy. And they weren't talking about a little touching and kissing.

This is what I think, lying here. So I don't think of things that really hurt, that I can't bear.

One eight-year-old boy describes how his neighbor put lotion on his own penis and the boy's backside so he could slide it into the boy's rear. An eight-year-old doesn't make up a thing like that. A boy doesn't know about lotion on a man's penis. Or does he? Could he dream it? Be told it?

There were policemen involved, teachers, an assistant principal. These weren't people with horns and tails. They didn't breathe fire.

It wasn't one or two kids either. This was twenty or thirty kids, and it was their own children they were passing around. Five-year-olds and ten-year-olds. Then they started talking about busing in kids from other places, and there was no evidence, nothing whatsoever. It was tissue paper. Written on tissue paper and told in whispers. Everyone had the same panicky dream. Induced memory. Panic, collective hysteria.

That's not even the worst of it, though, because darker things happen. You get the earthquakes and the plane crashes, and they'll have the film crews there when they pick up the bodies, the pieces of bodies, so we can all see.

The terrible catastrophic events. Live and in color. Smashed, hurled, shorn, broken, pierced, splayed.

They show that movie of the president getting shot, and you watch it over and over. They speed it up, they slow it down, they freeze the picture and use arrows to point. It goes by a street sign, and for a half second you can't see anything. Then it comes into view again, and everybody's smiling and waving. The sun's out, you're standing on a sunny street. You've got your home-movie camera, and you're making a movie of the president. This is something you'll have for the kids.

She's next to him, in her pink hat and pink dress. The governor and his wife are in the seat in front of them. The governor starts to turn, as though he's about to say something. He's about to say, "Isn't it beautiful today? Wasn't that a good breakfast? The people of Texas seem to love you."

Then they slow it down. The film goes *click click click*—sprocket by sprocket it creeps through the camera.

The president's elbows lift like he's swimming almost, and the black car keeps moving, and then you see the back top of the president's head shatter, you see a spray of bone and flesh and hair and brain, and he slumps forward, and all of this is held forever on the movie that was taken that day near the grassy knoll.

And the movie plays again and again, with arrows and sometimes with commentary. But you never hear the crack of the gun, the explosion, the echo in the plaza. It's like the crack is inside each of us, like the lines we fill in between the dots.

If only everybody could and would. Stay the hell home, alone, in their own damn rooms. Though God knows that would be damned fucking dull. Huh.

·

Joan had been a lifeguard in college, and she got me to swim and drift and float hundreds of yards from shore with her.

"C'mon, sweetie," she said. "I'll save you."

July was hot, the sky was always blue, and on the radio and television we heard about the drought, the worst in thirty years, and how food prices could soar by winter.

We lay on our backs in the water and saw trees far off on the edge of the lake, and the few clouds in the sky were white puffs and moved slowly across the sky like sails.

Joan's brother Todd was visiting from Atlanta, and he brought a woman named Megan with him. She had red hair and freckles, and was close to six feet tall.

"You like her?" Joan asked me, and I said I did.

"You?" I asked.

Joan nodded, then laid her head back in the water and said, "I wish it was always like this."

And we floated for a long time without saying anything. When I pushed my head far enough under, so my ears were covered with water, it was as though I could hear every depth of the lake. Every rock and weed, each fish and drop of water.

.

Around five on Sunday afternoon, Walter and Stephanie leave for Brigham's, an ice cream store. They come back by six with large white bags.

Inside, there are containers of ice cream and hot fudge. There are nuts and cans of whipped cream, there are bowls and plastic spoons, and all of us gather around a table in the front day-room.

"Okay!" Walter shouts. "It's Sunday!" he hollers, like a hawker at Fenway Park.

We take bowls and spoons, get ice cream, pour hot fudge over it, then squirt whipped cream on that. Then we sprinkle nuts on top.

"Beats the shit out of prison," Jerry says. "This kicks prison's ass," he tells us.

.

It'd be cold outside, and Schumacher would say, "Tell me." But by now, somehow, I am aware of the conjectural nature of our discourse. To reach a deeper, perhaps truer area of discourse.

Behind him the window would be covered at the edges by frost.

"About Joan?" I'd ask, and he'd glare at me like he was tired of everything. As I am getting tired too. Though scared, quite scared. But distinctly tired, and tired of his fucking tiredness too.

There is a third-grade picture that I have in my. In fuckwipe's possession. She, Joan Millis. Is wearing a light-colored dress with white piping on the throat and shoulders. Her hair is still light, still shining. Is parted on the left, and held back with a white barrette. Still smiling. Lovely smile, though slightly inquisitive this year. Eyes have that light of intelligence, kindness, curiosity, shyness.

"How much time you have?" I'd ask.

"As long as it takes."

"An hour? Two hours?"

He'd nod some more.

"She'd been out swimming at a lake," I'd say. "This was August, and the heat kept up. It was ninety-something by three that afternoon, but I didn't feel like going out. Maybe because of the crowds.

"So I stayed home, sat on the back porch, and I kept drinking beer, and sweating, and I was on my third or fourth beer when I heard the car door slam out front."

"Joan getting dropped off?"

"Right. She'd gone with this woman we worked with, Alison someone, who always wore too much makeup, and who I didn't like.

"So the door slammed, and I heard her at the front door. Then she called hello, and I felt her behind me.

"She leaned down and kissed me, and then stood there and looked at one of her plants that was hanging from the ceiling.

"She was still wearing her bathing suit, that was all she was wearing, and there wasn't much to it. A bikini is what it was. Just black patches, really, on each breast, and one on her butt and another in front, and just strings holding it all together.

"And I sat there and watched her, and I felt all kinds of things."

"Like?"

"Like I wanted to get up, and untie the strings, and take the patches off. I kept thinking of her nipples getting hard, and me licking and sucking them, and wanting to take a whole breast in my mouth."

Don't do this, I am thinking. It is not fucking true. You did not do this. Not in any literal sense. You fuckwipe. You dicklick, thick-brain, numbnuts. The conjectural nature of this. It prevents you from encountering the harsh, hurtful, maybe unbearable, unen-durable nature of the real thing. Which is much more common, more ordinary. About the nature of love. The quality of marriage, of human relationships. Their ephemeral nature.

"I thought about taking the bottom of her bikini off, and spreading her legs, and licking her cunt. Sucking her clitoris, and making her moan and squirm."

"So what'd you do?"

"I sat there, and I got harder and harder. I kept thinking that she had no idea how much I wanted her, and how sexy she was in that bikini.

"She went from one plant to another, and she'd ask questions like, 'Did you have fun here? Did anyone call?' And I answered her, but I felt like I could barely talk, my throat was almost too swollen.

"And then I started to think of her at the lake, and how she'd walk around, and all the men would look at her. I thought how they'd look, and start to get hard, and it excited me to think that.

"Then I started to think that she knew all this. That she knew I was getting hard, and that as she walked past the men at the lake, she'd notice the front of their bathing suits and would see their cocks swelling."

"And."

"And I kept looking at her, and I could see the outline of her nipples, and when she turned away from me, I got up and went to the kitchen, and took out a knife, and went to the cellar."

"What'd you do down there?"

"I just stood there with the knife, and I felt myself—felt how hard I still was—and I kept picturing Joan at the lake, and thinking of her looking at how hard she made all the men.

"So I yelled upstairs. I said, 'Honey, could you come down?' And my throat was swollen like my cock."

Schumacher would be looking at his hands again, only it would be winter outside, and we'd be able to hear the wind.

"She came to the head of the stairs and said, 'Earl?' "

Schumacher, leading the pathetic witness in his fancy. Thus to help him to the end of his story and byword. Thus, perhaps, to face the fear, the tenable, assailable anxiety and loneliness of reality.

"Could you come down here? I said, and I'd hear her footsteps coming down.

"The knife would have a four- or five-inch blade. It'd be a knife we'd used to cut tomatoes or rolls, a knife we used to put mustard on bread."

"So she came down?"

"And saw me, and didn't notice the knife.

" 'How'd it feel?' I'd ask.

" 'What?' she'd ask. She'd be confused.

" 'How'd it feel? At the lake?'

"Her skin would be white, and I'd see the bones at her shoulders, at the base of her neck.

" 'How'd what feel?'

" 'Making everyone hard? How'd it feel to walk around with your tits and your cunt hanging out, and to have everyone panting for you?'

" 'Earl,' she'd say, then she'd look down, and she'd notice the knife.

"And before she could scream or see how hard I was, I'd begin."

This somehow is where I interpose the picture of Joan Millis, my former wife, and the picture of her from the fourth grade. Wearing a sweater with a broad snowflake pattern, and silver cat glasses, and a broad smile. And eyes that just shine and shine. And see and see and know, that I could not, would not, never will nor could do the things that I am speculatively describing to Dr. Schumacher.

"I'd be surprised how easily the knife went in," I say to him. Am somehow going on with the narrative for its own sake. Can't seem to end it yet. "Once it popped the chest cavity, it slid in like butter.

"She'd fall, and I'd be on her, stabbing again and again.

"I'd rip the strings off, and her tits would be covered by blood, and I'd do it over and over."

"Do what?"

"Stab and fuck."

"Fuck?"

"The bottoms would be off, and I'd spread her legs wide, and I'd see the lips, and I'd take off my shorts."

"Would she be dead?"

"Yes."

"How long'd it take?"

"Few minutes."

"And then?"

"Hide her body."

"Where?"

I shake my head. "I don't know."

"She's gone, you know."

"Yes."

"She's left you because she needed to leave you."

Earl shakes and nods his head some more. Says that yes, he knows. Shakes head, nods head.

.

That spring—the spring I was in high school—Mom had pain in her back whenever she tried to stand up or walk. I took her to a doctor, who gave her pills for the pain and told her she'd have to use a wheelchair.

For a while it was me helping Mom to the bathroom, and on and off the toilet, then dressing her.

She wasn't so many years old, but she now weighed less and less and had a series of small strokes that seemed to take small parts of her brain away.

She talked about being a girl, about New Hampshire, where she had lived the first ten years of her life.

"My father never raised his voice," she said. "Not once in all the years.

"He worked over at the Davis Ice Company, and the men there loved him. They bought a beautiful wreath for his funeral, and they kept coming up to my mother and saying how they loved him, how they never heard him raise his voice.

"Now, Daisy Kelley," she said. "Daisy Kelley lived over on Emerson Road, the green house near the end, and she used to say to my mother, 'Gert, the day you want to leave your husband, you tell me and I'll move in.' "

I made breakfast, while Mom watched from her wheelchair, her big hands folded and resting on her lap. I made Cream of Wheat, and poached an egg, and made tea with milk and sugar.

Then I pushed the wheelchair close to the kitchen table, and I watched Mom eat a spoonful of Cream of Wheat, a piece of poached egg. I watched her fish the tea bag from the cup with her spoon, drop the bag in the saucer, and sip. Tea was the only thing she'd finish.

I went to school and called the people from welfare and Medicare and Medicaid and filled out every fucking form the fucking government could print.

Mom had a telephone next to her wheelchair, a remote control for the television, and she was able to wheel herself to the refrigerator and bathroom. It took her twenty minutes to move from the wheelchair to the toilet, but if nobody was there, she could do it.

When I came home from school, I undressed Mom, put her teeth in water, took her to the bathroom, then put her nightgown on and put her to bed.

"Stay and talk," Mom said to me, and sometimes Mom would talk until one or two in the morning.

"We used to ice-skate," Mom said, and I'd drift into sleep, and come back to hear Mom talk about swimming in the ocean in 1938.

Pretty soon welfare had people come in to help give her baths, and after that it was poof—off to the fucking sheltered apartment for you. Here's your bucket and drool rag.

As for you, fuckwipe. Mr. Sunny Fucking Jim. Interested in becoming a ward of the Commonwealth of Fucking Massachusetts? Not just yet.

·

There were four people in the house when they arrived. The man climbed through a window, then unlocked the front door and let the two women in, and I keep picturing their faces as they stand there, and I keep seeing the faces of the other people, the people who will soon be dead. Because this isn't a dream.

They had a gun, knives, rope, and a change of clothes for later.

A man was sleeping on the couch, and the tall man with the gun woke him up, pointed the gun at his face, and said, "Don't move or you're dead."

One of the women checked the bedrooms, saw a woman lying on a bed in one room reading a book. In a second bedroom a man was sitting on the side of a bed, talking to a woman who was lying down. The woman was eight months pregnant.

The killer woman went back to the living room and told the tall man about the other people. He threw her some rope, told her to tie up the man on the couch. When she was done, she went to the bedrooms with her knife and ordered the man and two women to go to the living room.

The tall man told them to lie on the floor on their stomachs, and the man who had been sitting on the side of the bed said, "She's pregnant. Let her sit down."

The tall man shot him, and he fell in front of the fireplace.

The tall man took some rope, tied it around the neck of the man he'd shot, then tied the rope around the necks of the two women from the bedrooms. He threw the other end of the rope over a beam in the ceiling and began to pull on the rope.

The two women stood up so they wouldn't choke.

The man on the couch got free for a moment, and one of the women who had come through a window began to stab him. Then the tall man stabbed him.

The women with rope around their necks said, "Please."

The pregnant woman said, "Please. I want to have my baby."

"Don't," they said. "Please."

The tall man began to stab the pregnant woman. One of the women with the knives began to stab the pregnant woman too.

They stabbed the woman from the first bedroom, the woman who had been reading, twenty-eight times. They stabbed the pregnant woman sixteen times.

Both women were on the floor. The tall man was no longer holding the rope over the beam in the ceiling.

The man from the couch was still alive, and ran to the front lawn. They caught him and resumed stabbing him. They kicked him. He was stabbed fifty-one times, shot two times, and hit on the head with a blunt instrument thirteen times.

The tall man told one of the women to go back inside and write something on the wall with blood.

When the woman got to the living room, she leaned over the pregnant woman. She heard sounds. She later said she heard "gurgling sounds like blood flowing into the body out of the heart."

She took a towel, got blood from the pregnant woman's chest, and wrote the word PIG on a door.

Then they drove away. They changed clothes in the car. They stopped the car on the side of a road overlooking a canyon. They threw the bloody clothes over the side of the canyon.

They stopped at a house and used a garden hose to wash the blood from their arms and hands and faces.

The owner of the house came outside and started to yell at them.

It was after midnight.

They said they were sorry. They said they didn't know anybody was home, that they just wanted a drink of water. They said they didn't mean to wake anybody up, didn't mean to cause a disturbance.

•

Walter and Stephanie are working tonight, the vents have been turned on, and outside the wind's moving the whole world around. Jerry is making noise in his sleep, two doors down the hall. Noise like words, but I can't make out what he's saying.

I get up, go to the door, then down the long hallway to the front dayroom. Walter waves when I pass the nurses' station, but he barely looks up.

Stephanie is at the back end of the hall, her flashlight beam bouncing over the walls and ceiling.

My feet hurt like I've walked ten miles, and clouds are moving in front of my eyes. They gave me a shot at nine, then another at midnight, but I can't sleep, can't slow down, can't stop.

"You're like a hen on a hot griddle," my mother used to tell me, and she'd make me go outside and run ten times around the house.

Tonight I'm underwater, I'm in ice or snow, and I still can't stop the rush and press of thoughts.

Dad always lay there in the living room with his mouth open, the air making its way into his nose and throat. He lay for five weeks once, until his beard grew and his skin was whiter than sheets, than paper, whiter than milk.

Dad said, "Watch out."

The dayroom is dark and empty, except for chairs and tables, except for the washed light that comes in from the windows. There's no noise but the wind and the air in vents.

I pull a chair to a window, and the glass is cold, is the color of ice. There is heavy wire mesh outside the window, and there is a spotlight on the back of the building across from us, pointing down at a parking lot.

I count bricks on the building until I lose their shape in darkness.

Joan's mother had a friend who went to lunch one day with another friend. The woman was fifty-seven years old, she drove a Volvo, she had two kids in high school.

They found her car in a parking lot, near the restaurant where she was supposed to meet her friend. The car was locked, there was an umbrella and a box of tissues on the backseat.

Nobody saw the woman. She became the same as the children on the sides of milk cartons. The school picture, the smiling kid. "Child Care: Missing," it said.

It gave a Child Case Number. Sometimes it said "Stranger Abd."

It said "Name: Jennifer Stacy Bourne. Sex: F. Date of Birth: 8-22-92. Date of Disappearance: 5-26-00. From: Hillsboro, Florida."

Under Additional Information the notice said, "Hair: Brown. Eyes: Blue. Pierced Ears. $\frac{1}{2}''$ scar under chin. Birthmark slightly darker than skin color across left wrist. Last seen walking home from school."

There was a toll-free phone number underneath. "This number is only to be used to identify children, or by children who are missing," the notice said.

Stephanie comes into the dayroom and flashes her light for an instant across my face.

"That you, Earl?" she asks, and I say, "Yes."

"You need anything?"

I say, "No."

"You want a shot?"

"Not now."

"Okay," she tells me, and I hear her feet sliding away.

I read the cartons of milk when I ate breakfast. I saw the ads in the Yellow Pages. There were children missing from Leominster, Massachusetts; from Longview, Washington; from Clark, New York; from Phoenix; from Wapato, Washington.

There were four-year-old boys missing, there were thirteen-year-old girls missing. The fifty-seven-year-old woman, the woman with the Volvo, worked for a church each night, serving hot meals to the needy. She had gray hair and wore glasses with brown rims.

A car comes into the parking lot outside, circles the lot, then passes behind the building with the spotlight. The car was a dark color, but I couldn't see a driver because of the headlights.

This is 2004. The girl from Hillsboro, Florida, has been missing for four years. The girl with the scar under her chin, with the birthmark on her left wrist. If she is alive, she is twelve years old. Bible: What is thy beloved more than another beloved, that thou dost so charge us? My beloved is white and ruddy, the chiefest among ten thousand. Her eyes are as the eyes of doves by the rivers of waters.

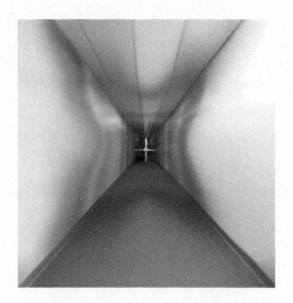

SIXTEEN

"Tell me," Schumacher says.

"Tell you?"

"How it happened."

I won't pretend to ask what. I'll no longer say, "How what happened?"

Each time I see him, he looks more tired, more worn out. He has a wife and children, a house in Wellesley. His wife is a psychiatrist downtown.

He's wearing a dungaree shirt, a red knit tie. He has dark patches of skin under his eyes

"She was sleeping," I'll begin this last time, for form's sake. Last because I'm arriving at memory and presence. A way of beginning. "The way she always did. Joan slept like death. Nothing could touch her, and that spring I never slept. Never until five or six in the morning."

"What about work?" he asks.

"I'd been fired by then," I say.

"So what'd you do days?"

"I slept till three or four or sometimes five. I kept the shades down and the curtains drawn, and I had the bed to myself. The whole place to myself.

"Once in a while, once or twice a week, the phone rang, but I'd never answer it. I started to think that burglars called to see if the place was empty. When I did get up I'd look out through the cracks in the curtains. I'd see cars go by."

"What else?" he'd ask. He'd have a can of Coke on his desk. He'd pick it up, sip, then hold the can in both hands. He'd look thoughtful. He'd be staring at the filing cabinet that was behind the door.

"After I got up, I'd make dinner, clean the house some, maybe look through magazines."

"And Joan?"

"This is the hard part. The very simple part. The very hard part, at the same time. It would be so much easier somehow to give you this version, still one more version, of how I killed her. I've killed Joan. I get very fucking anxious and fucking scared and confused. I begin to whirl, to spin. Because she's gone and dead and not gone and dead. Both at the same time.

"So she'd come in, and she'd look at the paper while I set the table and finished cooking.

"Then I'd say, 'Honey, it's ready,' and I'd hear her get up, and she'd kiss me when she sat down at the table.

"So we ate, and I cleaned up, and she usually had work to do.

"She'd been promoted to assistant principal in the winter, and she had way more work than before. I'd look up and see her asleep on the couch, her reading glasses still on, papers spread on her lap."

"So?"

"So I'd wake her up, and she always said she was sorry."

"Sorry?"

"For being so tired, for not being able to spend time with me."

He'd nod, would set the Coke on his desk.

"So she'd be in bed by ten, maybe ten-thirty if it was a good night."

"And what'd you do, Earl?"

"Nothing."

"Nothing?"

I'd shrug. "I'd look at my fingernails, at the sliver of moon at the bottom of each nail."

"It was ten-thirty, Joan had gone to sleep, and you'd been up five or six hours."

"Right," I'd tell him.

"So what'd you do?"

"I'd shut most of the lights in the house off. That's the first thing. Then I'd start to look out the windows."

He'd glance up.

"I'd go to the different rooms, to the different windows in the different rooms, and I'd look out.

"The front windows faced the street, and I'd look at the street-lights, at the trees and bushes and stuff, and I'd watch the cars go by. I'd follow them till they were out of sight, then I'd just stand there, and sometimes I'd press my face to the glass, and I'd wonder what I was doing.

"Then I'd go to the windows in the dining room and kitchen, or the windows out back, the windows on the porch.

"I could see the lights on in the house behind us. They stayed up till two or three sometimes, but I never knew who lived there.

"I'd seen a man in the yard before, but I didn't know if he lived there or visited or what.

"So the spring. That spring." Schumacher. He'd say, and he'd have the angry look on his face, the I-don't-have-time look.

"So around eleven I'd start drinking. Sometimes a beer, a little wine, sometimes rum, sometimes—most of the time—gin."

"Gin?"

I'd nod.

"I'd usually start slow, and I'd begin to feel happy and warm, and then I'd think of terrible things and I'd want to laugh."

"What things?"

"I'd think of the knives in the drawers, or the hammer I kept in a toolbox downstairs."

"And?"

"And that night I drank more than I usually did. I had two or three gins—strong ones—and I went to the cellar, and I didn't turn any lights on.

"I felt around with my hands, and there was faint faint light from the windows, and I found my toolbox in the utility room, and I took out the hammer and sat on the floor.

"I shut the door, so there was no light at all, and I stayed there and sipped more gin."

"What'd you think at the time," he'd ask. "What'd you feel?"

"Happy. Warm. I kept feeling I had something to do."

"And then?"

"Then I got up, and I went upstairs."

"With the hammer?"

"Right."

"And?"

"No. No. Not that at all. The poor fucking dicklick. We know him. We know him. He didn't do a thing like that. He hasn't got the balls."

Schumacher now is looking. Looking. And I am saying these things. Crying, or wanting to cry. And Joan weeping. Sobbing. Grief. Deep grief. Such sadness.

Kept slapping the head of hammer into left palm, and don't think he felt mad, or thought about Joan. His lovely spouse who had the courage, the gall, to love, to take in this pathetic, this isolated individual. For love means an other. A risk. An uncontrol. Something as in a gift given.

Stupid and alone and drunk in the apartment, I found an x-acto knife, and I began making these lines on my arms and chest and shoulders. Just what a fucklick would do. To call attention to the pathethic state of his emotional, spiritual, and professional life.

"I got to the hallway, and I remember I left the door open because I knew I'd have to go down there again."

"And?"

"I'd stare at my wrists and forearms."

He'd be holding the can.

"I went to the bedroom, and it felt hot in there. The blue light from her clock had this weird glow, and I started to swing the hammer at her head. Only it wasn't a hammer. It was a fucking x-acto knife. And it wasn't her head, because I'd already scared her off with my stories. My fucked-up, wacko stories."

"She never woke up? Never moved?"

"She'd moved out already."

I'd shake my head. He'd watch the top of the Coke can. He'd press the top of the can with his thumb, and the skin around his nail turned white.

"And then?"

"Started to draw lines. Light long lines on skin of arms and chest and shoulders and legs. Sides. Thin red lines. That stung. That felt not much of anything. That felt maybe a little good."

Took all my clothes off, stuffed them in a trash bag, got in the shower. And all the time, I left the lights off.

"Then I remembered that my other clothes were in the bedroom, and I stood there and kept thinking that I'd never be able to wear clothes again. That that was something I'd never be able to do."

Other side of me, side that was more in touch with reality—three spheres, as to person, place, and time—was sitting alone in apartment, resumed using x-acto knife. Cutting himself up in a not particularly dangerous way. But a way so as to make manifest the interior hurts, wounds, pains, as it were. Of being bereft. Arrive alone. Leave alone. Another dumb fuck whose wife had justly left him.

·

Ed and I rode our bikes to Crystal Lake, to Cambridge Reservoir, to Farm Pond, to Lake Waban, to Walden Pond. We wore cutoffs, sneakers, T-shirts, and no socks.

We rode down streets where trees grew on each side and formed a canopy overhead. We rode for a while without holding the handlebars. We rode from one side of the street to the other, leaning into each curve like a ride at an amusement park.

At the reservoir we hid our bikes under trees and bushes, covered them with branches and leaves, and went to a secluded place where we could take off all our clothes.

We swam at a spot near Route 128, but there were trees between the highway and the water. We were fifty yards from shore. The sky was blue, was vast, and the summer stretched ahead of us, bigger than an ocean.

The water slapped and slogged. It rocked us.

Ed said, "Earl."

I looked over at him, and he nodded to a place on shore.

A man was standing where we had left our clothes. He wore tan pants and a blue shirt. He wore glasses, and he was holding our underwear to his face.

He looked at us, waved, and went up the embankment, through the bushes, to the highway, our underwear in his hands. Out the window now I look at a star at night and think that Ed could see that same star. Though that is not likely. Ed and me seeing same star. Not fucking likely.

.

In Texas, near Houston, the boy was thirteen when he met the man. The man gave him candy, told him he was pretty. He became friend to the candyman, accomplice. Finally, after months and years he shot the candyman.

I love you, the candyman said to him at the end.

After a while the friend stood up. Then he let the boy and girl go. He watched them get dressed.

He called the police, and the three of them—the boy, the girl, and the friend—waited out front. It was the end of the killing for him.

After the police saw the body inside, saw the handcuffs, the board, the gun, the giant dildo, the friend started to talk.

He told about the boathouse. He told about the other friend, a teenager, and the place near Lake Sam Rayburn, and the spot by High Island.

They got the key from the owner of the boathouse, who had rented to the candyman.

Inside, there was a stripped car. They began to dig.

Six inches down they hit something wrapped in plastic. When they cleared the dirt away, they saw a boy's face, the eyes still open, a rope buried in the flesh of his neck.

They kept digging, until they had uncovered seventeen bodies in the boathouse. One body had no genitals. They were in a separate plastic bag.

They found four bodies at Lake Sam Rayburn, and another six at High Island.

The friend said there were more. More in the boathouse, more at High Island.

The police kept digging but couldn't find more bodies.

There were twenty-seven boys in all. The oldest was in college, the youngest was nine. Most were between the ages of twelve and seventeen.

The friend said it started a long time ago.

Don't worry, he told the police.

He said, He's dead now.

He said, I'm sorry. It's over now.

.

A young woman comes on the ward around three in the afternoon, and for a second I almost think it's her. Joan. She has the same hair, same face, same smile even.

But then I'm pretty sure it's the one who came in the second time. She's taller and older than Joan and has darker hair.

She stands outside the nurses' office awhile, talks to Jackie, signs some papers. She holds one of those nice leather folder things under her left arm. Smiles.

I look out the window. I see telephone poles with wires attached to them. I see a chain-link fence. Sky, trees, grass, birds. What have you. The whole big thing called life is out there.

Then I look at her, and I start thinking of who she might be. A social worker, or some kind of administrator. Or maybe someone like Joan. Who liked and even loved a person who was alone.

I look and look, and I notice she's wearing a wedding ring, and a watch. And then I realize that she does not seem to realize that this big, funny-looking man, this patient on a mental ward, has been looking at her for some time.

After a while she smiles and seems to say something like, "I have to run."

I watch her turn. Give a little wave with her free hand. Go down the hall, through the dayroom, and Jackie unlocks the front door.

.

Mom had three pillows behind her back and head. The light on the table next to her bed was on, and without her glasses, without her teeth, she looked both older and younger.

She said to me, "My father was the sweetest man I ever knew."

She folded her hands and licked her lips.

I looked at her. She looked at her watch. It was 1:26 in the afternoon.

"It was lovely then," Mom said. "My cousin Will, my aunt and uncle, Mother and Father, all of us at the house."

I nodded, closed my eyes, and listened to Mom's voice. It was rain and wind, it was surf hitting shore.

"That was 1952," Mom said. "That was before you were born."

Mom nodded.

"They wore the long skirts, the big sun hats. Ike was president, Ted Williams still played for Boston."

Mom drifted, and my eyes, as she talked, began to close.

"I don't know," she said, her big hands folding and unfolding. "It was different."

·

On the floor in the living room, Ed seemed to whisper something, but when I listened, he kept sleeping.

The curtains filled with air and lifted away from the window, then drew back to the screen.

A beer snapped open in the kitchen, and Dad cleared his throat.

"Don't worry," he said. "It's not as bad as all that."

Mom said something I couldn't make out.

"You, too," Dad said.

"Do you know," Mom began, then her voice went low again.

"All the time," he said. "Forever and ever."

·

An unremembered boy in a grave with long grass near Winder, Georgia, a hawk passing high overhead in deep blue late-afternoon sky. A nineteen-year-old girl with cancer in a hospital bed in Seattle, balloons and flowers on the table next to her bed, her head as white as a cloud. A boy on a bicycle looking up at sunlight reflected in a window on a street in Flushing, Queens. A nine-year-old girl with freckles adjusting her blue plaid bathing suit as she emerges from Lake Emily in Minnesota.

Can I've an ice cream, Dad? Fifty cents for candy? Twenty bucks for a T-shirt? Please, Mom? Can I, Mom? A six-year-old girl, yellow-and-white T-shirt, crescent scar on left wrist, gone missing on a trail in North Carolina? Last seen. DOB. Body of boy who went in search of his lost dog was himself found frozen to death in snowstorm three hundred yards from home. See you, Mom. So long, Dad. Be careful. Love ya. Mom. Dad. Ed. Mrs. M. Brandon. Joan. Gone all over. Gone for good.

•

Had he done it. Had I done it. Everything would be steel, is concrete, and everything echoes. The doors clang, the voices of the men echo, the bells ring again and again.

There is a tower at each corner, and twenty- and thirty-foot walls, and razor wire at the top. Each tower is glassed in, and there is a sharpshooter in each one.

They hold their rifles, sometimes raise them and point, and in the yard the men can feel the rifles.

Along the tiers the hands and arms reach between the bars, and looking down the length of bars there are hundreds of arms and wrists, of hands.

Late at night the steel and concrete echo even more. The footsteps on the tier, the CO checking beds, the vents, the clicks and scrapes and ticks.

.

Joan said, "Mom came in then, when I was just lying there, and she lay down next to me.

"I could hear her breathing, and I could smell the soap from her shower.

"She said, 'Honey, what's wrong? Why can't you sleep?' And I'd put my head against her side."

Over on Beacon Street the traffic moved by. It was midnight, but so hot that neither of us could sleep.

"She'd lie there," Joan said, "and she'd tell me about when she was young and couldn't sleep. How she'd wake her little sister up and make her talk. Make her tell stories."

.

I'm in a hospital in Boston, and spring is almost here. I can hear their footsteps in the long hallway. Though alone, I have my thoughts. Thou art all fair, my love. There is no spot on thee.

.

They'll come for me at dawn, and the priest will have left by then. They'll unlock the cell, and in a voice close to a whisper, they'll say, Earl.

I'll look up.

It's time, they'll say.

I'll stand up, they'll put the waist chain on me, the cuffs.

It'll still be dark, the sky in the east barely beginning to change.

I'll feel everyone sleeping, and as I walk the chain will click and ping. They'll have a guard on each side of me.

.

I weigh 227 pounds. I'm six-one. I have blue eyes and brown hair. There were and are so many boys and girls in so many places. Her eyes in those photographs. Such lovely skin, the hope in her eyes. The lifted eyes of my students. The children in Cicero, in Murfreesboro, in Stockton, in Charleston, in Queens and St. Cloud. Kids in baggy pants, tight spandex, pierced, bejeweled, tattooed, lipsticked, sunburnt. In T-shirts, thongs, sneakers, boots, barefoot. Wearing ties. Saying, "Dude," saying, "Fuck," saying, "Praise Him."

•

In the room they'll strap me to the wooden chair. My ankles, my wrists, my upper arms, my chest. Leather straps the size of thick belts.

They'll read the order, ask me if I have anything to say, and I'll shake my head.

Behind the windows, behind the half-open blinds, I'll see the outline of heads.

One man will pat my arm, and they'll go out.

I'll wait for the vents to close, for the chamber to seal. I'll wait for the pellets to fall into the solution, for the hissing sound, for the smell.

•

Joan baked bread, and she used to dance. She wore glasses when she read, she smelled like snow. She said: I was the best. The sweetest. Kindest. Nicest. Weirdest. Scariest. Most shy. Interesting. Unusual. Best-haired.

•

The chair will have straps, and my head and wrist and a place on my leg will have been shaved.

They'll put a petroleum-jelly-like substance on the shaved places, then they'll attach the wires.

I'll wait for the surge, the jolt, for when the lights go dim.

•

She said, C'mon, honey, I'll save you. She smelled of lemon, vanilla, cinnamon, cut grass, autumn wind, ocean, wet earth, morning, light.

■

They'll have sandbags behind the chair, and they'll pin a black circle over my heart. They'll give people cotton for their ears. Within, without.

I'll look up, and I'll see them. The four men. The rifles. Long black cylinders. Dull gleam.

They'll say, Ready. They'll say, Aim.

■

He knows somehow. In all three spheres. In some strange, some lonely and consoling way that he has not known before. That she is indeed and finally gone—but is also in him in this trembling, living way. And will always be in him because of how they were together once, a long time—back then.

He, Earl, me: I am nowhere. I am now here. As to person, place, time. Because something fails, something refuses to die. But instead goes deeper and wider and farther, like roots underground, like branches and leaves straining for light. Deeper down and higher. At the same time. Past and present.

■

Come inside, she said. She said, Hurry. She wrapped her legs around me. And stars. Stars. Stars. Black sky. So high and far. Stars. More stars. So as to illuminate heaven.